A FAE'S TWO ALPHAS

JEM ZERO

Copyright © 2023 by jem zero

All rights reserved.

No part of this book may be reproduced in any form or by any electronic or mechanical means, including information storage and retrieval systems, without written permission from the author, except for the use of brief quotations in a book review.

CONTENTS

Content Notes v

1. Innate Magic 1
2. Stay For Tea 8
3. If Dandelions Were Wishes 15
4. Dramatically-Timed Rain 23
5. Buckle Up 32
6. Desire by the Water 42
7. Look It Up 47
8. Firefly Moon 52
9. The First Notes of Birdsong 61
10. Embarrassment Over Scrambled Eggs 68
11. Always Time For a Misunderstanding 73
12. Poorly Placed Confessions 77
13. Problem-Solving is an Art 86
14. An Afternoon Exposition 93
15. Try Everything Once 100
16. Middle Cushion 110
17. Unexpected Tension 118
18. Over the Edge 125
19. Betwixt 135
20. Looking Out For You 141
21. When One Wants to Disappear 149
22. Because He Always Does 159
23. Unpleasantly Wet Pajama Pants 166
24. Emotions Bruise Too 173
25. Dirtiness is Okay 181
26. Prove It 190
27. In Which Two Alphas 197
28. Drink More Water 205
29. Making Demands 212
30. One Big Tangle 221

31. A Tether to Whom	228
32. Flames of the Unexpected	236
33. Dumpster Conflict	247
34. The Lost Dandelion Chronicles	255
35. Enthusiastic Homecoming	268
36. The Most Magical Solution	274
37. Possessed and Possessing	285
Acknowledgments	293
About the Author	295

CONTENT NOTES

Tropes:

- Sunshine one/Grumpy one/Sunshine one
- Hurt/Comfort
- Rival love interests
- Best friends-to-lovers
- Size difference (twink + two hunky alphas)

Potentially triggering content:

- Controlling/manipulative parent(s)
- Transphobia/dysphoria discussion
- Mild conflict & violence
- Bodily functions (including vomiting & bleeding)
- Depression & panic attacks

Shifter kinks:

- Explicit sexual activity

Content Notes

- Knotting
- Marking
- Double penetration

1

INNATE MAGIC

I ROLL the stem of a fluffy dandelion between my fingers, watching it bob and dip with each step I take. Long grasses bend beneath my boots—the ones I had donned with some reluctance, not thrilled by the prospect of wearing them in the mid-June heat. I don't often leave the college town I've begrudgingly made my home for the past year and a half, but desperation has pushed me past my usual boundaries.

After confirming our appointment, the magewolf told me how to find his cottage. It's located within the territory of the area's dominant shifter pack, the Harrises. A spelled marker at the boundary of the road and a wide field indicates the only place one can enter without being pounced upon by pack enforcers. I appreciate the option to approach without being growled at by wolf shifters, but it'd be even more considerate if the magewolf had beaten a path through the field. I'm sweaty in my long pants, but it's tick season, and even fae aren't invulnerable to the bloody parasites.

Not a half-fae without access to his magic, anyway.

Hopefully, with the help of this mage, a solution to the 'no magic' thing is incoming.

At last I reach the end of the field and greet the forest floor, pebbles and pine needles scattering the ground surrounding the cottage. It's a classic affair, rustic beams of dark wood crawling with vines and large, round stones that have been smoothed by time. Exactly the kind of place one would find a powerful wolf shifter capable of fixing magical problems.

I march up to the front door and knock with false confidence. The door swings inward before my fist can hit a third time, and my mouth rounds into a surprised *O*. I did my best to not make assumptions about what this encounter would look like, but the broad, silver-haired man filling the doorway is still wildly unexpected.

My grip on the dandelion slackens until it drops to the rough mat under my feet.

"Hi," I say, when he doesn't speak. "I'm Bennett Chiston. We set up an appointment?"

All the man does is nod. "Callum Truett. Come inside." I don't get any farther than the doorway before Callum rumbles, "Shoes off."

I oblige, happy to rid myself of the sweaty hiking boots. As I untie the laces I cast a covert look around the cottage interior. It's all one room, unpolished but organized. Bookshelves hug the walls to my left, wedged against more shelves containing various jars, boxes, bones, and twists of dried herbs. To the right, a kitchenette, hardwood table, and sitting area.

When I'm done stuffing my socks inside the discarded footwear, I find Callum sitting at the table, tapping at the keyboard on a laptop that matches the setting only because it looks like a relic from the past.

A Fae's Two Alphas

I pad lightly cross the room to sit opposite the magewolf, then take advantage of the momentary silence to study him. Despite the silver hair, short and tousled, Callum doesn't look older than thirty. Whether premature greys or magic, I don't know, but the pale stubble on his strong jaw creates a striking picture.

Unique hair has always appealed to me; my faded teal and purple fashion mullet can attest to that. In Faerie, the pastel oil spill painting my hair was all natural, but now, being deadlocked in a human body, I have to regularly dye it.

It's weird to stare, even in appreciation, so I clear my throat and begin after only a second of hesitation. "Mr. Truett."

"Callum."

"Callum. I don't know if you remember anything about my email—"

He pushes the laptop screen down halfway. "Start from the beginning."

Fine.

"My father is fae and my mother is human." I figure that's as close to the beginning as one can get. "I lived with them here, in the mundane realm, until they separated and I went to Faerie with my dad."

Callum leans back in his chair, propping one bare foot on his knee as he listens.

"I loved it there. I grew up in this tiny, shitty township in Wisconsin, and it sucked. In Faerie I finally felt like I belonged somewhere, which is why I'm so desperate to—"

"Please get to the point."

I huff, fighting a pout. I haven't had many opportunities to explain why being stuck in the mundane realm has been so devastating. I'm used to no one giving a shit about my feelings, though, so I smooth my palms down the crumpled cotton of my pants and summarize. "Not quite two years ago, my dad kicked me out of Faerie with no explanation, and he took my magic away so I can't get back."

Saying it feels anticlimactic. One minute I was in Faerie, doing something so delightfully irrelevant I don't even remember anymore, and the next I was in my childhood bedroom being mauled by my weeping human mother.

"I've been stuck here ever since. No way to leave, no way to contact him."

Callum taps one finger on the table. I'm surprised to see, in place of regular fingernails, a thick, blunt claw. "You want me to contact your father in Faerie?"

In my experience there's no reasoning with a fae who's made up their mind. Not when you've nothing to bargain with, and what could I offer my own father to change his mind, when he wasn't even willing to discuss it in the first place?

"No," I say. "I want you to fix my magic without his help." Then I can go to Faerie unassisted and holler at him in person.

Callum's thick brows climb on his forehead. "What is your definition of 'fixed'?"

"Being able to use it again...?"

The beat Callum is tapping against the swirling wood grain increases speed. He frowns at his hand, then up at me. "Summer Court?"

I open my mouth to give the affirmative, then close it. "Why did you guess that?"

Snorting, he tugs his laptop closer and flips the screen fully upward. "Do you think it isn't obvious? You're a summer fae. Half," he amends.

Irritation prickles my spine. "What difference does it make?"

Callum sends me a withering look. "All of it. Especially with the Summer Solstice coming up."

I *know* the Solstice is coming up. It's the most important celebration known by the Summer Court. I barely remember the events of any specific year, because we were always drunk on sunlight and high off the heady scents of sweat and flowers. Maybe that's why it didn't occur to me that what I'm requesting might be aided by the Solstice magic's thinning of the veil. Sighing at my oversight, I admit, "Yes, I'm from the Summer Court."

Callum clicks his tongue and shifts his attention to his laptop. He types rapidly, eyes narrowing, then moves his fingers over the trackpad. Enough time passes with him doing nothing but scrolling and clicking that I clear my throat, hoping for some explanation. He holds a finger up to still me.

When I've gotten almost unbearably squirmy, Callum closes the laptop, then says, simply, "I can't."

"You *can't*?"

"Fae magic is out of my domain, and I don't have any contacts that would be useful for this issue."

My heart plummets. "But you're the only mage in this fuckshit town." I don't usually beg for things I can't have, but nearly two years spent trapped in Marquette-fucking-Michigan has an effect on a person. I didn't spend eight years living deliciously in Faerie only to be stuck for the rest of my life in a college town known primarily for its ski resort and population of well-off retirees.

Callum sucks his teeth. "How much do you know about magic, Mr. Chiston?"

"Bennett," I correct, figuring if he wants me to use his first name, he can use mine too. "And I know enough."

"Internal or external?"

"What?"

He levels a frown at me. "Do you not understand the question?"

I don't, but I'd rather not admit it. "Maybe I don't know how concepts are phrased here."

Though Callum seems dubious, he explains without condescension. "Non-mundane people have internal magic. It comes from within, generated by their life force. That's how it'd work for an actual fae, but it might be different for you since you're half."

I bristle. "My magic comes from me."

"It's not the same for everyone," he replies with a shrug. "Theoretically, a halfling could be born without magic. You might possess the ability to use external magic but not generate any of your own. The magic you're used to could be drawn from your surroundings. Proximity to your father, or to Faerie, could fuel you. Not common, but also not impossible. Removing you from Faerie would leave him as your only source of magic, allowing him to cut you off at will. If that's the case, no external spell I can give you could force him to reopen the channel."

"That can't be it."

I've never thought in-depth about magic. It was close and reflexive, like breathing, and I didn't acutely feel its presence until it was gone. I've always been aware of my father's aura, though—the sharp bite of fae mischief I always lacked. If I was simply channeling full-fae magic, wouldn't I feel that in myself, too? Or would that be filtered out by the human influence?

Fuck.

Callum watches me, impassive in the face of my spiraling self-doubt.

I clear my throat in an effort to put myself back together. "I'm confident in my own innate magic."

"Sure." He picks up a thick pencil with a roughly-hewn wedge of graphite and scribbles something in a notebook of plain, unlined paper. I watch his hand move—large, masculine, the back dusted in silvery hair. The pencil is dwarfed in his grasp, but his handwriting is neat and precise, almost delicate. "The work I do is external magic. Spells, objects. I give someone who can't generate their own magic a resource that will do it for them. If you need a specific item I can help you, but I'm not comfortable extending my services beyond that."

"But—"

"That's how it is." Callum thumps the butt of the pencil rapidly on the open page and rubs at his stubble with the other hand. "Unfortunate, yes, and unpleasant to hear. I understand, but being upset won't change anything, and neither will lingering at my table, so you can—"

A knock at the door interrupts him. I look over my shoulder to see a tall man ducking through the entryway, not having waited for an invitation.

"Callum, you missed a meeting with Josie again this morning," the man says. "She sent me here to—"

Then he lifts his head, and the both of us go stock still.

2
―――――
STAY FOR TEA

"God damn it, Jesse, do you have any fucking manners?" Callum rumbles, but neither Jesse nor I break eye contact.

"*Bennett?*" Jesse chokes.

I stare up at my childhood best friend, unable to speak. Jesse Chen was never a small guy, but in middle school the both of us were equally gangly. I never grew out of it, though nowadays I prefer the term 'willowy,' but Jesse clearly did. The man in front of me is not only tall, but *built*. Stacked. Solid like this cottage, with biceps almost the width of my thigh. Instead of the businesslike cropped haircut he had when we were kids, Jesse's hair now flows down his neck in thick, black waves.

It only takes a moment after the shock passes for me to bounce out of my seat and fling myself at him, gasping when Jesse crushes me in those beautiful arms and squeezes me until I feel juiced. Laughing and gasping for breath, I break the embrace, drawing back to grin at him.

"You've grown up!" I chirp, scanning him up and down, from his distressed jeans and sneakers to his tight-fitting grey tee.

"And you... you kinda grew up, I guess." Jesse laughs, planting a big hand atop my head. "Bennett, what the hell? You look... different."

Oh, right. I scratch the shorn side of my head, smiling bashfully. "I'm a guy now."

I went to Faerie at thirteen, not yet changed by puberty. When Jesse last saw me I was a slip of a girly thing, wearing a dress at the fourteenth birthday party he shared with his twin sister, Josie. Then I came home and learned my parents were separating, effective immediately. I only started hormone replacement therapy a year ago, and aside from a lower voice, I haven't felt many changes. That Jesse noticed a change immediately has me even closer to walking on air.

Jesse doesn't miss a beat, which I'm grateful for. "It's good to see you, bud. The changes suit you. Should I call you anything different?"

I shake my head. "Bennett's fine." Out of all the things that bother me about being trans in the mundane realm, my birth name isn't one of them.

Behind us, Callum's chair scrapes against the floor. "Does this conversation have to happen in my home?"

"Don't be a dickhead, Cal," Jesse says with a roll of his eyes. "Bennett was my best friend when we were growing up."

"Happy for you. Celebrate your reunion somewhere else."

Instead of listening, Jesse wraps a large hand around the back of my neck and puppets me to the worn leather couch next to a large window. Callum huffs, but Jesse doesn't seem to care.

"Did you want tea?" he asks. "Callum, you didn't even offer him tea? Bennett, what kind of tea do you like?" Jesse doesn't wait for my response before walking to the small kitchen area on the other side of the table.

Callum stands, producing a low growl that reverberates off the windows. "Do I need to throw you out again?" The air stirs, and my amusement evaporates into alarm, but Jesse merely folds his arms across his chest and smirks.

"Is this really worth making a scene over, magewolf?" Jesse asks.

Callum steps into Jesse's space, his lip curling just enough to reveal the point of a fang. While Callum is a few inches shorter than Jesse, allowing Jesse to look down his nose at him, he clearly isn't intimidated.

I don't know if I should be scared. Unsure of what else to do, I say, "Jess, you didn't take your shoes off."

Their combined focus settles on me.

Callum's blue eyes are now lit with a faint glow, but rather than respond in kind, Jesse bursts into laughter. He claps Callum on the shoulder, unfazed when he's immediately shrugged away, then proceeds to wrestle his boots off where he stands. He tosses them at mat beside the entryway, though only one lands on it.

"Happy now, Cal?"

The magewolf grumbles. "Go sit down. I'll make tea." He steps out of Jesse's space and stalks over to a multi-tiered cart tucked against the wall. Each shelf is packed solid with bags of herbs.

Jesse plops next to me on the couch. Up close I notice lines of tension around his eyes, telling me I have explaining to do. "Where've you been, Bennett?"

"It's a long story." I swallow. "Or, not really, I guess. My parents separated and I left Wisconsin with my dad."

His welcoming expression fades. "You couldn't have kept my number?"

My teeth sink into my lip. I pick at the unmanaged cuticles over my fingernails and admit, "I wasn't anywhere I could have contacted you." Jesse waits. I wish he wouldn't, but it succeeds in forcing the words out of me. "I was in Faerie, Jess. My dad's fae."

In the kitchenette, Callum's puttering stops. I wonder if he's surprised my childhood best friend doesn't know about my heritage.

When I started school, my mom told me it would be dangerous to tell people I'm part fae. Hiding a part of myself from Jesse for all those years was difficult, but in those days I listened to everything my mother said.

Jesse examines me like I'm new, inspecting everything from the top of my spiky dyed hair to my bare feet, eyes lingering on my freckled shoulders. He used to tease me about how much they darkened in summer. Anxiety starts to set in, and I twist the tip of my pinky between the fingers of the other hand.

Finally, his smile returns. "I always wondered when you were gonna tell me."

My back straightens. "You *what*?"

"That you're not all human." Jesse grins. "I've known since we met."

I sputter. "How did you know? I thought I hid it well."

"I could smell it on you." He lets me blink owlishly for one beat, then two, before announcing, "I'm a wolf shifter, Benny."

Stunned, I lose myself in studying him again. It explains his adult size, but as a kid I wouldn't have known what to look for. I glance at Callum, still at the counter with his back to us. Callum is everything I'd expect a wolf shifter to be: big, growly, hairy. The stereotype. He even wears his claws and teeth out. In contrast, Jesse is clean-shaven, with neatly trimmed nails and no visible fangs.

I wonder what would make him drop them.

Jesse allows me to look, waiting with a patient smile as I process. A flush hits me when our eyes meet again, and I remember—abruptly, uncomfortably—the powerful crush I used to have on my *best friend*.

Before I have a chance to break the silence, Callum strides over, three mugs clutched in one big hand and a copper jug of water in the other.

"That was fast," I comment.

Callum arches an eyebrow at me, but remains silent as he lines up the three mugs on the coffee table and seats himself in a beaten-down, overstuffed chair. He catches my gaze, maintaining the stare as he tips the water jug. The stream splits into three, neatly filling each mug. Steam rises, when there was none before.

"Practical magic," he says flatly. With a dismissive flick of his fingers, he sends two mugs sliding across the table, coming to rest in front of Jesse and me. "A derivative of external magic."

"Thanks for the lesson," I grouse, reaching for the tea. A little satchel of fragrant leaves bobs in the dark liquid. When I take a sip I find it perfectly steeped. Hot, but not enough to burn. I am reluctantly impressed. Practical magic wasn't something I concerned myself with in Faerie, where things happened with barely a thought.

"So, why is Bennett here for magic lessons?" Jesse asks after a sip of his own tea.

Embarrassed, I muffle a groan in my hands.

"He came to ask if I would restore his magic. His father removed his ability to access it."

"Oh. What's the plan?"

"There's no plan. It's not possible."

Jesse blinks. "You're already giving up?"

"I can't be giving up on something that can't be done, Jesse."

"So you're just not trying at all. Got it."

My eyes flick curiously between the two men.

Jesse leans forward, elbows on his knees. "You've been doing magic for *how* long, and haven't figured out how to research a tough problem?"

"Would you tell a physicist to research how to violate the laws of physics?"

"Probably, seeing as they could go to a mage to explore magic as an alternate option. Hopefully they wouldn't come to you, though, since they'd only get an earful about all the shit you can't do."

"I'm not a scientist," I pipe up, "but isn't part of the point of science to, like, fuck around until you find new shit?" The arrival of Jesse as an unexpected advocate has tentative hope blooming in my chest.

Jesse points at Callum triumphantly. "Exactly! And magic *has* to be easier to manipulate than the actual rules of the universe."

A rolling growl rises in Callum's throat. "I gave you my answer and I don't have to defend it. Finish your tea and leave my fucking home." He begrudgingly adds, "And furthermore, magic *is* part of the rules of the universe. You can't go off breaking things just because you want to."

"But you're not trying to break the universe," I argue. "Just whatever lock Dad put on my magic."

"You don't even know the difference between internal and external magic, Mr. Chiston," Callum says sourly, folding his arms across his chest.

I roll my eyes at the use of my last name. To prove I'm

not intimidated, I do as he says and polish off the rest of my tea. When the mug is empty I set it on the coffee table with more force than necessary, and stand. "Thanks for meeting with me, Mr. Truett."

3

IF DANDELIONS WERE WISHES

As I walk away, I'm peripherally aware of Jesse jumping to his feet. He hisses at Callum, too low for me to eavesdrop.

I want to stop, get Jesse's new number, and ask what he's doing all the way in Marquette when we used to live in Wisconsin, but my pride won't allow me to linger. I try to appear unconcerned as I wiggle my feet into my boots and tie them tightly to keep critters from getting inside on my return trek through the tall grass. I'll find another way to get my magic back. I don't need a grumpy magewolf to dash my hopes.

The door swings open before I can touch the handle. I turn to scowl at Callum, who isn't even looking in my direction, but rather fixing his own scowl on Jesse. Whatever.

When I stomp outside, I see the dandelion I dropped still on Callum's doorstep. I close the door and pick it up. After a moment of contemplation, I exhale on a sigh and morosely watch the fluffy seeds take flight.

I'll find another way, I reassure myself.

Behind me, the door opens.

Alarmed, I turn, and am surprised to come face-to-face with Callum. He looks just as off-kilter as I feel, as if he didn't expect to see me still on his doorstep.

I swallow hard. "Did I forget something?"

Callum sighs and scrubs a wide hand over his face. "I can't promise anything."

Sudden elation curls my toes and runs up my spine, tingling the base of my skull.

"I'll accept the job, *but*"—he raises a finger—"only if you are prepared to accept that there are no guarantees."

"Of course," I say, breathless.

"Come back inside."

"Only if you promise not to kick me out again."

Callum's jaw flexes. "I won't," he says, and holds the door open so I can enter the cottage first.

"Long time no see," Jesse says with a smirk. He's moved to the table and when I sit down next to him, he claps me on the shoulder. "You owe me lunch." I grin crookedly, and try not to focus on how big and warm his hand is.

Callum takes a seat. He's holding a small bookkeeping journal and a pad for hand-written receipt papers. "It'll be five hundred for the deposit," he says, producing a comically old-fashioned ink pen.

"Five hundred?" I squeak. "Your website said two hundred."

It took me a while to scrape together, too. A while back I tried working at an artisanal smoothie place on the Northern Michigan University campus, but I couldn't keep it together and quit the second week. My mom gives me money if I need it, but I couldn't exactly ask her for two hundred dollars without explaining *why*.

"Two hundred is the price of a consultation," Callum says. "I price each commission based on complexity."

Panic makes my chest clench. "I can't afford that..."

Callum gives me a blank look, then closes the receipt book.

"Wait!" I can get a job, right? Online work? I can learn how to do things. There has to be something someone with no formal education beyond eighth grade and no work experience can get hired to do, right? Maybe a flower shop. I'm half-fae; I know a *fucktonne* about flowers. "I'll figure something out," I say, desperate.

Jesse cuts in before Callum can express the skepticism clear on his face. "I'll pay it, Cal, you jackass. Can't believe you're taking advantage of a helpless kid like that."

A surprised laugh bursts from my chest. "We're the *same age*!" I protest, laughing again when Jesse winks. I might be hysterical. "And besides, I can't let you do that. It's a lot of money."

"Consider it your belated birthday present for the decade I missed," Jesse says with a dismissive wave.

After leaving the mundane realm, I never crossed back, not even once. In the beginning, my mom visited me every week. She never seemed at ease in Faerie, and over the years stopped coming as often. By the time I hit twenty-one, it had been a year in mundane time since I'd last seen her.

As for Jesse, well. I missed him terribly. Eventually I told myself he'd be fine, and happy, and someone else would grow to love him like I did. I still hope that's true.

The mundane realm holds nothing for me, and it was worse when I was a child. There was constant dysphoria and fear. Couldn't be truly seen, couldn't be found out as fae *or* trans. I was one of those children who went into the forest to dance in a circle of mushrooms, trying to summon someone who'd take me away forever.

"Well?" Callum looks at me expectantly.

JEM ZERO

I glance between him and Jesse, my lips pressed together. Is the chance to return home worth accepting so much from Jesse after I abandoned him?

Maybe my answer is selfish, because yes. Returning home is worth anything.

"I accept," I say at last. "Thank you, Jess."

Jesse grins brightly. "That's my boy." He goes on to tell Callum he'll be back later with the cash, but I'm distracted by my face going fire-hot.

We were both bullied in school. Other boys targeted Jesse, taking advantage of his affable personality and conflict-aversion. I was small and shy, but the day my patience ran out, I gritted my teeth and took action. Tackling the nearest boy, I grabbed his hair and rubbed his face against the playground gravel until he hollered an apology. He came up with scratches all over his cheek, but was too ashamed to tell the teacher he got whupped by a girl, so I never got in trouble.

After recess Jesse had grinned and told me he was proud of me. *That's my girl*, he'd said. It made me burn then, filling me with a want I was too young to understand. Hearing him call me his *boy* this time—

Callum sets his receipt notebook in front of me, displaying a neat itemized list. Two hundred for the consultation, five hundred for the deposit, and... Something written in not-English. Squinting, I try to make out the script. Then I realize he's written the final item in a mostly-extinct coded language once used to form magical contracts.

"You know the old words of accord?"

"Of course. Do you recognize the writing enough to verify what it says?"

I wince, then shake my head. I'd actually tried to study

accords, hoping to better understand fae trickery, but quickly grew bored.

Callum taps the page. "It's a clause. In interest of fairness, if I fail to restore your magic, or if I back out of the contract, your payment obligation is nullified. If you back out, you'll be billed for the time I spent on your case."

I can guarantee I won't be giving up on my only chance at getting around this torturous banishment, so I'm unconcerned about the no-doubt massive amount that would be held over my head in that situation.

Callum continues: "If I restore your magic—*if*—you'll owe me a favor."

My eyebrows shoot up. "What kind of favor?"

"Open-ended. That will replace any financial payment. Will that be a problem?"

Despite past attempts, I'm no good at being sly. I don't know how to poke holes in people's words until I find a mistake I can exploit. No, I'm simple. I want to grow flowers in my hair and not worry about wearing an itchy, sweaty binder to compress the breasts I didn't have while using magic to keep my ideal shape. Since I never began medical transition, upon returning to the mundane realm, there was nothing masculine about me.

I've got no choice but to agree. "No, it won't be a problem. Anything else?" I hope I'm not making a mistake, but figure Jesse will intervene if Callum demands anything too unhinged. We've always had each other's backs.

Callum moves on. "I've made a note that Jesse will be handling the deposit, but if he for some reason reneges, it'll be your responsibility."

"I won't," Jesse assures me, rolling his eyes when Callum makes an irritated sound.

"If these terms are acceptable, please sign." Callum extends the old-fashioned pen.

I take it, half expecting twisted energy to burst out and entangle me in a dark, unbreakable blood oath. Instead I sign without fanfare, my signature scrawling and childish.

"One more thing," Callum says when I push the notebook back toward him. "I need your energy signature, to ensure you uphold the fae bargain."

My eyebrows shoot up. "Energy signature?" Is there going to be bloodletting after all? If my dad ever discovered I agreed to a blood ritual, he'd do more than take away my magic. More like he'd put me a cage and ground me for the rest of my mortal life.

Callum twirls his finger in the air, manifesting a brightly-burning candle. The wax is clear and oddly iridescent; attempting to study it causes a pang behind my eyes. He tilts the candle, allowing several drops of phantasmal wax to pool on the paper. When I don't move, he frowns. "Is something wrong?"

"No," I say too quickly. "I just wasn't expecting this."

"What, were you expecting blood?" Jesse jokes.

I remain silent, but my flushed cheeks are answer enough.

Callum huffs. "Your thumbprint, Bennett."

Nervous, but unwilling to back out, I press my thumb to the soft wax. I'm surprised to find it cool to the touch. It squishes under the pressure, sliding into the creases of my skin, memorizing its unique map. I might not have my own magic, but I feel Callum's like a knife grazing my nerve endings—a silent almost-threat that makes my hair stand on end. I withdraw as soon as the wax warms to my body heat, then rub at the goose bumps running down my other arm.

"Is that it?" I ask.

Callum plucks the notebook from the table, narrows his eyes at the page, then murmurs, too low to hear. I hold my breath. My heart pounds out the seconds until he nods and tears the yellow carbon copy off the back of the receipt, then hands it to me.

It looks like a normal receipt, with no evidence of the magic contract having transferred through. I fold it carefully and reach for my bloated wallet. I pry out a handful of mangled bills: a few twenties and tens, the rest a handful of fives and ones. I stare at the collection, trying to figure out why it feels off, and then remember the quarters. Those I dump from the change pocket, before shoving the whole mess at Callum. I nonchalantly tuck the receipt into my now-empty wallet, pretending not to notice his deep, bracing inhale.

Jesse beams at me while Callum sorts through the money, clearly enjoying his palpable irritation.

I, however, have no desire to anger the magewolf further. There are many questions I have for Jesse, none of which I want to ask while in Callum's presence. "We should go," I suggest.

"Only if Cal decides he can bear to see the back of us," Jesse teases.

"Come back in a week," Callum says to me. "And you," he adds, nodding at Jesse. "Get the fuck out of my house, or I'll throw you out. For real this time."

"Don't oversell it," Jesse says with a smirk. He knuckles the side of my neck. "You coming, Ben?"

A smile tugs at my lips. I got what I wanted from this trip, and more. The magewolf agreed to help me, albeit under duress, and I got my best friend back. I'll have to say goodbye again when I regain my magic and return to Faerie, but that's a thought for later.

"Yeah, let's go." I look at the front door, expecting to see my boots, but it dawns on me that I didn't remove them when Callum brought me in the second time. I wince as he makes the same realization. "I'll see you next week. Sorry about the shoes."

He grunts, offering nothing but a curt wave.

I trot out the door after Jesse, leaving the surly magewolf behind.

4

DRAMATICALLY-TIMED RAIN

There's so much I want to ask, but I have no idea how.

I go for something safe. "So what're you doing in Marquette?" Last I saw Jesse, we were living in that quarter-sized Wisconsin craphole. Now we're both twenty-three and walking through a forest in Michigan's Upper Peninsula.

Jesse makes a face. "You know the Harris pack is matriarchal, right?"

I shake my head. "I don't know much about shifters."

After a soft laugh, Jesse continues: "Well, by the time their previous alpha matriarch died, they'd failed to produce another alpha to lead the pack."

"Is that a big deal?"

Jesse stares at me for several appalled seconds. "Yes. Yes, it is a very big deal."

"It's not one of those phony wolf alphabet hierarchy things, is it?" My nose wrinkles with distaste.

"One of those *what*?"

"There was this scientist who thought wolf packs had alphas, betas, this whole thing where they fought for dominance," I say, all in a rush. "Except he was observing random wolves in captivity, not a wild family pack, so he made all these wrong conclusions. Even when he recanted they wouldn't stop selling the book because insecure straight men like it too much." My cheeks flush. "I read a lot," I feel compelled to explain. Not books, but whatever interesting detail the internet pops out for me when I'm trying to update myself on how the mundane realm works.

"I... wow." Jesse blinks, then shakes it off, lips curving as he looks down at me. "Well, I can't speak for captive wolves, but most shifter family packs operate on elder respect and familial hierarchy. The lead alpha in a pack has usually inherited the position, and will maintain it until they choose a successor—another alpha. We have stronger magic than the average shifter. A pack without an alpha is vulnerable, and the Harrises are the dominant pack in this part of the Upper Peninsula. Without an alpha they'd run the risk of getting overthrown in a potential pack war."

"And that has what to do with you...?"

"It has more to do with Josie than me," he admits.

My brow furrows as I try to connect Jesse's twin sister with the Harris pack's lack of a leader, but he doesn't keep me waiting.

"Josie and I are both alphas. Mom got two for the price of one."

I blink several times, scanning him from head to toe for the umpteenth time. "You're not only magic, but you're jacked up on pack leader magic?"

Jesse laughs, ruffling my hair. "Jacked up, sure. Pack leader, no. The three of us moved to Marquette about six months ago, after Josie accepted the offer to become the Harris pack alpha. She mated with the late matriarch's grandson, Andrew. So now we're here."

A Fae's Two Alphas

It takes me a while to contemplate this. "That's a huge change for you guys."

Maria Chen was a fierce advocate for her kids, but very shy. Imagining her as a wolf and the mother of powerfully magic twins is throwing me off, but when I think of Josie's personality, envisioning her in control of a shifter pack makes a lot of sense. Despite her young age, Josie did a lot of the speaking—not only for her twin, but her mother too.

"It's certainly been *something*," Jesse says with a rough shrug. He opens his mouth to say more, then hesitates. "The most interesting part is that your mom was the reason we learned of the Harrises' search for a female alpha in the first place."

I stumble to a halt. The bright green seed pod of a maple tree spins in the breeze, grazing my arm as it blows past. I rub the spot with my fingertips. "Mom knows you've been here? For six months?"

"She didn't tell us you were here, either. For all I knew you were still off wherever you went, and we never actually saw your mom in person. She just gave Mom the information to get in touch with the pack council and Josie did the rest."

"I've been living with her for two years," I say faintly.

My mother, Naomi Chiston, has always been cagey. It frustrated my father so much that he'd disappear into Faerie after particularly bad arguments—sometimes for several months. She openly distrusted him. They never married, and I doubt they even liked each other. I've never seen Naomi have a conversation she enjoyed. More than once I've thought I might be the only person she actually likes spending time with.

It was kind of her to reach out to the Chens. She's not a cruel person, so her being begrudgingly helpful doesn't surprise me, but discovering she brought my best friend's family to Marquette without informing either of us...

Why hide the truth? She had to have known we'd run into each other eventually, and it'd be reasonable to assume I'd be angry. Because I am.

The longer I stand here ruminating, the angrier I get. "This makes no sense. I walk around the city, like, all the time. Mom works night shift stocking this home goods store, so I'm alone during the day." Alone and restless, wandering endlessly, always daydreaming about finding another fae willing to whisk me away.

"I don't leave the pack lands much. That's probably why. Last time I went downtown I was picking up some groceries for Callum because he was too distracted with a client project to leave his damn cottage."

"Callum?" I'd almost forgotten the grumpy magewolf, but now I'm curious. Jesse *did* walk in without waiting for permission, and didn't seem bothered by Callum's threats. "Are you two close?"

Jesse snorts. "Hardly. He and Josie hate each other's guts and he deliberately ignores her calls, so I volunteered to be a go-between."

"Is he... *allowed* to ignore the pack alpha?" I wince as I say it, wondering how anyone would tell that beast of a man he wasn't allowed to do something.

A loud, undignified *ha!* springs from Jesse's chest. "First of all, Callum isn't part of the Harris pack. He's a lone alpha who was already living here when the previous Harris matriarch wanted to extend their territory. Callum refused to move, despite being up against an entire pack. Things could have gotten ugly, but instead of fighting a turf war over a little cottage, they came to an agreement. Callum would remain undisturbed, in exchange for monitoring and maintaining the wards around their territory border. I guess having enforcers guarding the land keeps the majority of nuisances away, so he tolerates the truce. Except like I said, he can't stand Joze, so I pass their messages back and forth to keep the peace. Gives me something to do."

I nod, distracted and disoriented. It takes me a moment to register that Jesse has gone quiet, at which point I also realize I've been scowling at the forest floor instead of walking. I was thoughtlessly following him, too riveted by our conversation to pay attention. When I scan the surroundings, I see a modest paved road cutting through the trees. "Where are you headed? Sorry, I was just trailing after you."

"That road leads to the pack house." Jesse tips his head to indicate the direction. "You can come along if you like. I'm sure Josie and Mom would like to say hi."

The thought about making small talk makes my skin crawl. Worse, I'm having trouble focusing on Jesse without my thoughts slipping away to ruminate on my mom's deception. Six months. I could have spent six months without this soul-sucking loneliness. With Jesse around, my desperation to escape might've been tempered. Not erased, but I could have had happy moments.

"I think I should just go home. I don't feel up for more company now," I admit.

"Okay." Jesse and I stare at each other, shifting awkwardly, until he asks, "Can I have your number?"

I exhale, relieved he didn't take offense. "Of course, Jess. We can make plans to hang out soon? Mom's house is on the other side of town, but like I said, I walk a lot."

We exchange numbers, then simultaneously look over our shoulders in the directions we're headed.

"I know you like to walk, but it smells like rain," Jesse says. "My car's just down there. I could give you a ride."

I smile, trying to make it as genuine as I can while feeling so untethered. "I'll be fine." I need time to think before I get home and see my mom.

"Okay." Jesse smiles and opens his arms tentatively.

I step forward, allowing Jesse to crush me in a warm embrace. We didn't hug like this before; maybe because I was still masquerading as a girl. Maybe we just didn't need it as much as we do now.

Pressed so closely, I revel in the way Jesse has grown. Still sturdy and unflappable, but now with a rock solid frame to back it up. I wonder what he feels while holding me. I haven't grown much. Haven't changed at all, other than getting taller and showing up in the mundane world with tits. Eyes closed, face buried in his shoulder, I focus on breathing him in and hoping he's doing the same with me.

Finally we part. The corners of Jesse's eyes crease, though his lips don't quite form a smile. He sets a hand on my head, skimming his thumb across my brow.

"It's good to see you again, Bennett. We'll be in touch."

I swallow hard. "Yeah. Thanks, Jess."

Then we turn to go our separate ways, Jesse toward the paved road and myself back into the tick-infested grasses. I force myself not to look back, but I hope he does, at least once.

Halfway into my trudge through the field, lightning splits the sky. I blink just in time to avoid taking a fat raindrop to the eye, but more follow, and within seconds I'm soaked. Maybe I should have taken Jesse up on that ride.

Conflicted emotions well up within me like the muddy ground beneath my feet. I trudge the last few paces until the field meets sidewalk.

A Fae's Two Alphas

There's no concrete in Faerie. It might sound counterintuitive, but that's why I don't leave the city often. Impersonal grey buildings, benches, and bridges are both my enemy and my escape; I hate them, but they create a harsh division between this realm and my true home. Walking to Callum's cottage, being surrounded by the field and the forest, reminded me of how long it's been since I smelled fresh earth.

Anger and hurt churns in my stomach, growing heavier with every step I take toward our street. Mom will be awake by now, which means I'll have to interact with her.

Resentment is overcome by a wave of yearning. I miss my dad. He always protected me from the uglier side of Faerie. Despite my mom's flaws, I felt protected by her, too, even when I didn't understand her reasoning. Now I have to face her knowing just how jealously she's kept me sheltered.

I stop on the sidewalk in front of our house, staring up the walkway until my teeth chatter from the cold rain. When I can't bear it any longer, I slink inside, chilled to the bone and dripping everywhere.

"That you, Benny?"

I inhale deeply, willing myself to be calm. Coming in swinging will not go well for me. "Yes, Mom, it's me." As I struggle out of my wet boots, she peeks around the corner of the hallway, a toothbrush in her mouth.

Naomi Chiston is an average looking white woman with brown hair and eyes, lacking distinctive features other than the bear tattoo that sprawls from the center of her chest down her shoulders. She watches me peel off my soaked shirt and socks, possibly waiting for me to say something.

I don't.

Finally, she disappears around the door jamb. I strip off the itchy, wet pants and leave everything in a sodden mass on the linoleum kitchen floor. Hair still dripping down my back, I pad into the bathroom.

Naomi silently hands me a towel. I scrub at my hair, glad the dye is so faded, because otherwise I'd be streaked with green right now. Setting the lightly-stained towel on the toilet seat, I set about trying to claw out of the chest binder that's stuck to me like an angry second skin.

"Need help?"

I freeze, regarding Naomi over my shoulder. Anger and hurt makes it hard not to scowl, not to demand outright, *Why didn't you tell me the Chens came to Marquette?* But her face is damp, expression vulnerable, and despite my anger, she looks nothing like a deceitful monster I can comfortably lash out at. She's just my mom.

"Yeah, thanks."

Naomi carefully helps pry the spandex binder over my shoulders and over my head. I sigh in relief as I massage feeling back into my chest, thanking her again when she hangs my binder on a hook in the shower.

"You're shivering, honey." She returns the towel to my hands.

I cover my chest, then disappear into my bedroom to finish drying off. I dress in a long t-shirt and boxers, then go into the kitchen to fry up eggs and tomatoes for our evening meal.

Cooking is usually my job, because Naomi frequently forgets to feed herself. Even as a child, when my dad was away it was either starve or learn how to prepare meals simple enough for a ten-year-old.

We eat in silence until Naomi asks, "Bennett, what's wrong?"

"Nothing's wrong."

Naomi gives me a skeptical look. "When I signed your

birth certificate, I made a vow to always notice when you're lying."

I barely repress the urge to roll my eyes. "Consider the vow broken, Mom. I'm too much of an enigma." I swipe a last bite of toast through the leftover egg yolk on my plate, shove it in my mouth, and rise to ferry the dish to the sink.

Naomi watches me with eyes of iron; I do my best not to crack under the scrutiny.

"You done?" I nod at her plate.

Naomi sighs and pushes it toward me. I wash that one too, ignoring the burn of her stare on the back of my neck.

I tense when she walks behind me and wait for her to speak. She only trails her fingers through the long hair at my nape, frizzing as it dries. "I'll help you freshen your dye tomorrow. Sound good?"

I offer her the most convincing smile I can manage, but I doubt it works. "That sounds good, yeah. Love you, Mama Bear."

With a pointed arch of her brow, Naomi kisses me on the cheek and trails off to her bedroom to get dressed.

I look out the kitchen window, watching the torrential rain shimmer against the near-dark sky. Waiting for my next appointment with Callum is going to make this a long week, but for tonight, I can sleep knowing I'm one step closer to returning home.

5

BUCKLE UP

"You didn't have to pick me up," I tell Jesse as he herds me into a nice-looking car. The outside is pristine, the inside clean.

Jesse gives me a good-natured smile. "I didn't want you walking through that field again. I keep telling Cal he needs to make a decent path. Guess it'd be too much work to actually accommodate his clients for once."

I snort. "It's a good test of how bad you want something. I almost turned around when I saw it." That's a lie, but I let the joke stand. I would have crawled through a field of broken glass if my magic was on the other side.

"Exactly." Jesse closes the door behind me and winds around to the driver's side. He hops in, then nudges me. "Seatbelt."

"Oh." I fumble with the buckle, struggling to fit it into the latch until Jesse holds it still for me. "Sorry," I say once it's secure. "I don't ride in cars much."

"I can't wait to see your calf muscles," Jesse says with a wide grin. "You must be buff as hell under those cottagecore pants."

The thought of Jesse looking at my legs warms my cheeks. "They're alright, I guess. It's not like I work out."

"Walking for miles every day is a workout."

Jesse pulls away from the front of the house. I glance back, paranoid Naomi sensed something amiss and woke up from her hibernation-like sleep to witness me sneaking out. I wouldn't have to tiptoe around if she'd be less suspicious and secretive, but that conversation won't go well no matter how right I am. Fortunately, she's nowhere in sight, and we make our quiet getaway in the direction of the Harris pack lands.

About five minutes into the drive, Jesse asks, "Do you want to get smoothies? There's this little place by the campus—"

"No!" When I see Jesse's alarmed expression, I scratch the back of my neck, sheepish. "Sorry. I actually used to work at that place. For two weeks."

A perplexed grin tilts Jesse's mouth. "What happened? A blender blow up in your face?"

"I couldn't handle it. I've got no idea how anything works anymore. I never went to high school, and the education I got in Faerie isn't useful here. While I remember mundane stuff from my childhood, I've forgotten so much. Mom made me get a GED so I could kinda-function, but a degree doesn't help you deal with customers, operate a register, or stop blenders from exploding." The memories send a shudder down my spine. "My phone is the only piece of technology I can operate reliably. Even my laptop confuses me sometimes."

"Gotcha. No smoothies, then."

We make scattered small talk for the rest of the drive. It's not exactly *awkward*, but it's been ten years of missed development. I want to ask about his interests and what he's been up to, but I don't have much to offer in return. Nothing I feel comfortable sharing yet.

The car passes under a gate with a sign identifying the land as Harris territory. Jesse waves at the guard stationed inside a small shelter. The area is warded, but I don't feel so much as a prickle of magic when we enter. The loss makes my chest clench. There are *humans* who can sense magic better than I can right now.

We drive past a huge building that looks more like a hotel than a house. Several pack members are milling around outside, and I slump in my seat so I don't draw their attention. From the pack house we continue through a network of cottages with fewer people outside, until we finally reach a stretch where the buildings thin and trees grow thick between them.

"Callum's place is coming up," Jesse says on the heels of my relieved exhale. "Are you okay?"

"Yeah, I'm just..." Not familiar with large groups of people and do my best to avoid them. "I don't want anyone to recognize me, in case word got back to my mom somehow."

"Right." Jesse pulls into a small notch of flat, stony ground beside a flowing stream and parks the car. "It's a much shorter walk from here, rather than that ridiculous field." He clicks the button to release my seatbelt, then winks.

I follow Jesse along the path we walked last week before awkwardly parting ways. Jesse strides up to the front of Callum's cottage and raps on the door.

Nervous, I hang behind. I'm not scared of what might happen, but rather what might not.

Callum is scowling when he opens the door. "What the fuck are *you* doing here?" The words are directed at Jesse.

Callum only glances at me before Jesse elbows him aside so he can enter.

"I gave Bennett a ride, since you're too much of an ass to make a decent path to your house."

"Kind of you." Callum follows Jesse, not bothering to invite me in properly. I trot behind them, listening as he continues to grumble. "Bennett doesn't need a babysitter. Go run around until he's done."

"Nah. I'm paying for this project, and it sounds interesting. Bennett doesn't mind me watching. Do you, Ben?" Jesse's smile looks dangerously close to baring teeth.

Pinned between the attention of two shifters, I start to understand why there are so many stories of people getting squirmy around alphas. I didn't feel any magic when we entered the Harris lands, but now the hair on my arms rises. I don't want to upset Callum, but I don't know how to say no to Jesse.

I focus very hard on taking off my shoes and lining them up on the mat beside the door. "I'm just the patient here," I say as neutrally as I can.

Callum and Jesse go back to not-quite-snarling at each other. I'm unsure if I should interrupt or wait for them to be done. Luckily, Callum notices my hesitation and composes himself.

"I'll be doing the examination over there." He gestures to a low cot set by the window, catching the late morning's rays. As I move toward it, I hear him mutter to Jesse, "Don't get in the way."

I lie down on the cot. Callum sits cross-legged on the floor beside me and inhales deeply. "The examination requires me to touch you. Is that alright?" When I nod, he hums in acknowledgement. "Signal if anything feels uncomfortable."

The first brush of Callum's callused fingertips against my arm makes me break out in goosebumps. It tingles, sending a thrill of warmth up and down my spine. He touches my joints—thumb, wrist, elbow, shoulder—before repeating the pattern on the other side. He taps pressure points on my neck and temples, feels around behind my ears, and finally strokes his knuckles across my forehead so tenderly it could be a caress rather than an examination.

I'm so overwhelmed by the contact, his strong and confident hands, that I nearly jump when he says, "Take off your shirt."

My hand flies up to fist in my shirt's lightweight material. The stretchy spandex of my binder slides beneath the touch. I can't bring myself to say a word, but Callum responds to my alarm with a furrowed brow.

"Cal," Jesse says from the chair he parked nearby. "He's—"

"It's fine," I force out. "Like going to the doctor, right Jess?" I sit up enough to slide the tee over my head, pretend-casual, and smile weakly when I toss it at Jesse. He catches it without a word. I lie back on the cot, hands folded lightly over my chest like it might stop them from noticing the stark contrast between the peachy fabric and my skin tone, tanned from all my time in the sun.

Callum proceeds like nothing about me is different from any other man. He sets his warm palm on my abdomen and applies slight pressure, circling in one direction, then the other, before moving to prod my hips, knees, and ankles. If he asks me to take off my pants next I might die, but he doesn't.

Finally, Callum sits back on his heels.

"What'd you find?" Jesse asks.

Callum shoots him a sour look, then addresses me. "I

can tell you're not fully human, but only because I know what to look for. There are no traces of magic, repressed or otherwise. If you had any innate magic, it's gone now."

Anguished fog fills my head until I'm unable to think. It leaves me dizzy, spinning, lost in words I can barely believe.

"What does that mean?" Jesse asks the question, but Callum holds my gaze when he responds.

"I have two theories. The first you've objected to, but it *is* possible that you absorb magic from your surroundings, and your father blocked that ability. That could be fixable, so we'll call it the best case scenario. Worst case scenario, your innate magic was excised, and your father is holding it somewhere. The easiest way to do anything about that would be creating a tether to your father's magic so I could compel him to release yours. However, creating a tether isn't easy, even for advanced magic users. Unless you're willing to risk asking him directly, I'd have to find another way to free it. If it's even still there."

"What do you mean by that?" I ask.

"Can't rule out it having been destroyed."

I sit bolt upright. "You can steal someone's magic and *destroy* it?"

Callum frowns at the hardwood between his feet, and he sucks his teeth before responding. "Doing so would require a complex combination of spells. I'd never condone such an action, but hypothetically, one could temporarily cut off a body's ability to absorb or generate magic, then siphon what was left until the existing reserves ran critically low. In that moment, a powerful enough spell could damage the core of one's life force enough to make regeneration unlikely."

My mind races. "I can't believe he'd do that. He wouldn't..." I trail off, because his actions have already proven I don't know him as well as I thought I did.

"Regardless of your father's integrity, this won't be easy. Even in the best case scenario, the results from my examination—specifically the *lack* of results—means you should prepare for the possibility that your magic is irretrievably lost."

"Please don't say that. Not yet." I grab for him with trembling hands, taking hold of his toned bicep. "I can't— I can't live like this." I try to steady my breathing but it comes out in quick, ragged gasps.

"Ben!" Jesse's voice is full of alarm.

"Sit with him." Callum extracts himself from my grasp. I hear him cross the room, but my attention is on Jesse, now crouched beside me.

"Bennett, are you okay?"

I manage to gasp out, "I'll be fine." Just a panic attack. Not that it feels in any way *fine* while it's happening.

Jesse runs his hand over my brow just like Callum did, except this time it's a real caress. I lean into his touch when he draws me halfway off the low cot so I can rest my head against his shoulder. His chest rumbles under my cheek, a hum so low it's almost a growl. The sound vibrates through me, wrapping around my bones and holding them tight, grounding me.

I draw a deep breath.

"It'll be okay," Jesse says, hugging me tighter while careful to avoid my bare midsection. "Cal's smart. He's been doing this for a long time. He'll figure it out, even if he's grumpy and trying not to get your hopes up. You just need to be patient and give him time to work."

I shudder, wishing he'd hold me even tighter; wishing I was bundled up in his lap rather than stuck with the edge of the cot digging into my butt cheek.

A Fae's Two Alphas

Callum appears with a steaming mug of tea. He kneels on the other side of the cot and holds it out. "Drink."

Jesse has to help me stabilize the mug so I don't spill, but I choke down the first few mouthfuls. The anxiety doesn't ease immediately, but whatever spell Callum infused the tea with has my chest relaxing and my breath slowing. When enough calm sets in, I reluctantly leave the shelter of Jesse's embrace. I settle on the cot by myself and swallow the remainder of the tea.

"Thank you," I say to Jesse, who smiles and squeezes my shoulder. Then I turn to Callum, flushed from embarrassment. Having a meltdown at the first sign of failure isn't a good look, and I don't want him to think poorly of me. "Thank you, too."

Callum meets my gaze for a second, then looks away. "Since I only have hypotheses to work with, I'll need to research options for theoretical magic. If you're okay with essentially being experimented on, then this project can commence."

"I'll do whatever's necessary." And I truly mean *whatever*.

"Alright. I'll begin my research and will be in touch when I have something prepared. Have a good day, Bennett." Callum's polite expression twists into a scowl when he looks at Jesse, but he says nothing, even when a knowing grin spreads Jesse's mouth.

Jesse tosses my abandoned shirt at me. I slip it over my head and stand up without wobbling. Part of me wishes I still felt unsteady, so one of them would touch me again. There's no excuse to linger, but I don't want to leave. It feels like giving up, even though we're just getting started on what will probably be a long, frustrating journey. I tell myself Callum will figure it out, because I can't bear the alternative.

Jesse and I take our leave. As we trudge silently toward his car, Jesse sends me worried looks, but I focus on clutching the small pouch of tea Callum gave me in case I "feel sick" again. When we reach the place I stopped last week, I halt.

"I can walk home." I'm not sure why I say it. It isn't that I want to be alone, or that I don't want to be alone with him, but another flicker of panic lights in my chest.

"No."

I scrunch my face at him. "No?"

"That's what I said. I'm driving you back." Like that solves the issue, Jesse cups the back of my head and ushers me forward, practically stepping on my heels until I have no choice but to move. I allow him to support me as we walk side-by-side. Before we reach the car, Jesse says, "Let's go sit by the creek."

There's no reason—or way, I suspect—to resist the suggestion, so I follow Jesse past the car, down a slight slope. I perch on one of several large rocks dotting the edge of the stream, and try to not look morose.

"I'm serious about trusting Callum," Jesse says after a moment. "He'll figure it out. And you—"

"Will be able to go back to my real home," I interrupt. "And never come back to this shitty fucking realm ever again."

Jesse falls silent for a bit too long, motionless by the edge of the creek. I open my mouth to ask if he's okay, but he abruptly yanks his shirt over his head, and I'm left speechless.

"Gonna go for a swim," he says, smile crooked.

I squint at the creek, which isn't anywhere near deep

enough for someone Jesse's size to swim in. It looks to be slightly above knee height on me, and would barely pass Jesse's calves. "If that's what you want to call it."

My skepticism takes a backseat when Jesse undoes the fastenings on his jeans and shoves them down. I stare at his well-muscled back, skin like polished oak brushed by waves of dark hair. His pants get caught when he tries to yank them over his shoes, leaving him hopping on one foot to remove one first, then the other.

I make a weak attempt at teasing. "You alright over there?"

Jesse manages to kick away his pants. "Just fine," he says without so much as a chuckle.

Despite feeling uncomfortably lecherous watching his thighs flex when he bends over, I can't look away until Jesse hooks his thumbs in the waistband of his black boxer-briefs. Before I can cover my eyes, Jesse blurs in and out of my vision. His surroundings warp as if they're caught within a mirage before snapping back into place. I don't fully register what's happened until a large brown and grey wolf splashes into the water.

6

DESIRE BY THE WATER

Jesse bounds into the creek, rolling under the surface to wet his fur. Upright once more, he sprints upstream, against the current, and disappears behind the leaves of an enormous, drooping willow.

I grow antsy waiting for him to come back into view. Eventually he reappears, picking his way over a tangled cluster of the willow's thick roots.

There's mud in his fur. He moves into the shallows, studded by a network of large river rocks, and rolls again, wiggling on his back until the mud is gone. Mostly.

Jesse leaves the creek, pausing on the loamy bank to shake moisture from his fur. Flecks of water hit my face and arms. It feels nice, especially when a breeze picks up, cooling the droplets against my skin.

Jesse tilts his head at me, tongue lolling from the side of his mouth. I don't know proper etiquette for interacting with a shifter's animal form, so I smile awkwardly.

"I don't suppose you can talk like that?" Jesse lets out a *woof* of lupine laughter, so like him it makes me smile. "I guess that's a no." I remain perched on my rock, wondering how to interact with him when he can't speak. It's not like I have experience reading wolf body language.

Finally he trots over, tongue still hanging out, and presses his wet head against my knee. I hesitate. Pictures did not prepare me for how truly massive wolves are—Jesse's head alone is the size of my torso. Curiosity draws my hand to his side, stroking lightly. When he leans into the touch, I work my fingers into the dense fur so I can rub behind his ear. From there I follow his spine, scratching firmly between his shoulders.

I don't expect the low, primal sound that rumbles through him. Jesse presses his wet head against my chest. Water seeps into my shirt, but I don't mind. I draw him closer so I can rest my cheek between his ears and wrap my arms around his thick neck.

After several minutes Jesse squirms out of my embrace. He licks my cheek messily, and barks in amusement when I sputter. Then he lopes back to the creek.

No longer content to merely watch, I remove my shoes and socks, then after a moment of consideration, my shirt. I cuff my pants over my knees, and wade into the water after Jesse, getting my bearings, then stop to breathe in the scent of nature. I've missed it more than I realized.

Jesse bumps the back of my knee with his head, urging me downstream. We explore together. I watch a crayfish snap in a pool of minnows and laugh when Jesse startles a nest of geese and is summarily honked at and chased for the offense.

When it's time to turn around, I'm reluctant. We reach the bank, and I trudge toward where I abandoned my clothes. I wipe my wet hands on my folded shirt before checking my phone, surprised to find it's been over an hour. I barely felt the time pass.

Then I see a text from my mom and every trace of my good mood dissolves.

"What's wrong?"

Startled, I turn to see Jesse in biped form, fully naked with only a rumpled shirt held over his crotch. I open my mouth to dismiss the concern, but his knowing look gives me pause. Even after a decade apart, Jesse still knows me.

"Just Mom. She wants to know where I am."

Jesse squints at the sky. "It's only a little past noon. Didn't you say she should be asleep?"

"She probably got up to use the bathroom and saw I was gone." It's weird, because I'm usually out of the house until closer to when she wakes up. We try to eat together in the evening before she goes to work. There's no way she knows I'm out with Jesse; if she did, she would have said so. Mama Bear isn't afraid of confrontation. "She can be clingy. It's probably fine, but I should get home to check on her just in case."

I turn so Jesse can put his pants on without me gawking and focus on shrugging back into my tank top. When I bend to grab my shoes, my foot, still wet, slips on the rocks. Before I have a chance to cry out, Jesse catches me under my shoulders. My back ends up pressed against his bare front; so close I can feel the contours of his powerful muscles. I have no idea how he made it to my side so quickly.

"Don't fall and break your head," he says, breath warm against my temple.

I huff. "I can't off myself *that* easily, jackass."

Jesse laughs, then makes sure I'm stable before letting go. He picks up my shoes, then hovers while I prop myself against a secure rock to put them on. I want to lean against him, but it feels different now that he's exposed. My gaze drops to his hand, the knob of his wrist, up his arms until our eyes meet. Jesse's wide chest expands with a deep inhale, black irises twitching as he searches my face. I swallow hard, holding still for his inspection until he disengages.

"I'm already hot again," Jesse mutters, scratching the back of his neck. His shirt is on the ground—he must have dropped it when he came to rescue me. Jesse snags it and pulls it over his head, then we walk back to the car.

On the way home, we sit mostly in silence. Unlike the awkwardness of the ride here, it feels comfortable. Sated. Jesse stops at a different place to get smoothies and buys me a giant marshmallow crispy rice treat, too. I grin the rest of the way to my neighborhood, before the unfortunate reality of the situation has me motioning for him to stop the car.

"Let me off here," I say, before he turns onto the side street.

"Why?"

I sigh. "Because if Mom sees me get out of someone's car, she's going to ask questions, and she's already in a suspicious mood." I don't want her to know I'm hanging out with Jesse until I'm ready for the conversation that will follow. Telling her it's a friend she doesn't know, or even a rideshare, would set off her over-protective paranoia.

Jesse purses his lips in clear displeasure. He pulls up to the curb and puts the car in park, then props his elbow against the headrest of my chair while I get unbuckled and collect my trash. "Don't worry about that, I'll take care of it." He removes the empty cup from my hand and tosses it into the back seat. "Bennett, I—"

"I enjoyed hanging out with you." I don't know what he was going to say, but if it's about Naomi, I don't want to hear it. "Thanks for giving me a ride. It helped to hold off the depressed doom-spiral for a while." I smile, but he doesn't return it.

"You know you're still great without magic, right?"

"That's not what this is about." I open the car door before he responds, hoping he gets the message. I don't want my unhappy mood to return. "Thanks again, Jess. Text me when you're home safe."

Jesse finally cracks a smile. "Shouldn't I be telling *you* that? I'll be fine. I'm tough." He flexes, chest and biceps tightening under his shirt.

I try to swallow, but my mouth is so dry my tongue sticks. Unable to speak, I wave goodbye and quickly slam the door closed, before turning on my heel and speed-walking away.

Hopefully it's an urban legend that shifters can smell desire.

7
LOOK IT UP

Naomi is sitting at the kitchen table, hunched over an untouched mug of coffee, when I enter the house. Her head snaps up as I open the door.

"Hey, Mama Bear," I say, kicking off my boots.

"Where were you?"

I bite the inside of my cheek to calm myself before replying. "Just walking. What's up? Did you have a bad dream?"

Naomi purses her lips. "No." She says nothing more, and I've long since learned not to push her to talk when she doesn't want to.

"You should get back to bed or you'll be exhausted at work." I stick her cold coffee mug in the fridge then nudge her with my hip, pushing until she flattens her palms on the table to resist.

"I'm not tired," Naomi grouses.

"You will be. Come on." Naomi leans on me as I lead her to the bedroom. I wait until she's crawled under the covers, then plop onto the bed next to her. "I'll stay until you fall asleep."

That appeases her. Not too much time passes before her breathing slows and she descends into restless sleep. I run my hand over her hair, hoping to ease whatever is plaguing her dreams. Eventually her fitful mumbles smooth into quiet snores. I could leave, but the emotional and physical exhaustion from earlier is getting to me. On top of the blankets, I lean against the headboard and close my eyes. It won't hurt to stay a bit longer.

When I blink next, it's two hours later and my phone has switched to power-save mode. Naomi doesn't stir when I slide off the bed and head for my bedroom. I plug in my phone, then shuffle down the hall to shower off the residue from splashing around in the creek.

Under the lukewarm spray, my thoughts spiral. Fear drips down my lips, insecurity pooling in my ears like disturbed tears. The air within the shower stall weighs heavy in my lungs, choking me until I'm desperate to escape.

I shove the sliding door aside, not caring when the spray follows me out of the suffocating stall. Then I throw the window open. After a few gasps of fresh air, I finally turn the shower off.

My hair is so faded no dye transfers to the towel when I dry myself. Naomi never helped re-dye it, which isn't surprising. It's not unusual for her to make empty promises.

I wrap the towel around my hips and enter my bedroom to get dressed. When I emerge, Naomi is awake, sitting groggily on the side of the bed.

"Told you so," I say as I pass her open door. She grunts.

I fetch her coffee from the fridge and stick it in the microwave. As the mug spins, a frown tugs my lips. When I first got the idea to hire Callum, I'd convinced myself it'd be a simple fix. Today has put into the complexity of this journey into perspective, and the magewolf warning me that we might fail hangs heavily over me. Frustration and helplessness simmer in my blood.

"Mama Bear?" I ask when Naomi staggers into the room. I set the hot mug in front of her, trying not to be impatient when she takes her time responding.

After swallowing a mouthful of scalding coffee, Naomi clears her throat. "Yes, Benny?"

I gnaw at the inside of my lip, realizing I didn't plan how to phrase the question. Naomi watches me so expectantly I blurt, "Could you call Dad for me? I miss him."

Naomi's eyes widen until I see a ring of white around her irises. "Why?"

"Why do I miss him?" I try to keep incredulity out of my voice.

Naomi swallows. It's fascinating watching her mind race, knowing she's searching for a way to argue. Can't tell me I'm wrong to miss my father, so she needs another excuse. I don't rush her, instead bracing myself for the bullshit.

My eyebrows nearly fly off my face when she says, "Okay."

"Really?"

"Was I supposed to say no?"

I don't dignify that with a response. "You'll call him then?"

A shifty look crosses her face—exactly what I was waiting for. "Well, I would. I will. I just need to find the rune circle first."

The first time my father ran to Faerie to get away from Naomi, he gave me a rune circle that could contact him beyond the veil. I attempted to use it a few times when he first sent me to the mundane, but he never answered. It's been ages since I saw it last.

I sink into the chair across from her. "You lost it?"

"I didn't lose it," Naomi says defensively. "I just... shoved it somewhere."

My jaw drops. "Mom, that's not something I can replace!"

"I'll find it. I'll look, Benny. I promise."

A desperate urge to demand answers nearly breaks me. Why didn't she tell me about the Chens? What triggered her waking up in the middle of the day to worry over where I am? What does she know?

I swallow the questions, leaving them to fester in my gut.

"Okay. Thanks Mom. I'm gonna go read." I barely avoid stomping down the hallway.

I try to read, but my eyes won't focus on the words. Instead I text Jesse. He chats amiably, asking if I had fun earlier, how I'm feeling, if Naomi is okay. I answer as honestly as possible and try to feel better. It almost works.

A few days pass, strung together only by my conversations with Jesse and one nightly text from Callum, always reading, '*Nothing yet. Will update tomorrow.*' Come Saturday night, when I hear the text tone for Callum's contact, I sigh in preemptive disappointment.

Then I actually look at the alert lighting the screen.

> Callum Truett: The Summer Solstice is tomorrow and fireflies are out. I've designed a ritual but it's time-sensitive.

My face goes slack with surprise. I rush to unlock the device and type a response with trembling fingers.

> Bennett Chiston: when should i come??

> Callum Truett: Now.

Naomi raises her eyebrows when I rush into the living room, squirming into my binder as I walk. "Going somewhere?"

"Yeah." I attempt to pull a T-shirt over my head while simultaneously shoving my feet into my boots.

"Where?"

"I don't have a curfew, Mama Bear," I respond tartly.

"Excuse me," she mutters. "I was just asking."

Just to keep her happy, I drop a kiss on her forehead. "The sky's really clear tonight, and I wanted to go look at the stars."

"You've developed a new interest in astronomy?" Naomi's tone is forced casual, but I can hear the suspicion underneath. I only shrug. "How long will you be out?"

"I'll text you." I blow her another kiss, then slam the door behind me and jog down the stairs.

I dislike being trapped around strangers, so rideshares are always a risky gamble. However, I'm so impatient that when I reach the 7-Eleven on the corner, I summon a driver to take me to the strip mall nearest the field. I walk quickly from there, only slowing when I pass Callum's spelled marker and the thick grasses bend beneath my boots.

8

FIREFLY MOON

Callum is already outside when I arrive. He's leaning over a worktable, digging in a large basket. It's past eight and the sun is dipping in the sky, painting the clouds orange and pink. The light warms Callum's silver hair and tanned complexion, creating an image so striking I slow to a halt several paces away. My lips part but I'm unsure what to say.

Callum looks up, eyes a vibrant cerulean against the riotous sunset. "You got here fast," he says in lieu of a greeting. "Sit here."

I plunk gracelessly onto the bench, still transfixed by the light playing over Callum's skin. It haloes the contours of his muscled physique, drawing my attention to the silver hair on his forearms and chest, exposed by the deep V of his collar. He doesn't acknowledge my interest, if he even notices past his laser focus on the materials he's lining up along the table. I watch his clawed hands, sure and precise, as he portions fresh and dry ingredients into a polished stone bowl, then grinds it into a chunky paste. He pours pale yellow oil into the bowl, swishes it around, then sets the bowl in my hands.

By now I know better than to ask questions, so I let Callum work without distraction. His process is fascinating. In my experience, magic was constant and involuntary, a reflex as subconscious as breathing. Witches, mages, wielders of tools and incantations—I had spared no time learning the intricacies of their crafts, because I hadn't needed them.

Now look at me.

As dusk darkens the sky, I notice winking spots of neon yellow. I can't help but ask, "What're the fireflies for?"

"They'll send the message through the veil." Callum removes the bowl from my hands. "Take off as much clothing as you're comfortable with."

My gaze drops to the ground, watching Callum's bare feet pad backward through stones and pine needles. Even his toes are clawed. Callum sits on his heels, gracing me with his full attention. With anyone else, I'd feel like prey, but Callum's unwavering stare is more protective than predatory.

I remove my shirt, shoes, and pants until I'm left barefoot in only trunks and my binder. "Is this okay?"

"I can work with it." Callum sets the bowl between his feet and dips his fingers inside, then begins to apply the mixture to my body. He starts with my wrists, then the hollows of my elbows, before moving to either side of my throat. From there, he circles his fingers behind my ears. Heat builds under my cheeks until I have to avert my gaze. I still can feel the puff of his breath against my jaw.

Next Callum hovers his hand over my sternum, blinking when he encounters the spandex of my binder. I watch him mentally recalibrate to avoid the fabric. He skips my chest entirely, proceeding to anoint the skin above my navel, followed by the dips of my narrow hips, then the back of my knees. I shiver when a drop of oil slips down my calf. Finally, when I start to think I might explode, Callum rubs the remainder of the mix onto the soles of my feet.

"Let that absorb into your skin."

I rest my heels on the ground, toes pointed upward, and wait. Callum disappears, leaving me sitting silently in a growing cloud of fireflies. A few land on me, one exploring my knee and another the tendons on the back of my hand.

Callum returns, his eyes tracing the glowing path from my knuckles into the fully dark sky. "Everything's ready. We'll be working over there, in the field."

I pause before standing. "What about the, uh, stuff?" I wiggle my toes to indicate my meaning. "Won't it rub off? And my feet will get all covered in pine needles. Could I put my shoes back on?"

"No," Callum says, nose wrinkling. "I'll carry you."

Stunned, I blink at him. Callum doesn't seem the type to be touchy outside of what's strictly necessary. My eyes flick briefly to his well-defined chest, which I'd been studying earlier, and my cheeks grow warm again. "Yeah, that would be fine."

Callum scoops me into his strong arms, holding me gingerly to avoid disturbing the drying herbs. He carries me to a woven blanket spread out at the edge of the grassy field.

I tense when he moves to set me upon it.

"What's wrong?" he asks, concern in his voice.

I curl against his chest, frowning at the tall shoots poking up on either side of the blanket. "I'm not going to get ticks if you put me in this grass, right? I'd rather not get ticks."

Callum huffs. "You will not get ticks. I'll examine you afterward if you're still worried."

A Fae's Two Alphas

With that reassurance, I allow him to lay me on the blanket. I wiggle, trying to get comfortable on my back.

"Try not to move too much," he murmurs.

Field grass and flowers rise around the edges of the blanket, reaching toward the moon. Without nearby city lights, the stars are brilliant alongside it, celestial promises sowing hope under my skin. A shiver runs down my spine. It's not because I'm cold, even though the night is cool and I'm nearly naked. Rather, it's anticipation, thrumming within my bones.

Callum produces an inkpot and a paintbrush with long bristles. When he dips the brush into the ink, it emerges a shimmery gold. When he begins to paint my skin, the touch is light enough to make me tremble. I jump at the brush running over the soft swell of my stomach.

"Shhh," Callum soothes me. "You're doing well, Bennett. Close your eyes. Focus on your breathing."

I don't want to close my eyes. I suck in slow, steady breaths, but keep my gaze on Callum. His face is lined with concentration, his neck and shoulders silhouetted by the moon at his back.

Maybe his touch lingers, claws tapping between lines of drying gold ink. Maybe I want his fingers to do more than graze my skin in points of simple contact. Maybe I'm delirious and drunk on starlight. It wouldn't be the first time.

When Callum's brush approaches my face I finally close my eyes, wincing as the cold ink takes shape on my forehead. The bristles trail down the side of my nose, creating a symbol over my cheek. Callum paints a different one on my other cheek, this one extending past the line of my jaw.

Then, stillness.

"I'm done."

I blink up at the sky. "What now?"

"We wait."

I make it ten minutes before I crack. "Can I get my phone or something?"

Callum makes an annoyed sound. "You can't sit with your thoughts for more than fifteen minutes?"

"How long am I supposed to sit with my thoughts?"

He takes a moment to respond. "It'll take a few hours."

"Hours?"

"At least. It could take all night for the ritual to work, so until it does, we have to sit here. The solstice means the sun will rise just after six, so you'll be waiting as short a time as possible."

"Can I sleep?"

"I'd prefer you to not."

I groan. "How am I supposed to stay awake just *lying* here?" I must have a point, because he doesn't argue.

"The phone's light will disturb the ritual," Callum says, leaving no room for argument. "But I will get something to occupy your mind." He moves quickly, silent as the night itself, and disappears into the darkness.

I breathe deeply.

Callum returns holding a single book with a cover of featureless dark leather. He sits on his heels, then thumbs gently through the pages. All of them are blank. He asks, "What would you like to read?"

"I have no idea," I admit. All I know right now is the weight of the moment, anticipation in the night. I'm not sure I'd be able to remember my own birthdate if Callum were to ask.

Callum shakes his head, before placing his palm against the cover. He murmurs under his breath, and a moment later the book comes to life. Silver strokes spill across the leather, rolling off the edge and dipping into the pages. The book throbs, as if it possesses its own heartbeat.

Wiggling up onto my elbows, I try to peer inside. Callum tilts the book so I'm able to inspect it without straining. I'm delighted to see the shimmer fade into neat black letters, the book's pages now populated with sprawling lines of text.

"What kind of spell is that?" I ask.

"This book is a conduit for spirits on the mundane side of the veil. I sent out a beacon requesting a storyteller, and the river spirit answered. Is that acceptable?"

I nod and extend my hand to take the book. Instead Callum settles beside me, legs crossed, and begins to read.

The tales of where water has flowed and who the spirit witnessed along the way are lovely, but I find myself distracted again and again by the relaxing cadence of Callum's voice. My eyelids grow heavy as the sound washes over me, raspy and low with rhythm in every syllable, tone pitching ever-so-slightly when emotions swell. I feel as if I'm in the river itself, feeling their adventures rather than hearing them.

Callum damn near fails his mission to keep me awake, until my attention sharpens with the beginning of a new story.

"There was a wolf, and he was running from something. He chased me far upstream, but that which he fought to escape did not give chase. I took him back to where he began, hoping he would find an answer. And he did, for the man on the bank met him at last, and together they sank into my waters."

A few lines later, I realize, with no small amount of embarrassment, that the river spirit is recounting my trip to the creek with Jesse. I'd assumed these were all old stories, but I suppose to an ancient river spirit, the passing of days is no different from centuries, with all visitors existing fluidly in the river's nebulous perception of time.

I struggle not to squirm as the river spirit recounts, in Callum's voice, the way I smiled, the way my pulse pounded in my palms and the soles of my feet. I wonder what Jesse was running from. I wonder what I was running *toward*.

"Are you alright?"

"What? Oh, I'm fine." I speak too quickly, and he raises a skeptical brow. "I'm definitely alright. Why would I not be?"

"You're breathing hard. Do you need water?"

Not necessarily, but it's as good an excuse as any. "I think so. Um, can I use the bathroom too?"

Callum glances at my feet, then sighs. "Try not to smudge the ink."

I tend to myself in the cottage bathroom, then clean my hands with a wet cloth, painstakingly avoiding the gold lines. When I tiptoe into the main area, Callum greets me with a glass bottle of cold water. He allows me a few mouthfuls before ushering me back to the blanket outside, setting the bottle within reach.

I successfully distracted Callum from the story about me and Jesse. I don't know if he would've realized the story was about us, or why I think he'd even care, but I didn't *want* him to figure it out. At the same time, I wonder if the river spirit might have told me more about Jesse's feelings, had I kept listening.

Though he doesn't pick up the book again, Callum spends the next hour entertaining me. I watch as he packs little cloth satchels; carves runes into small chunks of wood; and creates bundles with twigs and feathers, snakeskin and bones, and all manner of other ingredients I'd have never considered. He works silently, but notices whenever my interest piques. Then he tilts his project toward me so I can study the finer details. A few times he brings more water and bits of food I can pick at, but despite his efforts, I grow restless.

"Callum, if something... when whatever is supposed to work, um, starts working, what are we looking for?"

He eyes me. "The ritual is an attempt to call your magic from across the veil. The fireflies are meant to carry the message between realms, creating a beacon. Ideally, I'll locate the source where your magic is being kept." A sigh escapes him. "Or I won't. Bennett, it's still possible—"

"Don't say it," I plead. "We'll just wait to see what happens."

"Alright."

Inevitably, I begin to doze. Callum allows me to rest with my eyes closed, but when I descend too deep he nudges me back awake. The hazy night stretches onward, my earlier eagerness overtaken by discomfort.

"Isn't there something else we can do?" I move to rake my hands down my face, but Callum catches me by the wrists before I can smudge the sigils. "Sorry," I say, blushing.

"It's only a few hours until sunrise."

"I'm going crazy, Callum." The depth of my exhaustion hits me so hard I'm nearly overcome by the impulse to cry. My eyes prickle but I don't dare rub them.

Callum inhales sharply. Maybe shifters can't smell emotions, exactly, but I'm certain they can smell tears. "I'll make you some tea." He stands without waiting for a response, and stalks toward the cottage.

I breathe deeply, meditating on the hopeful feelings I'd felt at the beginning of the ritual. I can do this. It'll be worth it. I snuggle into the blanket and force myself to watch the stars for streaks of comets shooting across the wide canvas of sky.

The change happens so gradually that, at first, I don't notice.

Fireflies have been moving about the field, the males gliding through the air while females blink morse code in the grasses. None have shown interest in the ritual—not since Callum initially applied the oil and herb mixture.

Now, though, they're gathering. The first one lands on my collarbone, making me twitch. Another alights on my abdomen, running over my rib just under the hem of my binder. It tickles, but I fight back my desire to scratch. Yet another takes to my foot, and two land on my thumb. I glance down, awed to see them following the paths of gold ink Callum painted.

One by one they take off, replaced by others in a steady stream. Pinpricks of distortion cause the stars to ripple as the fireflies disappear across the veil.

9

THE FIRST NOTES OF BIRDSONG

BY THE TIME Callum returns with the tea, I'm practically vibrating with excitement. "Do you see?" I ask as he nears.

"I do." He lowers himself to his knees and extends a palm, eyelids fluttering as he searches for something I wish I could perceive. "Many have crossed the veil. They're searching for anywhere your essence might be hidden, or where it lingers. We will hear back by dawn."

Callum helps me sit up and holds the mug steady as I sip gingerly. I'm intimately aware of his calloused palm catching on the fabric of my binder. Once I've drained most of the tea, he lowers me onto the blanket. His claws graze my skin while he checks for any smudges in the ink. Exposed and vulnerable, I can't suppress a shiver.

"Are you cold?"

"No," I say. Then, quicker, "A bit, but it's fine." I hope he can't see my cheeks redden in the dark.

"Alright," Callum says without argument. That's when I notice his eyes drooping.

"Are *you* tired?"

He frowns at me. "No."

"What's your usual sleep schedule like?"

Callum's frown deepens. "Why?"

"Because I'm asking."

Callum regards me, mouth twisted like he's tasted something bitter. "I keep my schedule consistent."

"So staying up all night isn't great for you either," I conclude. Callum grunts. "Why don't you lie down?"

"No."

"Come on, just rest a bit. I won't let you fall asleep." I pat the blanket next to me and shimmy to the right to make room for him.

He sucks his teeth, but doesn't try to stop me. "Careful."

"I am being careful. Now lie down."

Maybe he's too tired to argue, but when Callum navigates his way onto the blanket, delight courses through me. He settles beside me on his back, holding himself stiffly with his hands folded over his chest. No part of him makes contact with me.

"How long have you lived here?"

Callum flicks his eyes toward mine, then away. "An odd question."

"It's a beautiful cottage," I continue, gesturing vaguely in its direction. "I was wondering if you built it yourself."

Chirping crickets and warbling tree frogs create a backdrop of sound. A firefly lands on my knee, its abdomen blinking slowly.

Callum inhales deeply through his nose. "I did," he says finally. "Twelve years ago."

"Have you always lived alone?"

"Yes."

"Do you get lonely?"

"That's a very personal question."

I tilt my head to smile at him. "So you do."

"It's not anyone's business." Deep furrows line his brow. "Should I ask you the same question?"

"You can. I definitely get lonely." I chew my lip, considering my next words. "I feel so different after missing eight years of mundane adult development. I know how to be fae, not human."

Callum is silent for a long time. "They call me feral."

"Who, the Harrises?"

He hums. "Everyone."

My brows knot as I contemplate this. "Do you feel like it's true? You being feral."

"I don't make an effort to present either way."

"Do you wish you had somewhere you fit in?" I prepare for him to sidestep the question, but take a chance on asking it anyway.

"The chance of that happening passed long ago," he says, tone neutral. "I feel peace here."

"You shouldn't say that."

"That my home is peaceful?"

"That you won't find somewhere you fit in. There are so many places in this world."

Callum scoffs. "Not many places where one can be a feral magewolf."

I nudge his elbow with the back of my knuckles and reprimand him gently: "Some people like feral magewolves."

Callum turns to look at me, blue eyes narrowed. At first I think he's annoyed, but no dismissal follows. "Not as many as those who might like a brightly colored half-fae."

One corner of my mouth quirks up. "You'd be surprised."

"So would you."

I become aware of his skin against the back of my hand,

and realize I've been stroking the back of his arm. I curl my fingers tightly into my palm and tuck my hand closely at my side. Maybe he didn't notice.

We descend into companionable silence. At least, I feel companionable. Can't say if Callum secretly wants to get the fuck away from me but has no choice but to stay. I can't think of anything else to say, and he doesn't volunteer anything, so we lie next to each other until I turn to ask about the time and see his eyes completely closed, silvery lashes resting against his cheeks.

"Callum?" He doesn't budge. I reach toward him, but stop just short of contact. Would he react poorly to being touched in his sleep? "Callum," I say a bit louder. "I said I wouldn't let you fall asleep."

I fail to rouse him with only my voice. While staring anxiously, not sure how to proceed, my awareness of Callum blooms into something I didn't expect.

He's incredibly handsome. I wasn't *un*aware of it before, but with Jesse around, I couldn't focus on Callum properly. Now, my gaze is drawn to him. From his brow, to his cheeks, to his lips, dark pink and surrounded by stubble. They part slightly as he breathes.

Sudden attraction, powerful and raw, leaves me frozen in place.

Callum is skillful and dedicated—especially for a man who insisted he couldn't help me. Despite his gruff demeanor, he's been kind. Attentive. I even coaxed a genuine conversation out of him. What he shared, though, makes my heart ache. Callum is as isolated as I am. If only there was a special place where he could feel comfortable and accepted.

The strong tea keeps me awake, leaving me with nothing

to do but watch Callum sleep. The fireflies slowly disappear, replaced by the first notes of birdsong.

Dawn.

No longer afraid of startling him, I sit up and shake Callum's shoulder. "You need to wake up," I say, splitting the peace of early morning. "Callum—"

The magewolf explodes into movement. He tears out of my grip and rolls onto all fours, teeth bared and eyes lit with a pale blue glow. My mouth hangs open as he flexes his claws into the dirt. Should I be scared?

Callum slowly comes back to himself, the glow in his eyes fading to normal blue. His eyebrows arch, and he rocks back onto his heels, resting his dirt-stained palms on his knees. "Bennett..."

"It's okay. I didn't want to scare you, but..."

He looks at the sky. "It's dawn."

"Yeah. It is." I bite my lip. "How soon will you know?"

Callum stands, expressionless, then reaches a hand out to help me up. "Go inside and wait for me," is all he says before busying himself collecting his accoutrements.

I obey, no longer walking gingerly to avoid disturbing the elements on my body. On the table is a bowl of water with wash cloths folded next to it. I sit and attempt to remove the ink from my hands, but it doesn't come off as easily as I'd expected. My brow furrows in irritation as I scrub harder, trying to peel away the gold residue.

Callum returns to find me jittery and flustered. "Bennett, what are you doing?"

Nose wrinkled, I scrub between my fingers. "Trying to get this off. With all your fussing I thought smearing it would be easier."

Callum rubs his thumb against one of the gold paths,

huffing when it doesn't budge. "Strange," he murmurs. Then, louder: "Stop rubbing, that won't work."

I drop the wipe. "How was it supposed to work? Did I do something wrong?"

"The ritual involved two separate spells. The first was simply a mix of elements to attract the fireflies. But the ink..." He traces another of the gold lines while his mouth shapes soundless words. Nothing happens.

"What about the ink?" I press.

"It was infused with my magic, giving the fireflies instructions on what to do after they connected with your energy. Without your magic there shouldn't have been any connection formed between you and—" His jaw snaps shut with an audible click. "It's hard to explain. Hold still."

My spine straightens when Callum goes to his knees in front of me. He takes my hand delicately. I don't know what to expect—more oil, an incantation?—but instead, Callum dips his head and exhales over the ink trails, warm breath tracing my tendons, tingling up my wrist. Bumps rise on my skin, and I shiver.

Callum follows the line of my forearm, blowing air as he goes, and the ink begins to flake, loosening from my skin to disperse in puffs of gold mist.

My gut clenches when I feel his breath on my throat, his lips only inches away; closer, when he cups his palm behind my head and draws me in to clear the marks from my face. I can't bear to look at him then, not with me nearly-naked and trembling and his mouth painfully near to mine. It's a relief—and also a regret—when he continues down my neck, skipping the expanse of my chest covered by the binder.

I think the worst part will be my thighs, with him resting between them, but it's not until he props my foot on his shoulder so he can treat my ankle that my stomach clenches and I have to cover my mouth to repress a whimper.

That catches his attention. His gaze lifts to spear through me.

"Just a tickle," I squeak, muffled beneath my hand. Callum hums in acknowledgement and the way his chest rumbles nearly undoes me. I keep it together for the last stretch of my other leg, and as soon as the last puff of gold mist dissipates I shoot to my feet.

"I'm gonna use the bathroom." Then I bolt without waiting for a response.

10

EMBARRASSMENT OVER SCRAMBLED EGGS

Before having an alpha shifter kneeling in front of me, I wouldn't have considered being turned on by someone's breath against my skin. It sounds annoying at best and gross at worst. And yet, when I slam the bathroom door behind me and strip my underwear, it's to find my thighs slick with arousal.

Flustered, I hop into the simple bathtub. I turn on the shower and move under the spray before it has a chance to warm up. The first burst of cold water makes me squawk.

Then I hear footsteps, quickly drawing nearer to the bathroom. Before I have a chance to say anything, the door opens and Callum's voice rings out: "Bennett? Are you alright?"

I clasp my hands over my tits, a shriek catching in my throat. The shower curtain is clear and hides nothing. Our eyes meet, and I wilt against the wall, flushing deeply under the still-cool water.

Despite the speed of his reflexes when I woke him in the field, it takes Callum several seconds before his face registers understanding of the situation. "You're—" He grimaces in the direction of the window, its frosted glass letting in just enough light to see by.

"The water was cold," I explain. "I'm sorry I didn't ask first."

"It's fine." Callum all but slams the door behind him, leaving me alone and trembling in the bathtub.

At least the water's warmed up.

"Fuck," I groan, knocking my head against the tile. *This* is not what I expected from this morning, but I resign myself to making the shower quick. I can't hide out in here forever.

I need to find out if the ritual worked.

Callum's explanation was curt, but convincing. Why shouldn't it work? If my father is holding my magic hostage in Faerie, Callum will be able to tell. Naomi will find the rune circle one way or another, and I'll be able to demand answers from them both. It's all laid out perfectly in my head. I'll tell my parents that I love them, make it clear they need to keep their weird controlling power-plays the fuck away from me, and go back to Faerie so I can feel normal again.

Perfect. All I need to do is face Callum.

Face him knowing he just saw me naked. And touched me, and shared his feelings with me. And fucking *breathed* on me, damn it. If my attraction to him hadn't made itself present while he was sleeping beside me, it'd be making itself known now.

My thoughts grow frantic when I exit the shower and realize that, in my haste, I neglected to observe the lack of available towels. Water drips from me onto the rug, as I scan the room like a caged animal. Maybe I can manifest something to dry myself with simply by being miserable enough.

No luck. I inhale deeply, toss a despairing look at the

simple hand towel, and tiptoe to the door. I open it a crack and call for Callum in a nervous, raspy voice. Chair legs scrape on the wood floor, and Callum appears in my peripheral.

I barely poke my nose out, trying to keep my body angled behind the door. "Um, there aren't any towels in here."

Callum's face twitches, then he waves a hand. I jump when something creaks on the other side of the bathroom door. I peek further out to watch Callum collect a towel from a narrow linen closet. Instead of handing it to me, he tosses it, leaving the towel to hover within my reach.

"Thanks," I say, snatching the towel out of the air before dragging into the bathroom with me.

Harrowed and exhausted from the long, sleepless night, I dry myself quickly. I shimmy into my underwear, but my chest aches from wearing my binder all night. I should give my ribcage a reprieve, so after a moment of hesitation I wrap the towel under my arms to hide my chest.

I creep from the bathroom, my binder balled up in my fist. Callum is in the kitchen, chopping something at the counter. I tiptoe over to lean my back against the refrigerator, relieved by the cool surface.

Callum sets down the knife and examines me. "Do you need anything else?"

I shake my head. "What happened with the ritual?"

The curious expression disappears, leaving Callum's face blank. "We'll talk over breakfast. Go sit."

That doesn't sound promising, but the promise of food is enough incentive for me to hold my tongue. A few extra minutes won't change what he's going to tell me. I notice my pants across the room, on the coffee table, along with my shirt. My phone is in the pocket, and I probably should check my notifications, but the thought of seeing a text from my mom keeps me in my seat, tracing the whorls of wood grain on the table's surface.

Callum sets a steaming plate in front of me. Breakfast is scrambled eggs cooked with peppers and onions, and a thick slice of toasted whole grain bread topped with cheese. He sets a fork and napkin beside the plate, and grunts in acknowledgment when I murmur a thanks. I twist the towel securely under my arms before tucking in. We eat quietly until about halfway through the meal.

Callum fetches a glass of water then stares at me until I drink. "Are you feeling better?"

"Yeah. I want to know what's up with the ritual."

I know it'll be bad news the moment he averts his gaze. I examine the knot between his brows, finding frustration and exhaustion that matches my own.

"It didn't work," Callum says.

My heart drops into my stomach.

"Rather, it *did* work. The message was spread, as intended, but I found nothing. No trace of your magic responded to the call."

I sink my teeth into my bottom lip, willing myself to be rational. This won't be Callum's sole attempt. He's only had two weeks. And yet.

My fork clatters to the table as I choke down a sob. I fold my hands over my face, ashamed but unable to hold back the surge of grief.

Callum stands abruptly. He steps toward me, but I don't want to be comforted. I stumble out of the chair and hurry toward the door, holding the towel with one hand while crying messily into the other.

The door opens before I reach it. I'd assume it was Callum's doing, except there's a large shoulder muscling the door wider, and thick arms supporting two full brown paper bags. Jesse's smiling face appears as he calls out, "Grocery delivery!"

Then he sees me and the bags go crashing to the floor.

11
ALWAYS TIME FOR A MISUNDERSTANDING

I JUMP BACK to avoid an avalanche of produce and wince when a carton of eggs is crushed underneath a bag of apples. An eggplant hits me in the ankle. I make a halfhearted attempt to retrieve it, but my fingers go slack when Jesse crosses the carnage in several long strides and clenches his fists in Callum's shirt.

"What the fuck did you do?"

I yelp. "Jesse!"

A low growl rises in Jesse's throat. Callum grabs his shoulders and shoves him back, but Jesse refuses to let go.

"Callum, you jackass, if you hurt him—"

I try again. "Jess, stop! It's ok, Callum was just—"

Before I can finish, Callum snarls and swipes at Jesse's throat. I clap my hand over my mouth to muffle a cry. I don't understand why Callum doesn't explain—or let me explain—that I'm not upset at him. Sure, ugly crying in nothing but a towel doesn't present the most reassuring image, but I was running away because I was disappointed, not because he hurt me.

All I need is for them to stop fighting long enough for

me to get a word in.

Instead, Jesse's eyes take on a bright orange glow, contrasting with Callum's pale blue. Jesse shoves Callum far enough that he slams into one of the kitchen chairs. Callum's clawed toes dig into the wooden floor, bringing him to a stop. His claws are longer than they were a second ago. Jesse's hands twitch, his own nails thickening as they lengthen into sharp points.

I want to run between them, but terror keeps me rooted in place. Then Callum lunges, and it's too late.

Jesse braces himself, his larger frame looming over Callum's crouched one, but when Callum rams into him, Jesse goes down. Blood blooms through Callum's shirt where Jesse's claws tear through his shoulder, but he shows no sign of slowing. Jesse lands hard on his back with Callum balanced on his chest, claws at his throat. In his other hand is a glowing ball of swirling white-orange energy. Jesse digs his claws into Callum's shoulder, but the other alpha doesn't flinch.

"Yield," Callum growls, his voice reverberating through the room. The sound resonates with unseen power, deep and rolling and commanding. I'm not the one under him yet I still feel the urge to lift my hands in surrender. The crackling orb in Callum's hand draws closer to Jesse's face, and he repeats, "*Yield.*"

Tension fills the spaces between their bodies, the stillness bloated with unknowns. I clutch the towel against my chest, afraid to even breathe.

Finally, the light fades from Jesse's eyes. He goes lax, his head dropping to the floor to expose his throat. Callum closes his fist and the ball of energy fizzles out.

I clear my dry throat, trying twice before I can speak. "Hey, guys. What the hell?" The tension strung between the alphas snaps as both turn to look at me. I smear my hand across my tear-stained cheeks and repeat, louder, "What the fuck was that? Are you fucking *kidding* me?"

Callum rolls off Jesse and backs away, posture defensive.

As soon as Callum is out of the way, Jesse jumps to his feet. He seizes my shoulders. "What did he do to you?"

"Nothing! He didn't do a damn thing, which you'd know if you hadn't gone apeshit on him the moment you walked in the fucking door."

Jesse's mouth hangs open, his voice catching in his throat. "He— But you—"

"I was crying because I've been up *all night* doing this *fucking ritual* and it *didn't work*. Callum was trying to comfort me." I ignore Callum's noise of protest. "I just wanted some fresh air."

Jesse turns to him for confirmation.

Callum has retreated into the kitchen, where he's posed rigidly like a threatened animal. His fangs are visible below his curled lip when he grumbles, "You heard him, pup."

When they don't say anything else, I prompt, "Jess, you could apologize."

The unexpected hurt in Jesse's eyes is piercing. Our gazes lock, but not for long. Faster than I can see without magic-enhanced senses, Jesse spins, crosses the threshold, and is gone.

I send Callum a pleading look. "You need to go after him." He doesn't speak, but his mulish scowl tells me more than his words could. I scowl right back. "Thanks for nothing," I say, then chase after Jesse.

It's too late. Jesse's shoes and clothes are scattered across the ground, and my best friend is nowhere in sight. Behind me, the door to the cottage slams shut.

Heaving a deep sigh, I collect the discarded items and

bring them to the outdoor table. My clothes, phone, and binder are all still inside. I abandon the towel in favor of tugging Jesse's very large, still-warm shirt over my head. It reaches halfway down my thighs, big enough for me to curl up in. I tuck my knees against my chest and wrap my arms around them.

Aside from being shaken, I'm physically fine. The aching tension in my stomach is from stress. For a moment I'd thought being upfront would neutralize the situation. Instead, I made it worse, but I'm not sure how or why. The fight wouldn't have happened if Jesse had asked what was going on before attacking, but Callum could have helped me explain rather than responding in kind. Chronologically, Jesse made the first mistake, but—

An uncomfortable thought rears its head.

Callum was defensive even though it wasn't his fault, and from a different perspective, the hurt in Jesse's eyes might have been betrayal. I realize that both of them expected me to take Jesse's side.

Of course I've known Jesse longer, and even a decade of separation and change hasn't erased our bond, but I'm trying to be fair. I care about Callum, too. Yes, he's prickly and stoic, but it's been a long time since anyone has taken care of me. I value his wellbeing as much as Jesse's. Supporting one doesn't mean I'm abandoning the other.

Unfortunately, I didn't make that very clear.

I drag myself upright and trudge over to the front door, wincing as pine needles prick my feet. When Callum doesn't answer my weak knock, I call out, "Callum? Please let me help you clean up." I test the knob, but it's locked. I raise my voice and try again. "My clothes are in there." Still nothing.

Groaning, I take my ass back to the table and ball up to wait until someone comes for me.

12

POORLY PLACED CONFESSIONS

I DOZE until a rustle awakens me. When I open my eyes I see a large brown wolf trotting toward me through the trees.

I glance at Jesse's phone. It's been about forty-five minutes, which is longer than I'd have expected Callum to leave me outside with none of my belongings. I uncurl and stretch my arms, then stand to work some feeling back into my stiff legs. Once I feel confident enough to take a few steps, I meet Jesse by the edge of the clearing. He looks smaller than he did the day by the creek, with his head down and his tail between his legs.

"It's okay, Jess," I say, ruffling the thick fur between his ears. "Your pants are on the table."

With that, I turn away and make myself very interested in the dandelions growing at the edge of the field so he has privacy to dress. Temptation to look over my shoulder prods at me, but I resist. My interest in the adult physique of my childhood best friend is not appropriate, especially right now. When I allow myself to look, I see Jesse seated on the bench with his head in one hand, the other draped over his knee. He doesn't look at me, even when I gingerly sit next to him. There isn't much space between his spread thighs and the edge of the bench, so our arms press together.

After a moment, Jesse says, "You were right. I should have apologized."

"Callum will get over it." Jesse scoffs. I jostle him reproachfully, but he hardly budges. "I'm serious."

"You don't know him."

"Do you?" I tilt my head, frowning up at him.

Jesse levels me with his own frown. "No, not really. I mean, he tolerates me, but that's because it's the easiest way to keep peace with Josie."

"I find that hard to believe. He doesn't strike me as the type to put up with something he genuinely doesn't like for the sake of convenience. Besides," I add when Jesse says nothing. "Every time I've been here, you guys do nothing but banter." *It's practically foreplay*, I don't say.

"Attacking him is a lot worse than 'bantering.'" His fingers hook to form sarcastic air quotes.

"I mean, real wolves snap at each other all the time, right? And you guys are both dominant or whatever."

Jesse makes an exasperated sound. "You don't— Look, shifter politics are way more complex than a regular wolf pack, because *we* aren't animals. If Callum and I were in the same pack, I could get kicked out, or if not that, face serious consequences. Even though Callum doesn't have a pack, he's older than me, and stronger. Hierarchies in family packs aren't established by fighting for dominance—you figured that out on your own. But we aren't a family pack. Josie mated in to become alpha of the Harris pack. Callum is a lone alpha by choice. And I…" He shakes his head instead of continuing.

I run my fingers along Jesse's arm, doing my best to understand. "You were trying to defend me, and Callum didn't have to escalate when I was about to explain the situation. I'm sure he'll see that once he calms down."

"Maybe."

Cautiously, I rest my hand on his back. Jesse doesn't pull away; he exhales and slumps further over his knees. I circle my palm over his skin, waiting for him to speak.

"I don't get along with the Harris pack," Jesse says in a tone that carries the gravity of a humiliating confession.

"But you're so..." Genuine. Likable. A joy to be around. I don't know how to say any of that, so I finish with, "Personable."

He snorts a laugh. "Doesn't matter. These people are majorly stuck up. I was only allowed to join the pack because Josie wouldn't agree otherwise. Mom prefers to keep to herself, so she manages fine, and Josie doesn't have to care because it's *her* pack now. She and Andrew aren't in love, but he'd come down hard on anyone who challenged her."

"You, though," I say quietly.

A halfhearted, bitter smile touches Jesse's lips. "Me, though. I can't stand it. And the feeling is mutual."

"I'm sorry."

He shrugs. "Nothing I can do about it. They're mean, Ben. Like, 'making your mom look nice' kinda mean."

"Wow." I purse my lips, trying to imagine a situation in which my mom could be considered *nice*. I love her, and I know she loves me, but that doesn't change the fact that Naomi is controlling, paranoid, and stubborn.

"They argue with each other just to argue," Jesse continues. "They constantly neg each other, and anyone else in blast range. Their whole mode of existence is bullying people and making it seem like a joke. Can't call them on their shit, either, because they're just teasing, and you're clearly overreacting.

The adults raise the kids like that, so no one learns to be better. They think I'm soft. I think they're jackasses."

"They sound like it."

"And they act like I'm useless! The elders suggested I go to the university for something more practical than Communications—which I already have a degree in—and they want me to live on campus instead of in the pack house with Mom and Josie. That didn't go over well, but it's not hard to tell they see me as an inconvenience."

My nose scrunches. "Fuckers." I hush in case Jesse wants to continue ranting, but he just runs his hands through his long hair. I cast about for a way to fill the gap. "I don't think Callum is like that."

"He isn't."

"So why are you scared?"

Jesse shoots me a withering look through the drooping strands of his hair. "I didn't just attack him—I *insulted* him on his own territory. I'm lucky he stopped fighting back when he did, instead of kicking my ass all the way to the pack house. He'd be within his rights to ban me from coming on his land again, and Josie would have to respect that."

Culturally, I'm out of my depth, but I want to give Callum the benefit of the doubt. After hearing what Jesse's been dealing with the past six months, I can't handle the thought of Callum cutting him off because of me. "He'll get over it," I say, trying to sound confident.

It's not that I know Callum after barely two weeks and one sincere conversation, but I feel as if I understand him. Callum is straightforward and focused, and witnessing that focus has been fascinating. Growly and gruff—*feral*—he resists camaraderie, but every time I needed him last night, he was there. I don't believe he'd put up with Jesse's presence without there being some thread of attachment.

"I don't think he dislikes you."

"Benny, you barely know him."

I sigh, giving up for now, but resolving to bring it up later. "Regardless of what Callum does or doesn't do, you know *I'm* here for you, right?"

At last, a genuine smile spreads across Jesse's face. "I do know that, yeah." He rests a heavy hand on my head. "I can't describe how glad I am to have you back. Missing you... I mean, it was ten years. It hurt less over time, but I never stopped hoping we'd get back in touch one day. I didn't think it'd actually happen, because your mom left Wisconsin right after you disappeared."

I scrub my wrist over my eyes, fighting an unreasonable desire to cry again. My nose itches with the effort of holding back tears. "I'm sorry I left you for that long, Jess. It wasn't that I didn't want to see you, but I loved Faerie so much I couldn't stand to leave. I asked Mom to tell you where I went, but..." Swallowing hard, I push thoughts of Naomi from my mind. "I missed you too, but time passes differently across the veil. I should've thought about how it'd feel for you on the other side."

Unable to hold back, I tilt my forehead against Jesse's strong jaw and lean into him. Half a second later he has me in a full embrace, ducking to rub his cheek in my hair. His lips are so close to my brow I can feel each exhale. A shiver races down my spine.

It's not until I've wrapped my arms around his ribcage that my brain fully processes our position. I'm pressed tight against Jesse's very, very bare chest, unable to move other than squirming against his smooth skin. Heat rises in my face as my awareness expands to his muscular arms and defined pectorals.

Then Jesse draws back just enough to cup my jaw in both his hands, long fingers curling behind my ears. "Bennett, this is a really bad time, but…"

I blink in disbelief, unsure of how we landed in this moment.

"Last time we were together, at the creek, I… I decided I'd tell you this next time we saw each other. I wasn't expecting it to be so dramatic, but I'll lose my nerve entirely if I don't say it now." Before I can get a word in, Jesse hurries on: "I've been in love with you since we were kids. I actually wanted to take you out or something before telling you, but… Shit. I'm sorry. This wasn't a good time to make a confession."

I stare up at him, eyes raking over his face like this might be an exhausted hallucination. Jesse licks his lips nervously.

A sudden grin nearly splits my face. This is *real*.

"You're ridiculous," I say, then lean forward to catch his lips with my own.

The kiss is brief, but meaningful. I've been running on magic tea and dwindling adrenaline, but when Jesse leans into the contact, an unbearable giddiness floods my senses. I don't draw back when I murmur, "Thank you for telling me."

Our lips graze once more, but the cottage door slamming open startles us. We tear apart, Jesse jumping to his feet while I remain splayed on the bench, clutching the edge of the table to brace myself.

Callum storms out of the cottage, eyes bright and teeth bared. "You," he says, jabbing his finger savagely toward Jesse, "get the fuck off my property. And you—" I shrink under the full force of his anger. Callum throws a bag at the ground before me. I jerk my feet onto the bench, before realizing the bag is stuffed with my belongings. "Leave. Both of you. Don't come back."

"But what about—"

"*Leave!*"

I barely have enough time to grab the bag before Jesse snatches my arm and drags me toward the road where he'd parked his car. I rush to keep up, hissing at the pine needles in my bare feet. My heavy boots inside the bag hit my thigh repeatedly, and when we reach the car I've the start of a nasty bruise. Jesse corrals me into the passenger seat, buckling my seatbelt before he slams the door and crosses over to the driver's side.

"Jess, is he going to be okay?" is the first thing out of my mouth when he opens his door.

It stops him in his tracks, and after I realize what I've said, it stops me too. I work my jaw, trying to figure out why my concern has nothing to do with Jesse or myself.

"I don't think that's what you should be worrying about right now, Ben," Jesse says quietly. He settles in his seat, brow furrowed as he turns on the car. He reverses out of the gravel pathway and onto the paved road, pointed toward the Harris pack house.

"He wouldn't hurt us." Even as I'm saying it, my mind calls up the image of Callum pinning Jesse to the wood. His expression was grim, full of more resignation than rage. I don't believe Callum would have gone through with inflicting any lethal wounds, even if Jesse hadn't yielded.

Before we go too far, Jesse briefly stops so we can resolve our respective states of undress. Jesse lets me keep his shirt, instead grabbing a spare from the back seat. I shimmy into my pants, still ruminating on the reason for our hurried departure.

"He doesn't really mean 'don't come back *ever*,' right?" I ask as Jesse drives through the main exit from the Harris pack lands.

"I don't know, Ben. I've been trying to explain to you how serious this is, but... I just don't know."

Neither of us speak during the rest of the drive to my house.

Though I'm quiet and still, I can't stop worrying about Callum. How must he have felt, being attacked in his own home? He was accused of hurting a person he cared— That is, hurting a *client* he had spent the night caring for.

I try to ignore the mental hiccup, but I can't. I want to believe Callum found something soothing in my company. Why else would he share his feelings with me, and allow himself to fall asleep at my side? In the tender hours of the night, I'd swear a bond had began to form between us.

The possibility that I already destroyed it causes pain to explode in my chest.

Jesse pulls to the curb in front of my house. I should have had him drop me off around the block like before, but even the length of the driveway seems an exhausting trek. If Naomi sees us, so be it. I unbuckle my seatbelt before Jesse can do it for me, and open the car door.

Then I hesitate. "You'll check on him, right? I don't think he meant it. That we shouldn't come back ever again."

Jesse flexes his fingers on the steering wheel. "You're the only person I care about right now, Bennett."

Message received. "Okay," I huff. After a moment of contemplation I lean over the center console and press a light kiss to Jesse's cheek. "I'll text you. Right now I have to go fall unconscious for the rest of the week."

He curls a lock of my hair around his finger, then

releases it. "Alright. I hope you don't get in trouble with your mom."

"She might not even be home yet."

One more breathless second passes without me exiting the car, then we move at the same time. Our mouths crash together in a frantic kiss.

I draw back before it goes too far, my whole face flushed and heart thumping messily in my chest. "Later, Jess."

It's hard to break eye contact when I step out of the car, but I force myself. With one more fleeting smile, I close the car door behind me and stagger up the front walk, the bag filled with my belongings hanging loosely from my tired fingers.

13

PROBLEM-SOLVING IS AN ART

ONE AND A HALF WEEKS LATER, after days punctuated by shy, intermittent texting, Jesse officially asks me out. It's the opening night of a local art show, he informs me over our video call. I blush hot, grin like a fool, and agree. Of course I agree. I've been wanting this since middle school, whether I could put it into words or not.

I wait until Naomi leaves for work before getting dressed in a pair of cutoff denim shorts and a slouchy shirt just shy of see-through. The lines of my binder are visible underneath the sheer fabric. In Faerie my transness was a nonissue; I assumed the features I felt comfortable with and wore what I wanted. Here, where visibility matters and outing yourself constantly wars with the sour taste of being misgendered, being openly trans is a hard choice.

As I fasten a braided choker in trans pride colors around my neck, I'm surprised by how attractive I feel. Even better, for this outing I don't have to wear long pants and boots to avoid catching bugs.

The weight that settles on my shoulders with that thought is, by now, achingly familiar. I haven't crossed the field leading to Callum's cottage since he sent us away. His nightly texts haven't reappeared; our message history is a graveyard of apologies, all unanswered. Yesterday I resorted to pleading in a long voicemail, after which I promised Callum—and myself—it would be my last attempt at communication, though he was welcome to reach out at any time.

Twenty-four hours later, I've given up hope.

I'm not sure what hurts worse: losing the already-fragile thread of getting my magic back, or the pang in my chest when I realize I'll never see him again.

I don't think Callum was solely angry at Jesse and I for defiling his workbench. He was angry, yeah, but it probably had more to do with how I ran after Jesse, leaving Callum bleeding alone in his cottage. I've turned the memory over countless times, obsessing over what I could have done differently. Not kissed Jesse in his front yard, for certain. Even giddy, wired, and sleep-deprived, I should have shown restraint.

There's something more than surface-level bickering between Callum and Jesse—I'm certain of it. Yet here I am, fucking it up. Not only did I ruin my chance at fostering a deeper connection with Callum, but I drove a wedge between him and Jesse. Whatever genuine feelings they'd been building are now gone, and it was my fault.

I sit at the kitchen table and shove my feet into a pair of rainbow chucks, then tug half-heartedly on the laces. My good mood is starting to to dissolve, but a text notification startles me out of my brooding. I snatch up the phone, still deluding myself into thinking Callum will text back. It's not him, of course, but what I see on the screen warms my heart.

JEM ZERO

> Jesse Chen: I've reached the rendezvous point where's my accomplice

> Bennett Chiston: letting my brain get the best of me as always. be there in a sec

My mouth settles into a smile as I send three different heart emojis. I shake my head clear, finish tying my left shoe, and grab my wallet on my way out the door. I jog toward the 7-Eleven, but before I reach the end of the block, Jesse's car turns the corner. He rolls up to the sidewalk and lowers the window.

I peer inside. "You're not where you're supposed to be."

"I got impatient." Jesse grins. "Get in the car."

I obey, though I bat his hand away when he tries to buckle me in. "I can do it myself."

With an affectionate roll of his eyes, Jesse leaves me to operate the latch on my own. I stick my tongue out at him.

He laughs and shifts the car into drive. "You're feisty today."

"All for you, Jess."

We joke all the way to the gallery. While we're waiting to pay admittance, Jesse whispers a joke about the snobby people in the queue, and I laugh way too loud, drawing dirty looks. After that, I elbow him in the side and hiss that we should focus on the art.

The exhibit is a collection of landscapes in a wide variety of media. There are traditional oil paintings, but also double-and-triple exposure photo collages, and found object assemblages. There's a map of the US made entirely from license plates, its many intricate layers taking up half of one large white wall.

For a good twenty minutes, Jesse and I browse, chatting about his Communications degree and his college friend whose work is in the show. He teases me while I marvel at the detail in a sculpture made entirely of wire and iron shavings. I know better than to touch art, but I can't resist hovering my fingers a few inches away from one of the peaks, seeking that tangy sensation of my fae half responding to the metal.

Nothing.

I try not to let it get to me, but despite Jesse's arm, big and warm and suddenly around my shoulders, my brain returns to its earlier state of morose pensiveness. It comes to a head when I stop in front of a painting. Thick acrylic waves protrude from the canvas, the riotous colors mixed with grasses and stones and other gatherings from nature. Though the work is beautiful, what halts me is the small ivy-covered stone cottage overlooking a distant lake. The landscape looks nothing like Callum's home, but even the smallest reminder makes my stomach ache.

Jesse's eyes follow my fingers as they trace the outline of the cottage in the air. "Has he responded to any of your messages?" he asks, correctly guessing my thoughts.

I shake my head. "Yours?"

"No. I even banged on his door."

I heave a sigh, then turn my face into Jesse's chest. His arms come up around me, but I still feel cold and incomplete. "We hurt him." Because that's the conclusion I've drawn after all my ruminating. Callum was *hurt* by how little care we showed him. Of course he wouldn't be interested in accepting any apologies.

Jesse sucks in a sharp breath, then exhales, ruffling my short bangs. "You mean *I* did."

"No, both of us." Before Jesse can argue, I follow with, "Do you think he'll ever speak to either of us again?"

Regret radiates off Jesse. We twine our fingers together,

neither of us moving until the couple to our right shifts impatiently. Embarrassed, I tug Jesse out toward the next piece.

"There has to be something we can do," I say. "He can't ignore us indefinitely."

"Pretty sure he can, Ben."

I frown at him. "I bet we could wear him down. He has to leave his cottage eventually."

"What're you gonna do, camp in the woods until he comes out?"

"Yes," I say in a deliberately childish voice that draws a soft chuckle from Jesse. The mood lightens a bit, but wheels are still turning in my head. "You could get Josie to request a meeting. That'd give you an excuse to bother him."

"Define 'trouble.' I can't make him do anything he doesn't want to, Benny. Callum might be agreeable enough when the council needs him, but if he doesn't want to interact with me he'll just refuse and Josie will have to do her own damn communicating."

"Which leaves us…"

"With no guarantees."

Sighing, I take a glum turn around the final length of the exhibit. "I'm done," I inform him, despite having barely looked at the remaining artworks.

Jesse leads me to the exit and we walk out, greeted by a wall of muggy air.

"Heat never felt this awful in Faerie," I complain. I wait for Jesse's responding quip, but he says nothing. "Jess?"

"There has to be a way to get him to answer us."

I don't resist revisiting our earlier brainstorming. "What if we went together?"

Jesse's gaze snaps to me. "Together? You don't think that

would piss him off more?" He takes my elbow, stopping me from taking a wrong turn while trying to find his car.

"No guarantees, like you said. But there might be a better chance if we're both trying to get his attention. We could be extra annoying."

He snorts. "Sounds risky."

"I feel like any attempt to get close to Callum is risky."

The conversation ends there, overtaken by the sounds of evening bustle. We reach the car and Jesse doesn't attempt helping with my seatbelt. Before he can turn the key in the ignition, I reach across the console and take his hand. His fingers curl around mine, squeezing.

I open my mouth, but nothing comes out.

Jesse saves me, asking, "Tomorrow, then?"

Sunday is Naomi's day off, so I regretfully shake my head. "Mom will be around. What about Monday afternoon?"

We spend the rest of the drive discussing our plan to entice—or annoy—Callum into opening the door. It feels like being in middle school again. Defending ourselves from bullies, in the classroom or on the playground, required strategic planning. This time *we're* the troublemakers, even if our intention is to help Callum rather than harming him again.

By the time Jesse reaches the 7-Eleven, I've convinced myself we have a solid plan of attack.

I move to exit the car, but stop with my hand resting on the handle. What does it say about Jesse and I that we spent nearly our entire date focusing on Callum? "We should do this again," I say, praying the air will have cleared by then.

"I hoped you'd say that," he says. He ducks his head toward me, then hesitates.

I want it too, so I lean forward, eroding the space

between us until our mouths meet. Our lips move slowly, carefully, with none of the first day's giddy impulsiveness. We totter together, our lives having intersected once more, creating a new path, rough and uncharted. All I have to do is follow it.

I move away first, regretful but in no shape to take things any further. "Text me when you get home safe?"

"You first," Jesse says, dipping in to give me one final kiss. "See you Monday."

I watch him drive off into the night. A glance at my phone's clock tells me Naomi should have already left for work, so there's no point in hurrying. Instead I follow the trail of jumbled thoughts across the street, hoping a long walk will help me untangle the threads.

14

AN AFTERNOON EXPOSITION

THE PICNIC BASKET IS HEAVY, so as we make our way along the path to Callum's cottage, I allow Jesse to nab it from me. He lifts it easily in one hand and offers me a weak smile I figure is meant to be encouraging. I attempt a more genuine smile in response, but no amount of pumping each other up will take away the nerves.

With Jesse close at my heels, I march up to the front door of Callum's cottage and lift my hand to knock. Before my knuckles can rap the wood, I falter. How hard should I knock? Should I start firmly so he has no way to deny hearing it, or start give him a chance to respond to a less insistent summons?

"Ben?" Jesse sounds confused. I throw him a helpless look over my shoulder. Jesse snorts, pats my shoulder, then reaches above my head to knock loudly.

I listen for Callum, but he moves so quietly there's no chance I'd hear him. Jesse can, though. He cocks his head, but I don't read anything positive in his expression.

I get over myself enough to bang my knuckles against

the door until it hurts, calling out: "Callum! You can't hide from us forever."

"Technically there's nothing stopping him," Jesse whispers in my ear.

I shush him. "I will stand here all week if that's what it fucking takes." Then I raise my voice again. "Please at least let us apologize? I know we hurt your feelings but I just wanted to see if you were—" The oak door swings open, startling me so badly I choke on the rest of my sentence.

Surprised, Jesse takes a step back, but I hold my ground. Gazing up at Callum's sturdy figure, I offer a smile. It probably looks more like a grimace, but I do my best.

Callum doesn't look particularly impressed. "What."

"We wanted to talk to you," I say. "I was worried, and so was Jesse, so we—"

Callum's gaze swings from me to Jesse, and I can tell the moment he registers the basket in Jesse's hand. His brow furrows. "You brought a picnic?"

"Yeah. I thought—"

"No."

Face scrunching, I step closer and reach toward him. My fingers stop just shy of touching his chest. "Won't you talk to us? I know last time we saw each other ended really badly, but we wanted to make it up to you. I'm sorry for..." I trail off, intimidated by his silence.

Callum studies me for an uncomfortable number of seconds. He spares Jesse a fleeting glance, then addresses me: "Your concerns are noted. Have a good day."

I lunge to catch the door, but Callum closes it so quickly I accomplish nothing but bumping my face against the wood. I reel back, rubbing at my stinging nose.

"That went about as well as I expected," Jesse says.

"I'm not done yet," I announce, loud enough for Callum

to hear me. He wouldn't have answered the door if there wasn't something compelling him in spite of his anger. "We're going to eat, and Callum is *welcome to join us* at any time." I pitch my voice so high Jesse cringes, but he doesn't argue.

I lead him to a patch of vines and clover just outside the sprawling vegetable garden. We spread a large blanket over the soft foliage, then pull out the food I spent all morning preparing. I also bought a handful of sandwiches from the corner store after determining I didn't have enough to feed two alpha shifters.

Jesse sprawls on his side, watching with a half-smile as I fuss with his plate. The smile turns perplexed when I open a container stuffed with a pale, hideous concoction.

"What's that?"

"This is a weird, absurdly sugary fruit salad," I explain. "It's got whipped cream, marshmallows, and a bunch of that fruit cocktail mix they made us eat during school lunch. The internet had the audacity to name it 'ambrosia.'"

"So you decided to make it."

"You bet I did. There's also potato salad." I spoon fingerling potatoes onto Jesse's plate, making sure they don't touch the ambrosia.

After I hand Jesse his full plate and fix my own, we try a few times to make idle conversation. The food is good, but knowing this isn't *just* a picnic weighs heavily on the atmosphere. I pick at the stuff I made, avoiding the processed ham and cheese sandwiches I bought from the corner store. I think they're gross, but I got them because they used to be Jesse's favorite.

"Who were you seated next to after I left?" I ask abruptly.

Jesse blinks. "Seated next to?"

"Yeah, in school. We met because..."

"Because Chiston and Chen were next to each other in alphabetical order," he finishes.

"Yes." I nudge him. "So?"

Jesse scratches the back of his head. "Well, I started high school the Fall after you disappeared. Uh, left. The high school had more people and most classes didn't do assigned seating. I wasn't 'next to' anyone."

I fall silent. "Did you make any other friends?"

A wistful turn plays at the corner of Jesse's mouth. "None that could take your place, Benny. Hey... Ben, wait. Bennett. You aren't going to cry, are you?"

I make a wordless sound of protest as I scrub my wrist over my prickling eyes, because I refuse to cry. "Jess..."

How could I have left you? How will I do it again?

Before I can interrogate the voice in my head, I notice something. A shimmer in the distance, like light hitting a prism and shooting in all directions. When my eyes adjust, I gasp.

"Look," I murmur. "He's beautiful."

Jesse lifts his head in question, and when his gaze lands where mine rests, he sucks in a breath of his own.

A massive wolf sits at the edge of the field, framed by tall grasses. Even from a distance, I can tell he's bigger than Jesse's shifted form. His size isn't what has us staring, though. With the high noon sun streaming in visible rays around the cottage clearing, Callum's thick silver fur glistens.

And he's watching us in silence, making no motion to cross the space and join us.

Jesse and I exchange looks, his eyes wide and worried. Despite his very justifiable anxiety, calm settles over me. I ruffle Jesse's hair, then push to my feet. The wind picks up, tracing the contours of my body in one wild, chilling gust that has Jesse scrambling to keep our plates from flying away. Then I take a step forward and the air goes still.

Not unnerving-still, just peaceful, the sounds of birdsong and chattering squirrels mixed with the whispering of pine needles.

I walk in careful, measured steps over to where Callum sits, only stopping to snag a sandwich from the open basket. I can't guarantee he won't bolt, but I don't fear for my safety. How could I? Not with how gently he held me, the warmth of his breath and pinpoint focus—serious, but in the right light, tender.

Stopping in front of him, I offer a shy smile. "I'd like you to come sit with us, Callum. I made ambrosia."

Callum's large head tilts. Even with him sitting down, we're nearly at eye level.

"It's full of sugar and preservatives," I add, "so I'm certain you'll hate it, but you can't judge if you're all the way over here." His ears are fluffy and white, and I want more than anything to pet them. So I do.

At first Callum stiffens, but when I circle my thumb inside the point of one twitching ear, he lets out a long, low *huff* that sounds so much like a human sigh I can't help but laugh. The space before me shivers, and with a ripple like the lifting of a mirage, the silver wolf unfolds into the man I've been waiting for.

Naked, of course.

I give Callum a moment to cover himself, but he doesn't. His piercing blue eyes study me. Though I have to put a great deal into refraining from gawking, I manage (just barely) to smile and hold out the sandwich, loosely wrapped in waxed paper.

"Turkey and brie," I say, gesturing with it. "I made it special for you. Jesse prefers ham."

Callum's gaze flicks to Jesse, then back to me. "Why?" His voice rasps, barely a whisper.

"Because we're sorry for... everything. And we wanted to see you again. *I* wanted to see you again."

His brows arch skeptically. "This has nothing to do with getting your money's worth, I'm sure."

I laugh. "That was Jesse's money. I don't give a fuck what you do with it." I press the sandwich into his hand, and wait.

Callum breathes out another sigh and shakes his head. He accepts the sandwich, inspecting it with a curious sniff. Without another word, he makes his way toward the rumpled blanket. Jesse's sitting upright, looking two seconds away from popping under the pressure from his bright red cheeks. When I get my first glimpse of Callum's gloriously toned backside, I feel very much the same.

Together we lower to the blanket, me landing cross-legged next to Jesse and Callum dropping into a crouch—one he could spring up from at any point.

I don't feel confident needling him, but I hazard a gentle nudge against his knuckles. "That can't be comfortable."

Callum scoffs, but obediently shifts into a more relaxed position. He then unwraps the sandwich and bites into the thick bread. I hold my breath until his brows raise in approval.

I grin at Jesse, mouthing, "*Told you!*" He grins back and pushes me over onto my side. I go down laughing. For a moment I lie there, sprawled on the blanket between the two of them, watching attentively as Callum eats.

Chewing slowly, Callum meets my gaze. He holds it, but I refuse to look away first. Finally he rolls his eyes skyward. "Stop it."

Jesse smothers a laugh under his hand, drawing Callum's attention. My focus sharpens as they study each other. I don't know what to expect, nor do I immediately understand what's happening when Jesse tips his head back, exposing his throat. Several seconds pass before I realize the submissive nature of the action.

Callum huffs something like amused resignation, then reaches across the blanket, a short yet endless expanse separating them. He brushes the back of his knuckles against Jesse's bared throat.

My lungs seize, stealing my breath.

When Callum withdraws, Jesse drops his eyes, and Callum huffs again, this time sounding lighter. "Eat, pup," is all he says before returning to his sandwich.

Between the two of them, everything is devoured except the atrocious fruit salad, which Callum abhors as predicted. Callum doesn't talk much, but he also doesn't protest when Jesse and I fill the space with nonsensical jokes and laughter. The whole while he makes no effort to conceal his body. I don't know if he notices, or cares to notice, our furtive glances. He doesn't even acknowledge when I fail to keep my eyes away from his cock—thick, uncircumcised, and surrounded by silver hair. Around the third time I avert my gaze with burning hot cheeks, I catch Jesse in the same predicament.

I shoot him a knowing smirk, and am greatly amused when he ducks his head so his hair hides his blush.

15

TRY EVERYTHING ONCE

With Callum having forgiven us, the fight to restore my magic is back on track. Callum more than makes up for the absence; nearly every day he calls me over for some new experiment. Jesse picks me up whenever he can, but eventually the large grass field begins to show evidence of a narrow path, beaten down by the number of times I've crossed it.

After a host of failures—bitter tea that left nothing helpful in its leaves; a magnetic magic cream that accomplished nothing more than attracting pixies and mosquitoes; and a motherfucking *séance*—I mentioned needing to do my T shot. It wasn't more than a side comment, but Callum had a good two dozen questions about the process. Baffled, I thought he just had a medical curiosity about hormone replacement therapy, until he conjured a radical idea about how to use it for our project.

The next time I enter Callum's cottage, it's to find him bickering with Jesse in the kitchenette. I haven't bothered with knocking for a while now, so they don't notice my arrival until I kick off my boots and make my way over to them.

"What're we fighting about?" I ask.

Jesse scoops me up in a hug, pulling my feet clean off the floor. Callum huffs; I wheeze. Once Jesse drops me back to the floor, he says, "Callum stood Josie up again."

"Why?"

Callum rumbles his displeasure, answering me without turning from his work at the kitchen counter. "Listening to the council nitpick the work I do is not worth my time."

"Did you at least call?"

He pauses, then repeats, "Not worth my time."

I elbow Jesse in the side, snickering. "He's giving you a workout with this go-between stuff."

"No more than usual," Jesse says, grinning despite the earful I'm sure Josie gave him.

"If we're done," Callum cuts in, finally facing us. "It's ready." My gaze strays to the little vial in his hand. *Testosterone Cypionate*, reads a tiny label. Callum tips his head toward the cot in the corner, surrounded by the usual magical accouterments.

My face heats as I make my way to the cot. Lately it's been hard to ignore my body's response to his touchy experiments. I do my best to conceal it, but Jesse confirmed a while ago that with their enhanced senses, shifters are able to detect many physiological phenomena that go unnoticed by humans. Any pheromone spikes I experience would be apparent to Callum, especially at such close range. He doesn't seem to be affected by them, though, nor does he show any signs of caring.

I strip down to my binder and trunks. Callum waits until I'm lying on the cot before sinking to the floor beside me. Morning light streams in through the window, drawing my attention to the familiar pattern of tree branches outside, swaying in the wind.

"Ready?" Callum asks.

"Yeah," I say, looking away from the window.

A quick glance shows Jesse in his usual chair, watching attentively. He sits far enough away so as to not crowd Callum, but while he's apologetic for assuming the worst of him, Jesse is still protective. His cheeks were flushed when he explained that he wants to be nearby in case something goes wrong, so I'm not left alone and afraid. I kissed him rather thoroughly after that.

Callum opens a small box filled with the medical supplies I use to administer my T shot. One syringe, two different gauge needles, multiple alcohol swabs. I make myself watch as Callum swabs the top of the T vial, then starts with the first needle—a larger gauge used to pull the thick oil out of the vial. He is methodical about tapping out the air bubbles before drawing the fifty milligram dosage.

When Callum withdraws the needle, I swallow hard. It catches his attention. "Everything alright?"

I want to smooth the furrow between his eyebrows. "I'm okay. I don't like needles very much."

Now his brows rise high on his forehead. "You have to do it weekly."

I snort. "Yep. That's what I get for wanting to look like a man without being able to shapeshift."

Callum looks like he might try to comfort me, but when he speaks, it's with professional detachment. "I infused the solution with your energy signature, copied from the contract you signed at the beginning of our arrangement. It might give you a temporary magic boost that would fade over time as the hormone cycles through your system. You'd have to continuously administer the enchanted oil to maintain a semi-regular wave of magic ability."

"Damn. How much will that cost me?" I mean it as a joke, but Callum merely scoffs and averts his eyes.

"Are you able to continue?" he asks.

I ball my hands into fists, and inhale deeply. On the exhale, I let my body relax—just as he taught me. "I'm ready."

Callum nods, then removes the eighteen-gauge needle from the syringe. He tucks it into the sharps box, then fits the smaller intramuscular needle onto the syringe. Holding it in his left hand, he tears open the package for a new alcohol swab with his teeth, then uses it to prepare the injection site on my thigh.

I take another deep breath. "I'm fine," I reassure him when I see his questioning glance.

With that, Callum positions the needle above my thigh with utmost care, squeezes a patch of skin, and pushes the needle in. The pressure is measured and even, not too hard or too soft, and the needle enters perfectly. It still stings. I close my eyes, counting backward from ten. Finally there is a slight tug as the needle withdraws from my flesh, and Callum makes a sound in his throat to indicate completion.

Blood wells up from the tiny prick. Callum sweeps a cotton ball over the blood, then rocks back on his heels. His eyelids droop as he runs his fingers in a wide circle around the injection site. I'm sure it isn't a caress—he's probably testing for success, or pain, or failure—but heat flares to life low in my belly all the same.

"When will we know?" I try not to sound as flustered as I feel. Even in a moment as tense as this, being around Callum is a ripe torture. He lights up my nerve endings with every touch, and his lapis-blue eyes draw desire from my core, catching behind my ribcage when I won't let it escape.

I'm *yearning*, goddamnit.

Callum purses his lips. "I don't feel anything yet, but it might need a while to circulate." He sounds dubious.

"How do you not feel it? You just put it inside me. Shouldn't you be able to feel the magic even if I don't have control of it?" I pointedly don't add a '*Yet?*'

"That's an accurate assessment," he says neutrally.

"So, what's wrong?"

Callum reaches for my hand and lifts me to my feet. "The magic is gone. Everything I put into the solution has disappeared without a trace."

I've been doing well at not breaking apart every time an experiments fails. I haven't had another crying meltdown like the one that triggered the fight with Jesse, and have tried my best not to rely on either of them to comfort me.

This, though.

It sounded like it would work. It didn't rely on finding my original magic, but simply infusing me with new, usable power. External magic, like Callum has explained at length. Something that comes from a spell or an object—an oil, in this case—that could be used by a mundane person. It would work perfectly with his theory that I might absorb magic from my surroundings rather than creating my own. I don't want that to be the case, but I'd accept it if there was no other option.

The plan made sense, right up to the point where every flicker of magic in my system disappeared into an invisible void. What if my father *does* have a siphon on me? Why would he do something so fucking cruel to his own son?

Callum must see the anguish on my face. He falls back

on his usual response to strong emotions, murmuring "I'll make tea," as he hurries over to the kitchenette.

Jesse is still in his chair, silent when he sends me a sympathetic look. He hands over my clothes when I reach for them, and turns to give me privacy while I'm dressing. Once I'm decent, I consider asking for a hug. I could snuggle into Jesse's comforting embrace while we wait for Callum to finish the tea.

Then I decide not to, because my thoughts are racing and my head is foggy. I need to be alone.

"I'm gonna go home," I say quietly. Both alphas perk up, alarm on their faces. "Sorry. I just don't feel good."

"I can drive you—" Jesse begins, quickly getting to his feet.

I wave my hand. "I want to walk."

"I don't think you should go yet," Callum says, sounding unsure. "Maybe it'll—"

"Don't fucking lie to me, Callum," I snap. "You know something's wrong, I know something's wrong, even Jesse knows something's wrong! We all fucking know this isn't working." I throw my hands in the air. "I'm so fucking *sick* of this."

All I can feel is cold, cavernous despair. I'll never go back to Faerie—my *home*. Naomi has yet to give me a way to contact Brann, and if I push she'll dig in her heels. Her suspicion will override her expert ability to skirt around important topics. She'll question me ruthlessly, and I don't know if I'll be able to withstand the pressure to confess.

And Callum, despite his greatest efforts, can't beat something he can't find.

"I really need to leave."

Callum takes a step forward. "Bennett, please. We can talk about—"

"I don't want to fucking *talk* about it!" I turn a snarl on the two shifters standing wide-eyed in front of me. In comparison to their size and power I may be a tiny, magic-barren half-fae, but I can match them through force of will, and I have no intent of backing down. "Neither of you have any idea what this feels like."

They don't argue, because I'm right. I can't imagine it would be easy to strip the magic from an alpha shifter, no matter who you are. The chances of either Callum or Jesse having to lose this part of them are slim-to-none.

Still, their shocked expressions fill me with guilt.

Regarding them, warring with my chaotic emotions, it dawns on me that the love I have for Jesse—a best friend, not quite a lover, not quite yet—and the rapidly growing fondness for Callum—fresh like a new bud, perfumed with desire—are the only connections I have. Naomi's evasiveness makes her a terrible mother. Meanwhile, Brann disappeared without a word after completely upheaving my life, lacking even the decency to explain himself.

It's been a lonely two years.

I open my mouth to... not take it back, but apologize, maybe. At least I can acknowledge what they've become to me and how much I appreciate it, before flouncing off to sulk by myself.

Before I can choose my words, Jesse says, "Ben, you aren't being fair."

Callum grumbles a warning. "He's allowed to be upset."

I should be glad Callum's willing to defend me, but it actually makes me feel worse. The thought is bitter and sharp, but in that moment I'd wanted them to hurt like I do, even though the pain centers around an act they don't condone and have tried doggedly to fix.

"Don't twist my words," Jesse says. He sounds so calm

this could be a normal conversation, but his face is completely neutral without even the hint of a smile. "I didn't say what he was allowed to feel, but he shouldn't be yelling at you."

"You think I'm overreacting?" I hate the vulnerability in my voice.

"I think you're treating Cal like this is his fault, and that's pretty ungrateful, considering everything he's done for you."

For a moment I think I'm going to yell again, but the spark of rage fails to catch, leaving me exhausted. My vision goes blurry, so I quickly hang my head, hoping to hide the moisture welling up in my eyes.

Jesse sighs. In my peripheral I see him reach for me, but he drops his hand before making contact. After an uneasy moment of silence, he swallows audibly and says, "I think we should put a plug in the project. It's not working."

"Jesse, that's not your call." Callum sounds about ready to pick up all the aggression I fought to put down.

"You've spent two months trying to crack this," Jesse says, his jaw set stubbornly. "Each failure is weighing on Ben, and it's gotta be weighing on you, too. This is neither of your faults, and maybe a solution will pop up somewhere down the line, but for now nothing good is coming from these experiments."

"You aren't thinking objectively," Callum argues. "Something is deeply wrong, and Bennett shouldn't have to live his life attempting to ignore it. There is no reason why this shouldn't have worked. The magic went somewhere, suggesting there *is* a siphon drawing on Bennett. What happens if it pulls on more than his magic? We don't know the consequences of letting this violation persist."

Jesse shakes his head. "I'm not disagreeing with you, Cal, but you might not be the person capable of fixing it. Maybe

Bennett should focus on getting in touch with his dad, and we can go from there."

I don't think that'll work, but I want to keep the peace, so I force myself to nod. "I'll talk to my mom again. Callum, I'll, uh... Figure out something about what I owe you. Just text me with the total when you've got it all—"

Callum waves his hand to halt me. "The agreement was that if I backed out, your obligation for payment would be nullified. I'll throw away the receipt."

I should be relieved that I won't be on the hook for some exorbitant sum, but I'm not. "Okay. Thanks, Cal. Now I really do need to get going. Sorry." I bite my lip and stare at my bare feet. My toes curl as my face crumples, the tension turning me into one great, throbbing nerve. "Thank you both. So much. I appreciate you two more than I can say."

Callum steps forward. "Ben, wait."

His image blurs when I look up at him. "You're amazing. You too, Jess. I just need to get a clearer head on my shoulders, okay? We'll talk later." On autopilot, I grab my boots and leave the cottage, hoping neither of them make an effort to stop me. I know they want to, but I'm glad they don't.

I make it halfway through the field before stumbling, pain exploding in my foot. The light is so low I can hardly make out the sharp stone I just stepped on. My boots are still in my hand, and I didn't pull my pants down, so the thick underbrush has left scratches all over my legs. Trembling, I fumble my bare feet into the combat boots, and continue to plod along until I reach the street. I'm anxious to know if any ticks hitched a ride on me, but I don't stop until I'm home, only narrowly missing Naomi by bolting into the bathroom.

I toss my boots aside, one thumping against the locked

door while I strip the rest of the way. Naked and shivering from adrenaline, I meticulously examine every single inch of my body. There are no ticks, but my foot is bleeding, and so are some of the scratches on my legs. Heaving a sigh, I slump into the hot shower and don't emerge until Naomi hollers that she's going to be late for work.

Depression comes, then.

It arrives with bared teeth and sharp claws, lacking the fuzzy ears or comforting warmth I've found in other predators. It takes me down like a newborn fawn, leaving me bleeding, weak, helpless, and so, so alone.

I sequester myself in my room for three days, only leaving to use the bathroom. Naomi throws some plastic-wrapped food items on my bed during one such trip, and those are all I eat. The fourth day, after she leaves for work, I wake up consumed by a thirst so desperate I bolt for the fridge to chug water directly from the filtered jug.

I'm gasping for breath with water dripping down my chin when I hear a knock at the door. Naomi should be at work by now, but maybe she forgot something. She wouldn't have been able to call me, since my phone died shortly after I got home from Callum's and I haven't charged it.

I unlock the door and open it without looking through the peep hole. Maybe that was a mistake, because I'm left paralyzed with shock at the sight of both Jesse *and* Callum standing on the porch.

16

MIDDLE CUSHION

"Callum? You left your cottage!" When they assume matching looks of alarm, I realize yelling at Callum and ignoring Jesse is not the way to greet them. Cringing, I add, "Hi Jesse. And Callum, I'm glad to have you here."

There's a pause.

"Why are you both here?" I feel like I should have put emphasis on 'both.'

"Callum was worried about you," Jesse says.

Callum bristles, but the glare he sends Jesse holds no heat, and his irises are their normal blue. He cuts back, "And Jesse wanted to apologize."

My gaze flicks between the two of them. "That's... very thoughtful." I don't know what else to say or do, so I take a step back and gesture for them to enter the house. Both alphas have to tuck in their arms to make it through the old house's narrow doorway.

Once they're inside I close the door and lock it. Nervous, I keep my hand on the handle. I'm not sure what seeing them inside Naomi's house will do to me. This is the first time I've had a guest over, because I'm not comfortable here. This place will never feel like my home.

When I finally turn, I'm left reeling at the bizarre sight of two large, beautiful men standing in the cramped living room. Watching, waiting patiently for me to stop freaking out.

I hazard a weak, wavering smile. "Thank you for coming. I've been okay." It's a lie, but I don't want to admit how deeply I've been affected by the failed mission. They probably know without me saying so.

"You weren't answering messages," Callum says, shifting his weight.

"My phone died."

Jesse lays a heavy hand on my head. Without my phone to distract me, I'd gotten bored enough to finally re-dye my hair, staining the overgrown fashion mullet blue, yellow, and pink, all mottled like an iridescent soap bubble. He runs his fingers through the freshly-washed strands, pausing to tug a wayward lock. "There are these things called chargers. Did you lose yours?"

I snort, opting for honesty over playing along. "No, I didn't. I just couldn't. Sorry if I missed either of your messages."

Callum shakes his head. "You're entitled to your grief. I'm sorry I couldn't..." He frowns when Jesse elbows him.

"You tried your best," Jesse says with surprising gentleness.

Grimacing, Callum steps outside the range of Jesse's prodding. I can't hold back a huff of amusement. Of course receiving reassurance would be uncomfortable for Callum.

Unsurprisingly, Callum doesn't acknowledge the faint smile tugging at one side of my mouth while I wait for him to continue. "I— We didn't want you to feel abandoned, even if the project failed." He hesitates, averting his gaze. "You're still welcome to visit."

My face bursts into the first genuine smile I've managed in days. "I will, yeah. Thank you." Just the idea of still being able to see him—something I'd been worrying about, but trying to repress—has my spirits lifting. I turn my grin on Jesse. "So, about that apology."

He snorts. "I should've been more tactful, probably."

"Anything else?"

"Not really." Jesse squishes my cheeks between his hands. "I don't want you to think I don't care about you getting your magic back and feeling comfortable in your skin. I do. But you were crushed a little more every time something didn't work. We all just need a break. Stopping for now doesn't mean an opportunity won't pop up later, you know? Just give yourself some time to heal." He bends to press our foreheads together.

I flush from my hairline to my collarbones. "I guess I can try," I mumble.

"That's my boy." Jesse's face splits into a grin. "I knew you'd stop being a twerp eventually."

I feign offense. "Cal, did you hear what he just called me?" What might be the tiniest, most fragile snort of amusement puffs from Callum's flared nostrils. It also could have been a hiccup, but the potential flutters in my chest, filling me with such affection I grow bold enough to nudge his arm with the back of my hand. "Aren't you gonna defend my honor?"

Callum returns the gesture. "There's not enough room in here for me to put him down like I normally would."

Unfortunately, the comment evokes a mental image of spilled groceries, blood, and snarling. The memory of being helpless and afraid lingers like a bad taste on my tongue. I push it firmly out of my thoughts. No one will be fighting today.

Jesse laughs and loops an arm around my neck, pinning me so he can aggressively scrub my hair. My hand falls away from Callum. Instead I push at Jesse, trying unsuccessfully to escape. His arms are like rebar.

"There might not be room for Cal to kick my ass, but there's plenty of room for this." Before I can respond, Jesse scoops me up and throws me over his shoulder.

I shriek in indignation. While pushing against Jesse's back I catch a glimpse of Callum's alarmed expression. I don't have time to say anything, because Jesse tosses me onto the worn leather couch. I bounce like a ragdoll, then use the momentum to launch myself at Jesse's middle.

Jesse lets out an *oof* when I tackle him, but he's otherwise unaffected. He goes low, grabbing me around the thighs. Next thing I know, I'm upside down.

I kick and howl in protest. "Fuck off! You don't get to call me a twerp then toss me around like a football."

"Who says? You're a great football. Very tossable." Jesse plops onto the couch and I end up sprawled in an undignified heap across his lap. I scramble across the couch until I can seize the nearest pillow, which I proceed to beat him with until he's crying for mercy with real tears of laughter rolling down his cheeks.

Finally I stop, flushed and smiling wide. "I'll give you a reprieve, but first you have to admit I'm not a twerp. Otherwise the beatings will continue."

Jesse takes my hand and yanks me forward. I catch myself against his firm chest, close enough for him to lean down and whisper in my ear, "You can beat me more later."

Before he withdraws, he catches my earlobe between his lips, letting me feel the tiniest point of a fang.

Then his mouth is gone, and I am *wrecked*.

Jesse leans back, settling smugly against the arm of the couch.

I'm going to kill him later.

Right now, though, Callum is frozen in the doorway, appalled. I grin sheepishly and beckon him toward the couch, but he doesn't move.

"We're done fucking around," I promise. I'm not surprised to see him thrown off by play wrestling. It requires trust and familiarity, and Callum doesn't seem to have either. "Come sit down with us. We can watch something, yeah?" I address the question to Jesse as well.

"Buddy, this guy doesn't even have a TV in his house."

"That's an even better reason for him to join us!"

Callum stays where he is, so I climb off Jesse and approach him. After a moment of mutual contemplation, I take his hand.

"C'mon, let's all sit down. Jesse will be good, and I'll stay in the middle so he can't bother you." Because that's obviously my only reason for wanting the middle cushion.

Callum doesn't respond—he simply examines me, caution in his blue eyes. I hold his gaze for as long as I'm able, waiting until I see caution shift to curiosity. Finally, he squeezes my fingers in his.

I'm used to him touching me, but Callum being receptive to my touching him back ignites hot, licking flames of desire.

Then Callum sighs and removes his hand from mine. Disappointment cools the fire in my chest, until I hear a soft shuffle and notice Callum awkwardly shifting his weight. I gasp when I realize why, laughter bubbling out of me.

"You're wearing shoes!"

Callum grimaces as he kicks off a pair of open-toed brown sandals. He sets them neatly by the door, then flexes his bare feet, the tips of his clawed toes digging into the mat.

Once I've stopped giggling, I offer my hand again. To my utter joy and fascination, Callum accepts, allowing me to lead him toward the opposite end of the couch. He throws a glare at Jesse—can't help himself, I suppose—before dropping into a tense, upright crouch. Contrasting with Jesse's unconcerned sprawl, Callum leaves one foot on the floor, tucking the other in front of him on the faded leather cushion. In this position he could leap upright in the blink of an eye.

I don't protest. He must be unnerved by the change of surroundings; even a powerful magewolf is allowed some fear of the unknown.

After snagging the remote, I wedge myself between them as planned. Both alpha shifters run warm, making me glad for the air conditioning. Maybe wolf shifters wouldn't mind being around a sweaty twink, but just the thought sends a wave of nervous energy through me. I try to ignore it, focusing instead on sitting primly with my knees together and one hand on my lap. I take care not to touch either of them, which is difficult with Jesse sprawled like a huge, lazy dog.

I lift the remote, intending to find something we all want to watch, but Jesse snatches it out of my hands.

"Jess!" I sputter, trying to reclaim the remote. He holds it out of reach. "Give it back!"

Jesse locks me behind a solid wall of bicep and begins to navigate through the channels. I try another angle of attack, but Jesse twists to effortlessly keep me at bay. I retaliate by sinking my teeth into his forearm.

Yelping like a puppy, Jesse jerks. It throws off my balance, sending me tumbling backward.

Into Callum.

Who catches me, because he always does.

I end up with my back against Callum's chest, his arms wrapped around my front. When I tilt my chin up to peer at his face, I'm not surprised to see him scowling at Jesse.

"Could you be careful?" Callum growls.

"He bit me!"

"Oh, yes. With all of his very sharp and dangerous teeth."

I squirm against Callum. "Hey. My teeth are *extremely* dangerous, thank you very much."

I've gotten used to the fact that Callum doesn't smile. Maybe his facial muscles lack the reflex, or his brain doesn't send the right signals. Even when he's at peace, or those rare times he shows amusement, the tells are all in his eyebrows, a slight lift or furrow that requires careful attention to interpret. A level of attention I should feel embarrassed about paying, but he's never commented.

I hope he doesn't comment now, because I'm staring openly, in awe of the softness that's taken over his features. Eyelids low, brows relaxed, blue eyes holding my gaze so I can look my fill. I almost lift my hand to brush my fingers against his silver-stubbled cheek.

"Thank you for the correction," Callum says, voice low, vibrating his chest in a way that makes me melt. "My apologies for the insult." I want to believe there's laughter in his eyes, even with his lips relaxed.

Quite content with how we've ended up, I snuggle against Callum's warm chest. Jesse is watching us with a crooked grin, and I can't help my giddy smile.

Callum doesn't dislodge me when he shifts into a more

comfortable position on the couch. Intoxicated by his warmth, I settle more securely against his shoulder, until our hips end up pressed flush. I seek out Jesse's warmth as well, stretching my legs so I can tuck my bare feet into his lap. Jesse winks and drops his hand to my ankle, thumb tracing half-moons over the arch of my foot.

17

UNEXPECTED TENSION

"I'm hungry," I whine. "We should order pizza."

Jesse squeezes my foot. "Sure."

"You're going to have to use your phone though. Mine is still dead."

He scoffs. "Twerp."

I jab my fingers in his side, receiving a light swat for my trouble.

"Watch it," Jesse says, withdrawing his phone from his pocket to order the pizza. "I picked something for us to watch, by the way."

"Is it gonna be awful?" I ask.

"No. Callum would leave if I played something too offensive. Just hang on."

We wait until Jesse has summoned a delivery driver on his phone before he opens the YouTube playlist. Thanks to Naomi's shitty Wi-Fi, it takes several seconds for the video to cast to the big screen. I close my eyes while it loads and focus on savoring Callum's warmth behind me.

Jesse nudges me. "Don't fall asleep."

"I wasn't falling asleep!"

He feints at tickling me, prompting me to draw my leg back and threaten to kick him in the face. Jesse laughs, catches my ankle, and kisses the sole of my foot. My heartbeat kicks into overdrive.

Callum shifts behind me, and the unexpected brush of his fingers against my throat has my blood throbbing with heat. On instinct, I lift my hand, seeking out this point of contact. My fingertips brush his knuckles while my gaze fixes on Jesse's parted lips and brown eyes, his dark pupils blown wide. His thumb traces the dips of each of my toes, until the television screen blinks and the three of us, as one, snap our attention forward.

I squint at the description of the YouTube channel, but Jesse fullscreens the video before I can read anything. "Stop acting so secretive," I complain, kicking him again. This time he lets it connect, not even grunting when my foot makes contact. It's like trying to break through solid oak. The contact lingers long enough for me to notice Jesse's strong pulse, his heart beating as rapidly as mine.

Unable to handle the flush taking over my body, I pull my hands and feet back into the safe haven of the middle cushion, scrunching my body until I'm no longer touching either of them. I focus as hard as I can on the loading video and try to ignore the heat radiating off the men on either side of me. When the image of a woman in a top hat and cane pops up, my brow scrunches in confusion.

"Welcome back to Practical Magicfest! Today we're going to be—"

"Magic tricks?" Callum says, clearly disapproving.

Jesse snickers. "Just give it a shot, okay? I love this channel."

I narrow my eyes at Jesse, half suspecting he's only pulled this video up to annoy Callum. He chuckles and puts a large hand on my head, twisting it back toward the screen. I bat at him, but don't shrug off his arm when he settles it around my shoulders.

"—exploring how you can use practical magic to enhance the most classic tricks. My name is Sarah, and this is Practical Magicfest. Let's get started!"

Sarah the Magician starts by giving a quick rundown of the usual formulas for magic tricks. She demonstrates non-magic strategies for identifying random cards selected by audience members and describes the most common forms of sleight of hand.

I watch with surprising enthusiasm. Sarah is charming and cheerful while thoroughly explaining the ways one can step up their performances using hints of real magic. Making a card disappear right out of someone's hand and show up in hers at the snap of her fingers. Turning foam balls into luminescent, sparkling illusions that float in midair when she releases them.

Then she launches into making things disappear. "Vanishing is a common technique. It involves plenty of misdirection and sleight of hand, of course, but using real magic can make seemingly impossible feats way cooler. And it's all easy!"

First Sarah demonstrates the French Drop by popping a coin into a sealed bottle, followed by making the bottle disappear. An assistant joins Sarah in the frame while she spins a quarter between her fingers, showing off a spot of red paint on one side. I'm surprised when she drops it into her mouth and swallows. Sarah then asks the assistant for a handkerchief that, just a moment ago, wasn't draped over their leg. The actor lifts the handkerchief, revealing the red-marked quarter tucked inside.

"Normally, this would be a planted audience member,

but I'm going to show you how to do it for real. If any of you play video games, you've probably heard the term 'hammerspace.' It describes the unlimited storage some games allow for all the items in a character's possession. You're going to be making your own hammerspace."

Callum tilts his head. "Creating a pocket dimension?" I send him a questioning look, to which he responds, "They're quite complex."

"You can find my tutorial on setting up your own hammerspace here." Sarah points at the corner of the screen where a video preview pops up. "These will only allow you to store an item for a few seconds. Fortunately, that's all you need to complete this trick."

She uses sleight of hand to hide the handkerchief while she shows off the quarter. Then she projects the opening of the pocket dimension—as Callum described it—just above her lips, to catch the coin when she drops it. Before the pocket dimension ruptures, she reaches for an audience member and releases both the handkerchief and quarter onto their person.

"Remember, you can't project this kind of hammerspace. You have to be quick and immediate about where you place it in relation to the spot you've linked the space to. Practice this technique over a table before you try it for real, so you don't choke yourself on your first attempt!" She laughs. "Once you've mastered the hammerspace, it's a great place to hide your drugs. Don't tell anyone I said that."

Sarah closes the video with the usual spiel—thanks for watching; like, comment, subscribe; tell your friends—but I'm more focused on Callum's muttering.

I bump him with my shoulder. "What're you thinking?"

"This is a dangerous skill to be teaching amateurs," Callum says.

Groaning from the other side of the couch, Jesse runs his hands down his face. "Fucking hell, Cal, you can't take something at face value just once?"

"It takes a massive amount of skill, concentration, and undiluted magic to create a pocket dimension worth anything. I doubt the average *magician*"—he grimaces at the word—"would have enough life force to maintain a hold on their drugs long enough to survive an encounter with law enforcement, but even a small trick can risk the dimension rupturing prematurely. It's not a good idea."

"You don't enjoy anything!"

"If you were aiming for enjoyment, an irresponsible magical tutorial was one of the worst things to pick, pup."

I place one hand flat on each of their chests, as if my skinny arms could keep them apart if they really wanted to tussle in my living room. "Boys, can we please keep it contained? If I wanted to see dogs snarl at each other, I'd have gone to a puppy training class."

"*Dogs?!*" Jesse yelps.

Callum merely looks unimpressed, though I suspect he's hiding offense so he looks better than Jesse.

Not put off in the slightest, I ask, "So, are *you* skilled enough to maintain a pocket dimension?"

"Of course I am." The hint of growl under his words does very, very dangerous things to my body.

I focus on the conversation, willing my libido to slow the fuck down. "What do you use them for?"

Still grumbling, Callum gently brushes my hand from his chest, then scrubs at the silvery stubble on his jaw. "Containing items when I shift, mostly."

Imagining Callum as that massive silver wolf once more, this time knowing he could be carrying his clothes in a little magic bubble, almost breaks me. "That is the most adorable thing I've heard all day," I say seriously. Behind me, Jesse bursts into delighted laughter.

Callum scowls. "How is that adorable?"

I pat his thigh, then turn to Jesse. "I have to agree with Cal. Your video sucked. I get to pick next."

Jesse rolls his eyes, but relinquishes the remote. "You guys are the ones who suck."

The three of us sink back into the cushions, and as I navigate to a wood-working channel, I can't avoid noticing how our limbs have relaxed enough to gravitate together. My knee against Callum's, Jesse's arm once again draped behind my neck, but this time close enough for his fingers to brush Callum's shoulder.

My mind wanders as I half-watch a YouTube artist begin shaping a vase from a block of resin and wood mounted to a spinning lathe. I usually play these videos when I can't sleep. That combined with the two hot alphas shifters I'm sprawled between has me drowsy and fighting yawns.

I muse on what Callum said about the difficulty of maintaining a pocket dimension, and how skilled he must be to have mastered the skill. The unspoken competence makes him even sexier. My head lolls onto Callum's shoulder, and his stubbled chin brushes my forehead when he looks down at me. I can't decipher his expression, so I offer a small smile and say nothing. Jesse squeezes the back of my neck, fingers threading through my hair.

The shadows in the living room shift as the artist on the screen buffs their project free of lingering snags before applying a coat of glistening finish.

Halfway through the next video—an antique restoration—the pizza arrives. We eat mostly in silence, and after I'm full, I flop completely horizontal onto the couch, content for once. My feet end up in Jesse's lap again; he massages them with warm hands that engulf my narrow bones. This puts my head in Callum's lap. I drape over his thigh, tensing in case he wants to push me off. He doesn't, though his breath stutters. I give his knee a calming pat, and when his hand lands in my hair, my body melts into a boneless puddle.

The video plays on, detailing an engineer's process reconstructing bolts from a rusted old tool. My mind drifts until I'm a fragile sliver away from sleep.

18

OVER THE EDGE

I'M disturbed when Callum moves under me. My eyes flutter open, flicking between him and Jesse, who's crouching on the floor in front of me with a hand on my thigh.

"It's time for me to go," Callum murmurs in a low, rumbling voice. "I've an appointment tomorrow."

I moan unhappily.

"C'mon Ben, it's late." Jesse tugs until I flop against his shoulder, giving Callum space to stand.

At the door, Callum sighs before nudging the plain sandals with his clawed toes.

I clamber out of Jesse's hold, swaying when I get to my feet, then wobble over to Callum. I stop an arm's length away. "Thank you for coming."

Callum hums, noncommittal. "You should sleep."

"I'm sure I will eventually."

He clicks his tongue in disapproval and says, somewhere between a suggestion and a command, "You'll take better care of yourself from now on."

I grin weakly, my exhausted brain fighting to keep up. "Are you gonna make me?"

After a moment, Callum looks past me. "I'm sure Jesse will," he says in a flat voice, then turns toward the door. He goes rigid when I catch him, locking my arms around his ribcage so I can press myself into his well-muscled back. One of my hands accidentally grazes the V-neck of his shirt, and I can't help but linger over the soft hair on his chest. I remember the picnic, where I was unable to stop myself from following the path of silver hair trailing down his stomach toward his cock. His beautiful, delicious-looking—

"I'm serious," I whisper. "Thank you for looking after me."

Callum folds his rough palm over my hand, pressing it against his heart. I count three intoxicating beats before he gently tugs my hands away. Sensing I've reached the end of his tolerance, I take a polite step back.

"You're welcome," is all he says. Then his brows tick up.

I look over my shoulder in time to see Jesse's crooked smile. "I'll see you tomorrow, Cal."

"Of course you will." Callum picks up the brown sandals and reaches for the door. Between one breath and the next, he disappears into the night.

Several beats pass, neither Jesse nor I moving. It's as if Callum's presence is taking longer to clear, even with him out of sight. Finally, the floorboards creak as Jesse walks up behind me.

I'm feeling weirdly shy, so I don't turn to face him. "Aren't you going to drive him home?"

"No, he needs time to decompress. I bet he's gonna shift and run back."

My lips curve into a small smile as I imagine Callum

peeling out of his clothes behind the sparse front yard bushes. "Thanks for bringing him."

"Of course," Jesse says. "I know you care about him."

I lean my back against his chest, tilting my chin up to study the angle of his jaw. "You care about him, too."

Jesse clears his throat and wraps his arms around me. "Maybe. What about you, though?

"What *about* me?"

Jesse dips to nuzzle my temple. "I care a *lot* about you."

A shiver runs down my spine. "The feeling's mutual."

"Good." Then he notches a finger under my chin and draws me into a brief kiss. He says his next words against my mouth: "Remember when I said you could beat me more later?"

My stomach tightens with anticipation. "I remember, yeah."

"Good. Because it's 'later' now." Jesse kisses me again, this time hot and disorienting. He scoops me into his arms and drops me onto the couch, not missing a beat before he descends over me.

One knee comes up between my thighs, and his mouth lowers to my neck. The earlier hint of teeth was nothing compared to the fangs he's now scraping down my throat. I throw my head back with a soft cry that turns into a moan when he grinds his thigh against my apex. I can already feel his cock swelling in his jeans.

We haven't fucked yet. Always too unsure, too hesitant, stuck wondering what it'll do to our rekindled friendship.

After being wedged between him and Callum for two hours, I'm far too worked up for doubts or fears.

So I buck against him shamelessly, tucking one leg over his thigh. It gives me better leverage, just the right angle to grind against his cock, now fully hard and pulsing. My blood throbs in time; I feel it in my ears, like listening to the inside of a shell and hearing the ocean.

Jesse catches me behind both knees and pushes them apart, spreading me until my back arches. "I've never wanted to tear someone's clothes off before," he growls, dangerously low.

"Please don't," I rasp. "I like these shorts." I shudder when he traces the shell of my ear with his tongue, my nerves singing at the slight tease.

Jesse kisses me hard, tongue and teeth prying me open, leaving me panting into his mouth. "What about the shirt? Can I rip that off?"

Delirious laughter bubbles out of me. Even hovering, hot and predatory, Jesse's still the same best friend I've always known and loved.

"Go for it."

With a vicious, triumphant grin, Jesse shifts his weight to his knees. It gives me a better view of his mussed hair, flushed cheeks, and the prominent line of his cock straining against his jeans. He yanks his shirt over his head, exposing golden-brown skin that glistens with the first beads of sweat. He lets me look, lets me run my fingers over the swell of one pectoral and down the hills of his abdominals, until I take the plunge and press the heel of my hand against his cock, grinding up the textured denim.

Faster than I can follow, Jesse catches my wrists in one hand and pins them over my head, against the arm of the couch. With the other hand, he tugs my hair until my neck is exposed. He goes for the throat, sucking and biting from my jaw to my collarbones—not hard enough to break skin, but definitely leaving marks. I whimper, excited by the sensation of being claimed. Jesse growls in response and takes hold of the collar of my tank top. It makes a satisfying

A Fae's Two Alphas

sound, ripping in a straight line all the way down to the hem.

"How was that?" I ask breathlessly. "Happy?"

Jesse chuckles lowly. "Never been better."

"Good." With that confirmed, I reach for the fastenings of his pants.

Now it's Jesse's turn to shudder. He leans back to give me a better angle, breathing in great, anticipatory gasps as I thumb open the button and tug down the zipper. I take hold of the waistband of his boxer-briefs and meet his eyes, wanting to see how he looks as we irreversibly cross the threshold between friends and lovers. Jesse's long hair frames his face like a wolf's mane, eyes glowing a faint orange that shadows the smooth planes of his cheeks.

Yeah, I think we're ready.

With careful, precise movements, I tug on Jesse's waistband and free his dark, swollen cock.

I do my best memorize the gorgeous visual: Jesse, bare and open, tensing as I wrap my hand around his cock and stroke the hot skin. It weighs heavily in my grasp, thick and throbbing, the whole length velvety soft. Jesse's body is taut, shaking from the effort of holding himself back.

I smile guilelessly, squeeze him, and ask, "What next?"

Jesse's hips buck, driving his cock through the hollow of my fingers; he half-winces, suggesting he hadn't meant to lose control. My smile turns wicked as I drag my hand all the way down to the patch of dark curls on his pubis, then up until I can circle my thumb over the head, collecting a bead of precome.

"Wanna see you," Jesse gasps. "Please."

I draw a sharp breath. Only fair for me to be exposed and wrecked like him, but...

My fingers graze the tight fabric of my binder. What

happens if he doesn't like this as much as he thinks he will? With my chest unbound and nothing of note between my legs? As far as I know, Jesse is bi, but that doesn't mean he finds men attractive in the same way he likes women. I even shave all my body hair, thicker and darker after months on increased testosterone. It's not a manly look, even for a twink.

Still, despite my fears, I trust him.

With a shaky hand, I guide Jesse further back onto his haunches so I can squirm out from under him. I shed the torn shirt, then grab the bottom of my binder.

Jesse's eyes soften in the face of my trepidation. "It's okay if you don't want to, Ben. I don't want you to be uncomfortable—"

"I just need to ease into it," I say faintly.

"Can I help?"

I nod, already beginning to tug the strong spandex. Jesse catches the band, helping to stretch it, so I have an easier time pulling it over my head. I shake out my hair as the garment falls to the floor in a whisper of forgotten fabric.

It'd hard not to cover my chest when Jesse looks at me. He tilts his head, a tiny smile curving one corner of his mouth, and asks, "Would it be better if I didn't touch them, or...?"

At the end of the day, and the night, and any other time, Jesse never once questioned me when I showed up a decade after his fourteenth birthday and told him I was a guy. Retroactively fearing his opinion is more than a bit silly.

I grin, mostly meaning the confident way I lean back on my hands, baring everything to his hungry gaze. "You can do whatever you want, as long as you're touching me instead of worrying."

Then Jesse tips me over, bringing our mouths together

again and again. He drags his big hands from my shoulders to my hipbones, then brings one to press against the small of my back until I arch toward him. The other palms one of my tits, thumb drawing a teasing circle before he rubs my nipple between it and his index finger.

I make up my mind about this development being a net positive.

Jesse makes short work of kissing down my body, sucking my nipples and massaging my hips on his descent, until he's sitting on the floor between my splayed legs, staring up at me with his hands on my knees. I no longer have the wherewithal to tease or deliberate; my fingers fumble open my shorts, and Jesse kisses me while pulling them down, dragging my trunks along as well.

Without hesitation, I part my legs for him, but Jesse doesn't immediately dive in. He doesn't even look, at first. Instead he grabs me under my knees, keeping me in place with my bare ass hanging halfway off the couch cushions. Jesse busies himself sucking a mark onto my hip, refusing to touch my cunt. I writhe against his firm hold, struggling to find some kind of stimulation.

Once satisfied, Jesse meets my eyes and kisses just below my navel. Then I watch his eyelashes fan over his cheeks as he finally looks between my thighs. Hunger sharpens his face, and a rolling growl that bursts to life in his chest.

"*Jess*," I plead, twitching my hips and spreading my legs wider. He doesn't make me wait any longer before diving in, tongue catching me in one long, obscene lick. My back arches as I moan with relief.

Jesse firms his grip on my knees, parting my legs as wide as they'll go as he spears his tongue inside me. It thrusts so deep I hear him struggling to breathe through his nose.

My clit aches with the need to be touched, so when Jesse

leans back just enough to suck in air, I change the angle of my hips. He doesn't take the hint. Growing desperate, I seize a handful of his long hair, trying to direct his mouth toward my clit.

It's not until he smothers a laugh against my inner thigh that I realize he's playing with me.

"Jackass," I gasp.

Jesse bites my thigh, then sucks so hard it's almost painful.

I writhe, imagining how dark the bruise will be. It excites me, the pain radiating until my whole cunt is pulsing. "Touch me, goddamnit!"

"Touch you where?" Jesse laves his tongue over the stinging spot.

"If you don't stop fucking around and suck my—"

Jesse pinches the hickey. I yelp, but the sound dissolves into a moan when he finally circles his tongue around my clit, and draws it into his mouth. Testosterone has enlarged my anatomy, leaving the head of my clit exposed. Jesse's tongue flicks over it so hard it makes me thrash.

The aggressive stimulation evens out into the perfect balance of pleasure and agony. Jesse fucks me like he knows my body, its wants and its limits, where to push until I'm just shy of breaking. My eyes fill with tears, overstimulation swirling with fondness. In this moment I feel wholly understood, acutely aware of the barriers that are crumbling between us. Barriers I used to consider impenetrable.

I wish I could suspend myself in this space forever, but Jesse is, unfortunately, too skilled to allow that.

Catching my hips, Jesse yanks me a few inches forward. I wrap my legs around the back of his head, heels digging into his shoulders. Keeping him there.

I wonder what he's feeling. Does he sense every part of

me, the way my blood rushes for him? Is he still hard, growing more desperate with his cock hanging untouched in the cool evening air? I want to tell him how deeply he's affecting me, drowning me in relief, but speech is far beyond me, so I run my fingers through his hair and beg with dizzy, incoherent moans.

"Close?" Jesse asks, his thumb rubbing a slow clockwise path around the head of my clit.

Still unable to speak, I nod and whimper. Both my hands fist in his thick hair, pulling in an attempt to ground myself.

Jesse laughs, then dives back in, mouth working with reckless abandon as I thrust into the stimulation. It doesn't take much longer... and fucking *stars*, does the surge overwhelm me.

With a fractured scream, I reach climax, coming hard and fast and all for him. Never-ceasing flicks of his tongue guide me through the mire of agonizing pleasure, joy infusing my veins until I find my voice just long enough to cry out: "I love you, Jesse. So much—" before another intense wave shuts me up.

Jesse draws back to kiss the scattered pinpricks of broken capillaries he bestowed upon my thigh. My hands relax until I'm merely petting him, apologizing for how hard I pulled his hair. Wordlessly, we soothe each other.

But Jesse isn't done yet.

I open my eyes enough to see his hand disappear behind the couch cushion, shoulder hitching as he touches himself.

My voice comes out quiet, barely a whimper. "I want you to fuck me."

Jesse's gaze snaps to my face, his pupils dilating. "Bennett..." I watch in awe as the orange glow creeps over his irises, painting faint yellow highlights over the angles of his cheeks.

"Please?"

Jesse growls in that low, wanting way I'm becoming obsessed with, and surges up to kiss me. I feel his cock, hard and unbearably hot, rubbing precome against my knee. My legs ache from the position Jesse held me in, but I try to wrap them around him anyway.

I don't expect him to stop me. My eyes widen with concern. "Jess?"

"Do you have condoms?" Jesse asks.

My jaw drops. "C-condoms..."

"I can't—" He gestures weakly. "It wouldn't be responsible to not use one."

The thought didn't even cross my mind. "I've never used a condom in my life," I admit, my head dropping against the cushion. "We didn't need them in..." I'm sure he'll get the picture without me elaborating.

"Sorry, but I don't want to risk it."

"You think I'll give you some magic STD?" I try to keep the offense out of my voice. Despite having come barely a minute ago, my cunt throbs with the need to have him inside me. I want to feel his release.

"No," Jesse says, already drawing away. "I don't know anything about your reproductive cycle, and I don't think either of us can risk a pregnancy right now."

I slap a hand over my face and mumble, "Technically, I shouldn't be fertile anymore after being on T for... Okay, fine, whatever." Anything to keep Jesse comfortable.

Jesse gives my thigh a final pat before he extricates himself from between my legs. "I have an idea." Then he stands up, leaving me sprawled on the couch, cold and confused.

19

BETWIXT

In this moment, there's nothing I fear more than Jesse getting up and leaving me. I start to scramble toward him, but he stops me by grabbing both my calves and pressing my legs together.

"Jesse?" My voice squeaks.

He kisses the arches of my feet and smirks over my toes. "Don't look like a neglected kitten; I'm not going anywhere." When I cringe from embarrassment, Jesse nips my ankle. "Don't look like that, either. Brace yourself."

Then he tugs me down the cushions, not stopping until my ass is resting on the arm of the couch. The position, my hips raised above my shoulders, is awkward and confusing until Jess props a knee on the couch arm next to my hip and murmurs, "Spread your thighs a bit, sweetheart."

I figure it out then. A shudder runs through me as I obey, parting my legs just enough for Jesse to push his cock between them. It gathers the slickness from my orgasm, allowing a smooth, indulgent glide. Jesse wraps an arm around my thighs, squishing them together, and tucks my ankles against his shoulder. Then he starts to thrust.

I've never tried intercrural before, but the look on Jesse's face when he eases through the tight space has me sold. Groaning quietly, he kisses my ankle, then looks down at me, eyes clouded with lust. "This okay?"

"More than," I murmur.

Jesse's cock is big enough that when his hips are flush with my ass, I can see the shiny purple head peeking through. I feel him in ways I'd never have considered; tingling friction as he thrusts in and out, bringing a slight twinge of pain where I'm bruised. Though his dick isn't in direct contact with my cunt, the rhythmic slap of his balls provides its own unique stimulation. Before I know it, I'm groaning along with him.

I wedge my fingers between my smushed-together thighs, struggling until I find my wet, throbbing core. Once I get my fingers inside myself, Jesse's thrusts push them deeper, and they find my G-spot perfectly. I push the heel of my hand down, bucking so my clit has something to rub against.

"Feel good?" Jesse asks breathlessly. I nod. "Perfect."

A silvery string of precome leaks from the head of Jesse's cock and lands on my stomach. I sweep the fingers of my free hand through the pearl of moisture and bring it to my lips, sucking off the taste of him.

Jesse watches me with laser focus. "You like that?"

I give my best attempt at a crooked grin. "Love it."

He shudders, then starts moving his hips faster. "You feel amazing, Ben. Can't wait to fuck you for real."

"You'd stretch me— ah! So much. *Fuck*." Jesse's groans fuel me. "Want you to fill me up, push inside me. All hot and huge. Wanna feel you come."

"Good news," Jesse says, seconds before his voice

dissolves into a strangled yelp. He slams against my ass, giving a few short, powerful thrusts, and then freezes as a thick string of come bursts from his cock and lands across my wrist.

It smears as I pick up my pace, fingerfucking myself as more and more of Jesse's come streaks my arm and chest. One final groan later and Jesse's on his knees again, prying my legs apart, allowing him to lick between my fingers. I spread them wide, holding my labia open to give him plenty of room to fuck me with his tongue while he rubs his thumb hard against my clit.

My second orgasm hits like a tsunami, catching my whole body in a violent spasm. I cry and buck and gasp through the onslaught. Jesse's palm slides through the come on my stomach, pressing over my pubis so we share each pulse.

At last, the waves even out, leaving me a wreck of come and sweat. While I'm still shuddering through the last aftershocks, Jesse bites me, teeth covering the already-tortured hickey. It sends another spasm through my body. I writhe until I find my voice enough to beg for mercy.

At last, Jesse pulls away. He kisses up my body until he's looming, wetness from our combined release making his lips glisten. I watch them, licking my own lips, and relish in the taste of *us* when he swoops in to claim my mouth.

We continue tonguing each other down until my back starts to protest the awkward position, at which point Jesse plays gentleman and helps me adjust until I'm on the cushions properly. He examines me, smiling faintly, then tucks his fingers under my chin so he can kiss me gently.

"We'll get you cleaned up."

Jesse disappearing down the hallway. I squirm—not in

the good way—when cooling semen drips down my chest. Fortunately Jesse reappears quickly, armed with a damp washcloth.

He kisses me again, then proceeds to wipe me down, gentle with my abused nerves as he cleans my crotch, before moving to my abdomen to scrub off drying streaks of ejaculate. Too worn out to protest, I watch him with hooded eyes, lying boneless until he's done. He leaves again. I hear water running, then a few minutes later Jesse reemerges, damp and clean.

Jesse never took off his jeans—would have interrupted, put too much space between our bodies—so he has an easy time tucking himself away and zipping them closed.

I whimper, still splayed naked on the couch. Jesse laughs quietly as he snags something off the floor, and then I'm greeted by his wonderful-smelling t-shirt. I shamelessly wriggle into it. Before I settle, Jesse nudges me aside and flops on the couch, settling on his back so I can stretch out on his broad chest.

"Was that okay?" Jesse asks out of nowhere.

I bite the crook of his shoulder, but my teeth really do lack any sort of threat, so all I get is a soft inhale of surprise. Without removing my teeth, I mumble: "What do you think?" Then I turn the bite into a series of kisses along his collarbones.

His laugh rumbles underneath me. "Just wanted to make sure."

"Mngh. We shouldn't lie here too long." I make no attempt to move.

Jesse hums. He doesn't seem inclined to move either and, in fact, wraps his arms around me, squeezing until I can barely breathe. The pressure doesn't release until I'm just shy of gasping for air. Jesse keeps me in the embrace, one hand coming up to stroke the sweaty back of my once-pristine fashion mullet. I haven't touched the sides up in so long it's basically a nothing-style, but it feels amazing when he runs his fingers through the long strands.

We're silent for a long time, just resting, listening to each other's bodies: His chest swelling with each inhale. The steady, strong beat of his heart. The flex of his throat when he swallows and the way he tilts his head when I ghost butterfly kisses over his neck.

It's well past midnight, but I don't ask Jesse to check the exact time. His phone is probably on the floor anyway. I'm exhausted, but just before I give in to the weight of my eyelids dragging me down, I whisper, "I meant it."

"Meant what?"

I press my lips to the soft skin under his ear so he can *feel* the words when I say, "That I love you. I do. I'm... so, so glad we found each other again. I love you, Jesse."

"God, Ben. Bennett." Jesse sucks in a shuddering breath. "Thank you. You're the most important person in my life. I'm so relieved you're back. Please don't—" He stops, hiccupping. The TV screen has long since gone dark, no longer illuminating our bodies, and whatever he'd been about to say melts into the night.

I can barely make out the lines of his face, but the furrow between his brows concerns me. I reach up to smooth it, receiving a soft kiss on my wrist for the trouble.

"You have to know I love you too, Bennett. It's never been a secret. I wish I'd told you before." Jesse swallows. "Close your eyes, sweetheart. Rest for now. I'll get you up before morning."

I'm too tired to protest. Jesse massages the back of my

thigh, squeezing my ass in a warm palm, the fingers of his other hand working down to my scalp, drawing dizzy circles. Powerless, I succumb to the soothing touch and descend into a contented sleep.

20

LOOKING OUT FOR YOU

As promised, Jesse shakes me awake a few hours later, scattering kisses over my face when I grumble in protest. "Get up," he whispers, puppeting me upright. "Gotta put you to bed properly."

I don't understand why I can't stay wrapped up in him forever, but I reluctantly allow myself to be guided down the hall to my bedroom, leaning on Jesse for each step. He tucks me in, then leans over with his arms on either side of my head, and kisses me until my nerves are singing, and I'm begging him not to go.

"I have to," Jesse whispers, brushing my shaggy bangs out of my face. "Your mom will go apeshit if she finds me here."

I blink several times, trying to clear my bleary confusion.

Right. Naomi, who doesn't like strangers in the house. Who withheld important information about my friendship with Jesse for reasons yet unknown.

Displeased with the unpleasant reminder, I groan and flip onto my side. "What time even is it?"

Jesse fumbles his phone out of his pocket. "It's almost five AM," he says, just as his phone vibrates.

"What is it?"

"It's a text from Cal."

I perk up, pushing the covers away. "What did he say?"

Jesse gives me a wry smile. "Don't be too nosy, now."

"Okay, sure, whatever. Tell me what he said."

With a roll of his eyes, Jesse shows me the chat.

> Callum Truett: You're not back yet. Is everything alright?
>
> Callum Truett: Josie is looking for you.

There's about an hour and a half between the messages. When I look back to Jesse, he's wincing.

"Not away often?" I ask.

"Never. And I sleep next to Mom's room. She must have noticed that I wasn't in bed."

I can't help it; I start laughing. "You can't even stay out long enough to get laid without worrying literally everyone."

"Shut up," Jesse grumbles, giving me a little shove.

My laughter tapers off as I watch Jesse type out a quick "*I'm ok*" to both Callum and Josie, whose slew of messages fill up the whole screen.

Callum responds immediately. Jesse reads it, then sighs. "Fucking Christ. Cal said Josie wanted to send pack enforcers to look for me. The only reason she didn't is because Callum told her we'd been together." He rakes a hand down his face. "I can't stand them sometimes."

"At least Callum was able to help?" I give Jesse's head a comforting pat.

"Yeah." Jesse swallows and looks away, a frown tugging

the corners of his mouth. "Should we feel bad about tonight?"

Concern makes the back of my neck prickle. "Why would we feel bad?"

Jesse nervously scratches at his bare chest. "Well, Callum..."

"You think he'd care?"

Jesse scoffs. "You're really asking that, Ben? He's smitten with you."

My face scrunches as a barrage of questions go feral inside my head. "I don't know if I believe that." Hope surges inside me. I turn aside because I don't want Jesse to see it reflected in my expression, but I suspect he can sense how my heart just began to pound.

"Think what you want. Do whatever. I'm just telling you what I've seen." Jesse frowns hard at the blue sheet covering my legs. "He'd never do all this for anyone else."

My teeth dig into my lower lip. "Callum's aware that you and I were going on dates. He had to know something would happen eventually."

"I don't know if that makes a difference," Jesse says.

Was it wrong to press against Callum like I did if I was going to run into Jesse's arms the moment he left? I know I was shameless about hanging off both Jesse *and* Callum. What would I have done if Callum hadn't left when he did? Explode?

I'm silent for too long, lost in not knowing what to say. At the end of my rumination, all that comes out is, "Jess, do you have feelings for Callum?"

He tenses. "Do you?"

"Is our answer gonna be the same?"

Too long, again, Jesse holds his breath. With all these pauses, it's going to be daylight before we finish this conversation. Birds are already singing outside the window.

Finally Jesse exhales, and sounds exhausted when he says, "I think so. I'm sorry."

"Why are you sorry? It's not like we're exclusive."

Shrugging, Jesse turns to sit on the edge of the bed. I plaster myself against his back and wrap my arms around his middle, trying to squeeze a response out of him.

"I don't want to get between you and something you want," Jesse admits.

Shocked, I sit upright. "You aren't between me and anything. Why would you think that?"

"Why wouldn't I?"

"Jess..." I thunk my head against his shoulder blade. When he doesn't acknowledge me, I do it again. "It's not just about me, you know."

"In what way?"

I try to figure out how to say what comes next. "I'm not gonna be here forever. Eventually, I'll figure out how to get my magic back. I'll yell at Dad. Or beg. I'll do *something*. But I'm going back to Faerie one way or another, and when that happens, I don't want either of you to be alone." The words hurt, but I force them out because he needs to understand. "You shouldn't hold yourself back from Callum if you get the chance to... to connect."

Jesse's body tenses in my grasp. "I should say the same to you," he says neutrally. "If you and he get a chance to '*connect*.'"

"C'mon, Jess. Don't say it like that."

I scrub my forehead against Jesse's skin until my bangs are mussed. Abruptly, he stands. I almost tip over and go sprawling off the edge of the bed. When Jesse makes no move to catch me, I know I've seriously fucked up.

A Fae's Two Alphas

"I'm heading out," he says. "Goodnight, Bennett. Try to sleep."

"Wait!" Jesse pauses with his hand against the door. I study the way his back muscles flex before tugging his shirt over my head and tossing it at him; he catches it without looking. "Didn't want you to drive home shirtless," I explain in a small voice.

"Thanks." Jesse slides into the shirt and, before I can interrupt a second time, slips from my bedroom, closing the door behind him.

Naked and shivering, I squirm under the covers and pull them tight around me. I squeeze my eyes closed, seeking enough calm to go back to sleep.

A scream pierces what's left of the night.

I shoot upright, bolting for the door. As my hand closes around the handle, I realize I'm still stark naked. I'll be no use to anyone running around without a scrap of clothing, so I grab a pair of pajama pants from the floor of my closet and hop into them. The shirt I select ends up bunched against my chest because just then the screaming escalates and I can't waste any more time.

The problem isn't that I don't know what's going on—it's that I think I *do*.

I burst into the hallway, hissing when I see that my mom has backed Jesse against the refrigerator. A small light over the sink illuminates them. Naomi is armed with nothing but her purse, but her bear tattoo is visible, snarling between the straps of her white tank top. For a moment, I almost believe she's a genuine threat. Then Jesse, an *actual* predator, sends me a panicked look.

It helps me find my voice. "Mom, what the fuck are you doing?"

Naomi turns toward me, her eyes wild. "What is *he* doing? Here. In my house!"

"I live here too," is my first objection, but she appears unmoved. I try again: "For fuck's sake, Mom, stop cornering him!"

"I have a right to corner anyone sneaking around my home in the dark."

My groan is long, loud, and exasperated. "Mom, he was just leaving. We were... hanging out." Hopefully, she didn't catch that hiccup, but by the way her gaze swivels back to Jesse, I suspect my hope is misplaced.

"You know better," Naomi says, not taking her eyes off him.

"I'm allowed to have people visit me *where I live*. Jesse is my oldest friend." My eyes narrow. "Unless you've conveniently forgotten? Mom, look at me."

"It doesn't matter," she finally says.

"It damn well does!" I gather the shirt more securely over my chest. If I put it on now, Naomi might take advantage of my distraction and hit Jesse with her purse, or something equally appalling.

I storm over and push my weight against her, trying to bodily force her out of the path between Jesse and the door. Unfortunately, she doesn't budge. While I'm taller than Naomi, her stocking job has made her way more buff than I could ever be.

"Mom, he's not a home intruder. Let him leave."

"He'd better not come back," she snarls, stepping out of the way so quickly I overbalance.

I have approximately half a second to decide if I'm going to flail to prevent myself from falling or if I'm going to keep my tits covered at the expense of crashing to the floor. Jesse, whose reflexes are far faster than mine, catches

A Fae's Two Alphas

my shoulder before I can succumb to the worst of both options.

The moment Naomi sees him touching me, she lunges. This time I abandon the shirt so I can catch her arms and shove as hard as I can. "Mama Bear, you need to calm the fuck down. Stop! Just stop." It's not until I take Naomi's face between my hands, forcing her to look at me, that she goes still.

"Bennett..." Her tone reeks of distrust, posture tense like she's about to bolt.

It hurts more than the paranoid freakout. I release her and take a step back, sparing a brief glance at Jesse. His expression is hard, arms crossed over his broad chest.

"Why do you hate my best friend so much?" I croak. "Why didn't you tell him I went to Faerie? Why didn't you tell *me* that you brought the Chens to Marquette?" I rake my hands through my tangled hair, then scoop my shirt off the floor, covering myself again. "Seriously, Mom. How the fuck did you think I wouldn't find out?"

"I didn't lie about anything," Naomi snaps.

"Okay, on a fucking technicality, you can't be dishonest about something you *don't say*, which is why they call it lying by omission! What do you have against my friendship with Jesse?"

"It's not my job to tell you everything I do just in case you want to know. I don't have anything against any of your friendships." The nasty scowl she shoots Jesse says otherwise. "I'm just watching out for you."

I shake my head, both exhausted and *tired*—not just physically, but in my soul. "I can't believe you." Turning away, I finally put on the shirt. Then I take Jesse's arm. "Let's go."

"Go?" Jesse tilts his head.

"Yeah. We're going to Callum's." I glare at Naomi, standing alone in the kitchen, posed like something feral. "Mom, I'm... really fucking disappointed in you. Don't wait up for me. Just go to bed."

I expect her to howl, or protest, or *something*, but I get nothing. Naomi stays stock still, watching Jesse, who's now refusing to look at her in favor of tracking my every movement around the house. I grab my phone and charger from my bedroom, dip into the bathroom to snag a clean pair of underwear and my toothbrush, then return to the living room to pick my binder off the floor and put on my shoes.

When I'm ready and waiting at the door, Jesse finally gives up his ground. He pointedly turns his back to Naomi, ignoring her completely as he follows me into the early morning air.

21

WHEN ONE WANTS TO DISAPPEAR

CALLUM IS WAITING in the front yard when we get within eyeshot of the cottage. Jesse had draped a protective arm over my shoulders during the trek, but when I see Callum I peel off and run to him. In the heat of my emotions, I'm unable to think better of faceplanting into Callum's chest.

I feel him gasp when my arms tighten around his ribcage.

The air is cold, and Callum is frozen in my grasp. I breathe deeply against his breastbone, trying to collect myself. Callum is more compact than Jesse; easier to cling to, but just as strong. I hope he doesn't freak out about being jumped, and relief floods me when one large hand comes to rest between my shoulder blades. He doesn't move otherwise, but the pressure is steady and comforting in a way completely unique to the way Jesse overwhelms my senses with each embrace.

Not better, not worse. Just different.

"Bennett," Callum says in a low voice. "What happened?"

"My mom. She just— I can't—" I make a desperate,

frustrated sound. "Callum, you have to try again. I can't fucking do this anymore."

"Try again?"

I'm sure he knows exactly what I'm referring to, but I still clarify: "My magic. This is torture."

Callum looks past me. "What's torture?"

I bury my face in his shirt so I don't have to see the way he questions Jesse with his eyes. They've only known each other for seven or eight months, but I have faith in their bond. What's there now will grow stronger with time and trust; Jesse and Callum will find themselves drawn together eventually, inevitably. They won't be alone when I leave.

"Being here. This horrid fucking realm," I hiss. "I want to go *home*. Away from all the ways humans have made the world suck." Especially the human who birthed me.

"What would you like me to do?" Callum keeps his voice level.

Hurt by his reticence, I withdraw, inching away from both of them. I wrap my arms around myself so I don't miss their touch, separate or combined. "There are other ways, right? You don't have to give me my magic back to get me into Faerie. Humans go over all the time. If I could just... get there. I could find Dad on my own. Work it out between the two of us."

"Okay," Callum says, still infuriatingly calm. "How do you plan on crossing the veil?"

"You aren't going to help me?"

"It's not that I don't want to, Bennett—"

Sudden fury scorches me from the inside out. "Don't bother explaining; it doesn't matter. I'll figure something out myself. Sorry for bothering you."

Jesse calls out when I turn toward the forest behind Callum's cottage. It's the only direction I have left; the other options take me toward the Harris pack house or the too-visible, too-familiar field between here and the unfeeling city concrete. Pine needles rustle under Jesse's feet, but Callum says something too low for me to hear, and Jesse stops.

Cheeks flushed with shame and despair, I trudge into the forest, refusing to look back.

Now I understand, with crushing finality, that there's nowhere I truly belong. Not even here with Jesse and Callum, despite everything that suggested otherwise. If they truly cared they'd understand.

At first, I wonder if they'll come after me. A good chunk of time passes before I stop twitching at every crackling leaf and twig, expecting to see Jesse beating a path toward me. And Callum... Why would he prevent Jesse from coming after me?

Smitten, Jesse said. What bullshit. The way he caught me last night, his arms strong and secure, that wasn't... And just now, feeling safe in his unwavering embrace...

Jesse's wrong, is the point.

Stomping my boots against the forest floor becomes tiring. I have no anger left to burn, leaving me feeling defeated and abandoned. I don't know how long it's been either, since my phone is still dead and useless in the pocket of my pajama pants.

Staying in the mundane realm forever would be a waking nightmare, but Jesse and Callum could make life here... tolerable. Enough that I could ignore the longing sometimes. When the lack of freedom and self-expression inevitably became too much for me, I'm sure they'd find a way to talk me off the ledge.

But after storming off like I did, I don't blame them for not coming after me. Jesse and Callum might not be stereotypical arrogant alpha males, but shifters have that hierarchy bullshit. I can't imagine a person imbued with alpha magic would let themselves be ordered around by some powerless twink in a snit.

My fit of sulking comes to a halt at the same time as I do. I look at the puffy head of a white puffball mushroom half an inch away from being caught under my boot.

Taking a step back, I examine the unexpected scene in front of me.

The leaf litter and pine needles making up the forest floor have thinned out in favor of a bold carpet of green moss. Scraggly wildflowers in bright colors poke through, swaying in a breeze I can't feel. They grow wilder near a large, decomposing tree trunk that has fallen directly through the center of the small clearing.

As I investigate further, I see more mushrooms, and in greater varieties. Ribbed brown dryad's saddles the size of dinner plates, growing from the base of the decaying wood. A sprinkle of green-capped pinkgills and tiny orange chanterelles are bathed in dappling of golden daylight, just beginning to push through the leafy canopy. Ruffled orange coral mushrooms that look like shag fabric intersperse with dozens of tall honey fungus, their cream-and-coffee caps turning up at the ends.

I step back, surveying the space as a whole. Then I practically rip the laces off my boots to get them untied, because I know a damn faerie circle when I see one.

With my boots tossed haphazardly behind me, I breach the boundary of the circle. A shiver runs through me when my feet, sore from all the walking, sink into the cool moss. I trace the boundary of the ring, sketched out in staggered rocks and flowers and mushrooms, wondering what I'd have to do to summon another fae through the veil. Sing? Dance? *Scream*?

Nothing happens until I look up, thinking I've heard something, and miss a wayward branch protruding from the line of foliage. I trip, hurtling forward, and only barely manage to catch myself against the soggy wood of the fallen tree.

My ankle throbs, leaving me no choice but to sit my ass on the damp surface, wincing as moisture seeps through the seat of my pajama pants. I drop my head into my hands and contemplate crying. Contemplate that screaming hypothesis. Wonder what I'll have to do to get back to civilization, since I'm stranded out here with a twisted ankle and a dead phone.

I squeeze my eyes closed until stars flicker behind my eyelids, and when I open them, all I see is the large, dark snout of an absolutely gigantic wolf two inches away from my face. I reel back with a shriek and fall gracelessly over the other side of the trunk.

It doesn't hurt, but the ground is wet, and my phone fell out of my pocket on the way down. I lie flat on the moss, staring up at the leafy canopy and waiting for death, not even shifting to stop my phone from digging into my side.

Death doesn't come. Instead, Callum's strong, tanned shoulders and silver head unfold from his wolf form, leaving him peering at me over the rotten wood.

"Are you alright?"

"No," I answer honestly.

Callum tilts his head. "Are you going to stand up?"

"Also no."

"Okay." He walks around the tree trunk, boldly and unconcernedly naked, and lowers himself to sit cross-legged next to me on the mossy ground.

JEM ZERO

I close my eyes again. "Why are you here, Cal?"

"I wouldn't let you run off with no way to get back." When I don't respond, he says, matter-of-fact: "You found the faerie circle."

"You knew it was here?"

"I did, but it was abandoned long before I built my cottage. The land remembers the magic, but the circle is otherwise inert."

"Oh, great," I say, voice dripping with sarcasm. "I'm so *very happy* to hear that. Don't you have any faefolk contacts? I refuse to believe you don't know a single fae you could call over the veil for a favor."

Callum snorts and gives my shoulder a light, reprimanding nudge. "None I'd trust."

"Right. We can't be trusted, but—"

"And I wouldn't risk your safety gambling on fae court relations at any given moment," he continues. "Most of my business is done within the Unseelie Court."

Finally, I open my eyes and blink at him. "You've made bargains with Unseelies and still have all your organs?"

"Exactly."

I contemplate what he said in the pause that follows. "I'm sure I'd be fine," I state with deliberately false confidence.

"No." Callum adjusts his weight on the mossy forest floor. I wonder if his ass is getting cold. "Bennett..."

"Am I gonna like what you're planning on saying next?"

He breathes a quiet scoff and shakes his head. "Likely not. I think you're being selfish."

The statement has me sitting straight up. "Selfish how?"

"You don't listen to yourself." Callum fixes his piercing blue gaze on me. "Do you realize how much you hurt Jesse whenever you talk about hating everything about the mundane realm?" He puts subtle stress on 'everything.'

I hunch my shoulders, curling in on myself. "I don't mean to upset him."

"There's no way to avoid it," he admits. "But you could be more tactful in his presence."

"You, lecturing *me* on being tactful?"

Callum tilts his head, eyebrows raising. "Jesse and I have a different sort of relationship than what he has with you. Do you disagree?"

I grumble, "No. But you still tell him you can't tolerate his existence, like, all the time."

"Maybe. He knows where we stand."

"Where is that, Cal?" I tilt my head, attempting to mirror his expression, but it probably looks silly rather than questioning.

"Jesse is welcome in my home when he's not being obnoxious," Callum says, as if he's being magnanimous.

"Which is why you tell him to fuck off and look actively displeased every time he comes near." I nod in fake-understanding. "That scans."

Callum pushes his wrist against my knee. "Enough of that, faeling. I couldn't keep him out even if I made a genuine attempt."

I contemplate him, studying the ice blue of his eyes and trying to suppress my reaction to his touch. The back of his knuckles linger against my leg, delicate like the wingbeat of a hummingbird. It's close enough to the lurid love-bite Jesse left that I almost squirm, but I'm afraid Callum might pull away if I do. Instead, I blurt what isn't the *worst* possible thing to say, but is still pretty damn awkward.

"Jesse has feelings for you."

Callum's gaze drops to the forest floor, silvery eyelashes brushing his cheeks.

I duck to reestablish eye contact. "You don't look surprised. Because you've known for a while, right?"

I can tell he doesn't want to face me, but Callum isn't a coward, so with a brief shake of his head, he looks back and says plainly, "I know."

"That's good." I put my hand on his knee. "You already have each other. You just need to let Jesse in, so neither of you are alone."

The corner of his mouth twists. "Relationships are rarely so simple, Bennett."

"What's stopping you?" Callum doesn't respond, so I push harder. "I'm serious, Cal. Why won't you acknowledge his feelings? Unless… you don't reciprocate?" The thought didn't occur to me until just now, and my chest tightens in dismay. "You don't feel the same. Oh my god."

"Bennett," Callum says with a frustrated sigh. "This really isn't your concern."

"The hell it isn't! I want to go *home*, Cal, but I don't want you and Jesse to be left alone." I swallow hard. "Why don't either of you understand that?"

"You have no idea what I do or don't understand." He doesn't snap or growl, or even raise his voice, but the coldness in Callum's tone gives me pause. I'm treading on dangerous ground, but I need him to see where I'm coming from, because I know Jesse won't.

More cautious this time, I ask, "Do you have feelings for Jesse? It'd be okay to admit you did. Do. If you do, I mean. I just think he needs someone. He's so alone, Cal. He's alone and I'm afraid he won't be okay when I leave."

"You say it with confidence. 'When.'"

I scowl—not at Callum, but at the hopeless space in

front of me, nothing but a dead circle of fractured dreams. "I'll find a way over the veil eventually. No matter what it takes. And when I do, I'm never coming back."

"That's your decision," Callum responds placidly.

The neutral tone makes me squirm. "You don't have anything else to say?"

"Of course I do. If you were open to truly listening, I'd ask what you expect to bargain. What do you have that another fae would find appealing enough to do you a favor? How would you guarantee someone with good intentions would find you? How many bones in your hands would you sacrifice to go 'home,' Bennett?"

As he speaks, Callum's voice raises in volume. Not quite to a yell, but enough that the restless not-breeze filling the ring stirs the flowers from their peaceful waving.

"How powerful is your father, a man who would take everything from his son with no word of explanation, when it comes down to defending you from your own reckless actions? Will he save you? Who will suffer the consequences for the inevitable chaos—him or you?"

My voice cracks when I admit, "I don't know. I have no fucking clue, Callum. All I know is that this place is killing me."

With a heavy sigh, Callum extends a hand to brush my bangs out of my eyes. He traces the outline of my face, the textured pad of his thumb ghosting over my lips. "How?"

"What do you mean?"

"How is it killing you? Make me understand."

At first I freeze up, and all I can think of to say is, "There's so much fucking concrete. It's horrid. And I had to work at a smoothie place and it was the worst thing I've ever done." Then my brain comes back online, and the real emotions come pouring out. "I feel useless, especially compared to you and Jesse. Unable to use magic and meet you as equals..."

Callum inhales deeply through his nostrils but doesn't interrupt.

"My body is all wrong and out of sorts. I haven't been physically mundane since I was thirteen, then I suddenly reappeared in what might as well be a human adult body. Do you get how weird that is? Even after two years, I still feel clumsy and awkward. Also, I was able to control my appearance in Faerie. I made myself into a beautiful man and no one cared about me being trans, but here... Everyone but Mom sees me as a girl. No one outside of you and Jess knows me well enough to acknowledge my gender.

"And, fuck, it'll take forever for me to get anywhere in a hormonal transition. If I don't want to wear a binder I'll have to get top surgery, which sounds awful. And for the rest of my life, I have to stab myself once a week and *hope* I get all the changes I want, while feeling completely helpless the entire time. I don't know how human trans people deal with it.

"It's like being chronically sick, and there's no cure, no hope of one, except for maybe one doctor who is trying his best and still can't figure it out. So I have to live every single fucking day like this, desperately wishing I could feel okay again. Just okay. Not even great." I close my eyes, wrinkling my nose against the burn in my sinuses. "I just want to feel okay."

22

BECAUSE HE ALWAYS DOES

AFTER I FINISH MY RANTING—OR, maybe, after I've worn myself out like a toddler having a tantrum—Callum watches me for a length of time I can't approximate. Despite the circle being abandoned, it feels like time is shifting restlessly around us.

The pressure grows until I'm wriggling on the wet moss, which has thoroughly soaked my pants, leaving my butt and thighs cold even as the temperature of the new summer day rises. I don't know if I should beg Callum to say something or flounce off in another fit.

When he speaks, it's preceded by a long, mournful inhale. "I believe I understand, on some level. And..." Color rises in his cheeks. I lean forward, staring like a fool because I'd never considered Callum *blushing* before. "If there was anything I could do to assist with your transition..."

"You'd do that for me?"

"There are many things I would do for you." Before I can turn that over in my mind, Callum continues: "Transformation spells exist. I might be able to, hm. Work something out. I'll look into it."

My eyes glisten with tears I can't hold back anymore. "Thank you," is all I can say.

Callum's eyelids drift low, allowing me to admire the vulnerable contours of his sharp, masculine features. In the dappling of sunlight through the swaying branches above, his image is one of all-consuming beauty. I wouldn't be able to look away from him if I tried.

God, I want to touch him. Hold my palm against his cheek, find out whether his stubble is coarse or soft. Run my hands down his toned chest and watch him emerge from his isolated prison cell, growing warm and needy, full of want and *wanting*, until he's hard, wet, and desperate. So desperate. Until his heart carves itself out of his chest and I can cradle it between our bodies and swear on all the blood flowing through my veins that I'll treasure it. Treasure *him*.

"What are you thinking about?" I ask, trying to rid myself of the silly, impossible fantasy. Callum's shoulders are drooped, his usual confidence faded. Concerned, I give in to the desire to brush my fingers over his arm. "I'm sorry if I said something wrong."

Callum catches my hand and squeezes it. "I've been living in this cottage for twelve years. I acquired the land when I was nineteen, because I needed… I wanted to build a home for myself."

The outburst was unexpected, but I don't call attention to it. I want to hear what Callum has to say. "Why so young?"

"Because that's the age I was when I was exiled from the Truett pack."

The admission wrenches a horrified sound out of me. "You were barely an adult. Why would they do that to you? I thought…" What did I think? That pack was better than family and stuck together no matter what? That a pack member would only be exiled if they did something truly horrendous?

"My father was the lead pack alpha. I was his pride and joy growing up."

I bite the inside of my cheeks to prevent myself from interjecting any nervous commentary.

"When I was eighteen, I entered my first romantic relationship." He swallows, tendons in his throat bulging. "With another man."

My nails are digging into Callum's skin, but when I try to ease my grip, Callum tightens his. "He didn't like that?"

Callum shakes his head, and for the first time ever, I see him smile.

It's not a happy smile.

"Father didn't approve. I was supposed to find a strong mate—a *female* one—and sire strong children. He told me my infatuation would be a phase, and that I was expected to abandon it as soon as possible. I told him I was gay, and—" His voice hitches. "And that was the end."

I stroke the back of his hand with my thumb, following the lovely network of tendons and veins. "What happened to your partner?"

Callum pinches the bridge of his nose, his expression pained. "He helped me build the cottage, then left just before I turned twenty-one. I've been on my own ever since."

"Ten years," I whisper.

"Yes."

I clasp his hand in both of mine, drawing it close so I can press my lips to his knuckles. "I'm so sorry, Callum."

"It's no wonder I've become feral. Me and my magic."

The bitterness radiating from him forces its way into my center, triggering sadness so deep I feel the acid churning in my gut. "It's unfair, but it isn't hopeless." My breath fans over the hair on his knuckles, making him shudder. "We love you, you feral magewolf. Just as you are. Growly and blunt and— and *kind*, and thoughtful. You make me feel valued, Cal."

Callum snorts. Dismissively; then again, breathy and tired. "It's a nice sentiment."

"You don't understand." I roll onto my knees so I can face him better. The moss squelches under my weight, but I ignore it. "It's only been a few months since we met. This isn't a confession that comes from ages of yearning, but I want you to know—and accept—how much I care about you."

He shakes his head in an utterly hopeless way. That ache deep inside me radiates through my chest, the pain so sharp I press his hand over my heart in hopes of easing it.

Desperate for him to believe me, I say, "Jesse loves you. *I* love you."

"And you and Jesse," Callum spits, "are together."

Pain radiates up my ankle when I jump to my feet, but I power through it. "Every time Jesse and I go on a date, we end up talking about you. And last night after you left, we were *still* talking about you, worrying about your feelings. So before I escape this fucking realm, I plan to ensure you and Jesse will be okay without me."

Callum rises gracefully. "You're a presumptuous little imp."

"I'll take it," I say with a roll of my eyes.

"Then take this, too: I'm not something you can tame. You don't get to tell me what to feel and who to interact with, or how. How can you ask me to accept your feelings, then immediately promise to leave? What about that benefits me?" A growl rolls in his throat. "No one's ever tried to save me, Bennett. No one's going to succeed now."

I bare my blunt teeth—the ones I assured him were dangerous just last night. "I'm not trying to save you! I'm trying to *love* you."

"You'll get over it."

I snarl like the animal I most definitely am not, and lunge. Callum could stop me easily, could have subdued me before I even moved, but he doesn't. In fact, when I tug his arm and sink my very-dangerous-indeed teeth into his shoulder, he doesn't budge at all. He merely stares in bewilderment.

"What are you doing?"

"Mnnhg mm," I say, teeth still in his arm. I only let go when I become afraid of drooling on him. I wipe my mouth and mutter, "I just thought it'd be the wolf-like thing to do."

A sharp sound escapes Callum. One piercing note, like a bird's cry, rich in a way I almost can't define until I realize it's *laughter*.

I made Callum laugh. Holy shit.

Emboldened, I face him head-on and run my palms up his bare chest like I've wanted to do for so long. The curls of silver hair are soft and I never want to stop petting them. "I'm not giving up, you know."

Another sound, one I peg as a hysterical abortion of a laugh, forces its way from Callum's throat. He turns his face away, which does nothing to hide his reddening cheeks. "You're stubborn. Don't worry, I've noticed."

"Good, so you won't be surprised when I—" My plan of pushing up onto my toes fails spectacularly when the pain in my twisted ankle becomes too much to bear. I yank my foot off the ground with a yelp, then immediately lose my balance.

And guess what? Callum catches me. Because he always does.

He scoops me up and places me on the driest part of the tree trunk, which is a nice sentiment, but I'm already soaked, and now the temperature has increased enough that I'm starting to sweat. Callum drops to his knees and lifts my foot, clicking his tongue in disapproval when he examines it.

"You twisted your ankle? Ridiculous boy," he sighs. Whatever he does next hurts, but not too much, so I let my gaze roam around the forest, looking at everything but Callum. "There," he says at last. "You shouldn't be tromping about in those boots."

"Horrid things, aren't they?"

Callum hums.

I attempt a smile. "I wish I could always be barefoot like you."

"Seeing as you just did *this*"—he runs his thumb lightly down my foot, igniting the nerves—"I'm inclined to discourage future attempts."

"Can't have everything, I guess."

Callum levels me with a stare, hot with intensity and, I'm surprised to note, thinly-veiled anger. "Exactly. And there's no use dwelling on what cannot happen."

"Right, so you shouldn't use that as an excuse to reject what *can* happen," I say desperately, knowing he isn't talking about me frolicking barefoot like an imp.

"You don't understand, and I won't sit here arguing while you refuse to listen." He shakes his head again, more hopeless than I've ever seen him. "No one understands," he whispers.

"Cal," I say, so sharply he has no option but to look at me, blue eyes laser-bright among the shadows covering much of his face. "I've been mostly alone for nearly two years, and admittedly I can't imagine ten of them. But I'm not here to save you, and I'm certainly not interested in trying to change or tame you. Be feral if that's what makes you comfortable. I want it: every growl, every predatory footstep, every time you do that weird eye-glowy thing. All of it. Just— Just let me in."

And then, because I don't want to hear any further attempts at rejection, I dip my head the few necessary inches to bring my lips to his. Only long enough to get my point across without forcing myself on him, since he's right. I can't order Callum to accept, or even want, my love.

When I try to lean away, Callum catches my face and refuses to let go. His mouth is impossibly hot and tastes of need—of surrender. I don't suppose either of us expects me to fling myself at him, but that's what I end up doing.

23

UNPLEASANTLY WET PAJAMA PANTS

I END up a messy heap in his lap, but only for a second before Callum lies back, pulling me down with him. I squirm with delight, my hands roaming his chest and shoulders. Callum's palms frame my jaw, keeping me in place while he pants raggedly into my mouth.

I kiss him with teeth, as if I'm the feral one, and Callum responds by sucking on my tongue. Despite being fully clothed on top of his naked body, I feel exposed and vulnerable.

"Touch me," I instruct, taking his hands and placing them on my hips. Yet even with my guidance, Callum seems unsure. Not with his mouth, though. He kisses with messy abandon, growling when I tug his lip between my teeth. I barely pry myself away to gasp for breath, and take advantage of the break to rub my cheek against his, savoring the rasp of his stubble.

The combination of forest-damp clothes and beads of sweat forming on the back of my neck is beginning to irritate me. My wet clothes are uncomfortable, and the sun warming the clearing isn't enough to dry them off. Seems as good a time as any to strip.

My t-shirt comes off easily. I'm not sure I execute the technique as flawlessly as Jesse, considering I have no rippling musculature to reveal as I yank it over my head. My arms and shoulders are tan from all my walks, but the skin underneath my binder is a ghostly white. Speaking of my binder, I try to yank that off too. Not only does it not peel off to reveal sculpted gold-hued muscle, it doesn't come off at all.

I make a strangled sound, trapped in the sticky binder I should have known better than to remove carelessly. It's a struggle to escape even when I'm dry.

"Bennett," Callum sighs. Hopefully, that tone is exasperated-fond rather than exasperated-turned off. I can't judge by his facial expression because my arms are pinned to my face in two very different but equally awkward angles.

If it's embarrassing to need help removing my undergarments from two different lovers in the same twelve-hour period, I don't let myself dwell on it. Callum gently pries me out of the spandex, leaving me to sort the tangle of hair and limbs left behind. I attempt to fingercomb my hair into a less chaotic formation. My bangs hang limp over my forehead; I close one eye to avoid being poked by my split ends, but the longer strands of my hair catch around my fingers when I try to brush the bangs aside.

"Bennett," Callum repeats, warmth in his voice. "Slow down. Just stop moving."

I hold still, allowing him to put me together, smoothing my hair and squeezing my shoulders to bring warmth back into them after the adrenaline has me reduced to nervous shivers.

"That was horribly unsexy of me," I say in a flat voice.

Callum presses his lips into a thin line. No smile fights to tilt the corners, but his eyes crinkle as he looks back at me, and that's more than enough. "I hadn't expected this to be a sexual encounter, I'll admit, so I'm not let down. If that helps."

I giggle, then nestle my cheek into his palm, cherishing how it molds to the curvature of my face. That's when my freshly-exposed skin itches, as it often does when I've just removed my binder, and I thoughtlessly reach to itch under my breast. The center of Callum's focus drops by several inches, and just like that, I'm flushed from my eyebrows past my collarbones.

I resist the urge to hide them. Callum saw me naked that time he accidentally burst in on me showering, but I'd prioritized covering my tits over my crotch, so this still feels different. I manage to not fold my arms over my chest like a trembling virgin, but it's a near thing.

Callum doesn't seem aware of my internal struggle, instead looking rather lost in his own.

"Um," I say, not knowing exactly how to ask. "Have you ever... seen tits before?"

His expression loses its wariness and moves into full incredulity. "Bennett, I've worked as a doula for pregnant people. Do you really think I reached thirty-one years old without seeing breasts?"

I throw my hands up. "I don't know! You said you were gay."

Callum rolls his eyes skyward. "You try my patience."

"Same," I grumble. Then I knuckle him in the side. "In a sexual context, though."

Flushing almost as dark as I did, Callum puts his hand over his eyes. "No. I haven't."

"Gotcha. Do you want me to stop?"

Callum tenses, and is silent for so long I remove my hands from his body. He uncovers his eyes, blinks up at the sun, and then gently takes my wrists, guiding them back to his chest. When I uncurl my fingers, he flattens his palms over the back of my hands, pressing down until I can feel his lungs swell with each nervous breath. The trust is sweet-to-aching, so I take his mouth in a slow kiss. It fails to adequately express my feelings, but it's the best I have.

And Callum allows it. Welcomes it, if I'm feeling bold enough to hope. Wanting to extend the same trust, I gently switch the position of our hands and lead Callum to my own chest, stopping just short of contact.

At first, he sweeps his calloused fingertips underneath the curve of my breasts, thumbs following the valley between two ribs. I shiver, loving the rasp of working hands and the edges of his thick claws. He's careful about keeping them away from my skin; they may be blunt and worn, but he could still tear someone apart. It doesn't scare me, though. I love how his power contrasts with such gentleness.

Callum shies away from touching my tits properly, hovering over them like the wrong side of a magnet. But then he rubs one of my nipples between his thumb and forefinger, pinching it gently, and I react like I've never been touched before. I squirm and whimper, arching my back in encouragement—like, *please* keep going.

"Good?" he asks, gruff tone exposing nervousness at the corners.

"Yeah," I say in a shuddery voice. "Very."

"Okay." So he does it again, this time adding the other one, too.

My nipples are puffy, prominent even when they aren't hard. It embarrassed me when I was younger. Now, Callum explores with such interest that it eases my insecurity. Once

I'm stable, whining from need, he finally presses his warm hands against the swells of my breasts and gives them a cautious squeeze.

"Are they okay?"

Callum freezes. "Did you just ask if a part of your body is *okay*?"

"Are *you* okay, I meant." I didn't realize how insecure I would sound until he turned the question back on me, and now I'm twice as jittery.

By the look on his face, Callum isn't buying the correction, but he lets it go. "I wouldn't change anything." One hand follows my sternum to my collarbones, then further, until he can drag me in for another kiss. After that, his hands start to roam properly, the way I tried not to fantasize about during his torturous physical examinations. Instead of brief, clinical contact, Callum explores my body like he wants to memorize the shape of me.

I tease my tongue along the shell of his ear and relish in the tiny gasp that catches in his throat. Callum's hands are so wide that when he holds tight to my hips his fingers brush together across the small of my back. It leaves him enough leverage to press his thumbs into my hipbones, catching a tender spot left by Jesse's mouth only a few hours ago.

The feeling of Callum's touch over Jesse's marks sets something aflame within me. Merely kissing him has been lovely, but the combination of *them* puts me in such a state I'm not sure what I'm going to do with myself.

Callum kisses my neck without a hint of teeth. I wouldn't mind if he were to bite me, but his lips and tongue are enough for now. I adjust so I can worry the crook of his shoulder with my teeth. The new position brings me in contact with firm, satin-smooth heat.

A Fae's Two Alphas

Thick and dripping, the head of Callum's cock prods the hickey on my inner thigh. I haven't looked at it yet, but the bruise hurts so deliciously that pleasure has me arching my back, bearing down harder to amplify the pain.

Callum tightens his grip on my hips, stilling me. "Bennett..."

It takes massive amounts of self-control to not struggle, when all I want to do is grind against him. "Is everything okay?"

"I'm fine," he says. "Are... are you sure?"

Surprised that he'd have to ask, I go for full disclosure. "I've been wanting this since Summer Solstice."

Callum inhales sharply. "Of course you have."

With a shaky laugh, I sit up to straddle his waist. "Anything else?"

Callum plucks at the back of my soggy pajama pants and grimaces. "These have to go."

"Right. Oh, fuck. Cal, yanking them isn't helping!"

To Callum's credit, he doesn't ask to rip them off like Jesse did. It would be hot as hell, and I'd consider telling him to do it if I had anything else to cover my ass. He growls against my neck, but waits until I've levered myself through the complicated series of angles required to remove a pair of wet pants without climbing off someone.

But then it's over, and I'm naked on top of him, struggling not to move because he's just... *Looking* at me. He skims his fingertips over my skinny limbs and sore tits, leading down, down until he stops at my pubis. I haven't shaved in a few days, but I don't think Callum will care about the stubble.

When he tilts his head, I shift to give him a better angle, exposing my cunt. Other than some T-growth in my clit, it's not particularly impressive. Except there's this raw hunger in Callum's eyes, like my body isn't the uninspiring collection of angles I view it as.

When Callum touches me there, it's with such care my heart nearly shatters. He circles my clit slowly, then when I wriggle, impatient and growing desperate, increases the pressure and speed. Then, despite my protest, he withdraws.

"Callum?" I try to swallow down the worry threatening to choke me. What if he changed his mind? Thought he could deal with the lack of dick, but—

"Hush, Bennett." Callum taps two of his claws together and frowns.

"You won't hurt me."

"I told you to hush," he says, then cups both sides of my ass and urges me forward.

I want to ask what he's doing, but he told me to hush twice, so I silently allow him to position me with my knees on either side of his head. I clench one hand in the moss while the other grips his hair, barely able to process what's happening. Then Callum draws my clit into his waiting mouth and sucks, rhythmic pulses of suction that make me feel like I have an actual dick, which is, um. *Wow*.

For someone who's never eaten pussy before, he's doing amazing. I'd tell him so, but my mouth is too busy fitting itself around a scream as he brings me to one of the fastest orgasms of my life.

24

EMOTIONS BRUISE TOO

I SLIDE OFF HIS FACE, landing on the moss in a graceless flop. At least it's mostly dry now, just moist enough to be a relief from the day's mounting heat.

"Fuck, you're good at that. Are you sure this is your first time?"

"Positive," Callum rumbles, the sound predatory and full of purpose. He rolls onto all fours and prowls over me, inhaling deeply before he licks sweat from the side of my neck.

"You're going to fuck me next, right?"

Callum's breath is hot against my skin. He nips my jaw, making me squeak. "Your patience needs work."

"Which means yes?"

He growls, rearing up so he can manhandle my legs around him. His cock comes to rest in the hollow between my leg and crotch, sliding through the combination of spit and come that gives me remarkable flashbacks to Jesse fucking my thighs last night. Which reminds me...

"Fuck." I slap a hand over my face.

"What?" Callum sounds startled.

JEM ZERO

I pet his chest in reassurance. "Nothing's wrong, I just... don't have any condoms. Obviously." In fact, the only thing I had on me—my phone—is still lying on the moss somewhere.

Callum arches an eyebrow with such effortless grace I might as well come all over him again. "Are you afraid I'll—"

"Give me some magical STD? No," I reassure him. He seems scandalized by my phrasing, so I hurriedly finish my thought. "I'm just, uh, don't want to... Pregnancy."

Callum presses his lips together, and this time I *do* believe he's fighting a smile. Or remembering how, maybe. Either way, his eyes dance with amusement when he says, "I used magic to give myself a vasectomy out of spite when I was in my early twenties. No pups for me."

"Oh." I blink, turning that information over in my brain. "Cool. So, fucking now?"

"If you insist," Callum says, nuzzling my cheek.

I wiggle happily and lift my knees, before noticing Callum's furrowed brow. "Sorry, forgot you've never done this before. Can I touch you?"

"Why would it not be okay for you to touch me?"

"Oh my god, just come here."

Callum watches with unveiled fascination as I ease his foreskin back, swirling my thumb over the head of his cock to gather moisture, and position him properly at my entrance.

"Okay, just... Push in. Slowly, slowly. Yeah, I—*fuck*."

When he's fully inside me, I'm more than ready to go, but Callum holds up a finger. His forehead is creased, and he looks sheepish. "Just give me a moment." Callum's hips twitch forward and his eyes fall closed.

There's no point in being tactful, so I ask, "Does pussy feel different from fucking an ass?"

"I wouldn't know."

"You've never fucked anyone before? Ever?"

"It's usually the other way around," Callum mutters.

I'm still wrapping my mind around Callum being a bottom when he hazards his first tiny thrust. All thoughts disappear from there. I haven't been fucked in two years, and breaking that drought by getting railed by a bone-meltingly sexy alpha in the middle of a faerie circle is exactly what I need.

It takes a bit more careful rocking before we settle into a rhythm, but I wouldn't trade this fumbling exploration for anything.

Part of me wonders if Callum is the "silent during sex" type, but I learn otherwise. Callum's meticulous control dissolves more with each kiss, our tongues sweeping lewdly in time with his thrusts. Finally, we're moaning together, cries muffled in each other's mouths. Callum's noises are fragile things, shuddery inhalations and soft grunts. Once, a surprised hiccup, after he hits my G-spot for the first time and I jerk like I've been shocked.

On the cusp of coming again, I wrap my arms around Callum's shoulders and squeeze my legs around his hips. The increasing volume of Callum's moans suggests he's getting close, too.

Unexpectedly, he slows down.

My eyes pop open. "Are you okay?"

"Yes. I just want to warn, um. Fuck, I don't know... Do you want me to come inside you?"

I blink up at the canopy of trees, squinting against the sun's glare. "Is that a real question?" His expression is serious, so I say, "Yes, Callum. I want you to come inside me." I'd have hoped saying those words would come out more impassioned, but concern is putting a damper on my arousal.

"This is a shit time for an anatomy lesson, but wolves have a... sexual quirk."

I don't mean to get frustrated, but Callum's hesitation is making me unbearably anxious. "Just tell me!"

Callum clasps a hand over my mouth; I whimper against his palm. "When I orgasm, part of my dick will swell up inside you, which will keep us together for several minutes after sex ends. Yes or no."

My eyes could not possibly get wider. I study his face for any sign—however unlikely—that he's fucking with me rather than just fucking me. When I find none, I figure there's no way Callum would entertain anything that would hurt or scare me, with or without my permission, so I nod enthusiastically. I hope the agreement will get him going again.

And *oh*, it does.

Callum slams into me, hips working with punishing intensity. He drops messy kisses over my cheeks and forehead. I moan in response, bucking up to meet him.

"*Fuck*, Ben." Callum buries his face in my hair, driving his cock inside me with measured, powerful thrusts that have me sliding on the moss.

I push my fingers into the earth, still clutching his hair with the other hand. The connection between Callum and I, nature's vibrance and the circle's dormant magic, makes me feel more alive than I have in years.

"You close?" My sweaty fingers slip down his nape. I hold on, nails digging into Callum's skin, refusing to let go. He isn't escaping me. Not ever again.

Callum's response is a strangled sound. I don't expect him to take me in his arms, one braced under us while the other clutches me close to his chest. I cling, melded against his sweat-slick skin. One breathless second later, he's coming so hard I feel his cock pulse with every spurt.

Then it happens.

"Holy shit," I wheeze, unable to process anything but the firm... something... expanding inside me. Callum jerks his hips a few more times without pulling out, and I realize it's because he can't. Whatever's connecting us has stretched inside me so thoroughly it's tied us together, our hips flush.

Callum adjusts me against his chest, then nudges my leg out of the way so he can roll onto his back, settling me on top of him so I'm not at risk of being crushed under his lax weight. He runs his hands up and down my spine, squeezing my ribcage and shoulders as if he's trying to assure himself I'm real, present, and stuck with his dick inside me.

And that is such an intensely *arousing* thought, I can't help but wriggle, just a little, just enough to realize if I arch my hips, the swollen thing mashes into my G-spot. "Holy shit," I say again, flexing my pelvic muscles. "What is this?"

Callum groans, bucking upward as I rock on his dick with mounting desperation, aware of nothing but him. "It's called a knot," he rasps.

"Holy fucking shit." Usually I can't come without focusing on clitoral stimulation, but at this moment I'm devastatingly, painfully turned on by rubbing his knot against my G-spot. I'm seconds away from losing myself again.

Callum cups my ass, one finger dipping between my cheeks, and steers me with such determination that when he whispers, "Stay with me, Bennett," I snap like a torn branch in a windstorm.

He kisses the crown of my head and plays with my hair until I stop twitching and my breathing evens out.

"That was... incredible," I wheeze once I'm able.

Callum hums, sounding utterly content for once.

I meditate on the feeling of us, together. Clinging to each other in the middle of the forest.

For a very weird, but not exactly unexpected, moment, I wish Jesse was here to... what? Watch? No, not just seeing us, but lying next to us, maybe kissing Callum's temple or squeezing my ass. Both.

To distract myself, I blurt, "How long will it last?"

"I can make it go down sooner if you like." Callum sounds defensive.

Does he think I'm eager to get away? I squeeze my arms around him and kiss his neck softly. "No, I was just curious. I love this. Now you can't escape me."

Snorting, Callum tightens his grip as well. We relax as, silent until his knot begins to shrink in size. Finally, he pulls out, both of us sighing as we separate.

"Are you okay?" he asks as soon as I roll off him, bracing myself on my hands and knees.

I can't deny swooning a bit, but I manage to mumble, "Totally fine. Perfect. Great." Something warm runs down my thigh, which I identify (after an embarrassing number of seconds) as Callum's semen dripping out of me. I shudder, tucking my hand between my legs like I need proof. It unbalances me, and rather than fighting it, I let myself sprawl onto the moss.

Callum rolls onto all fours with much more coordination and creeps forward to check on me. "Still alright? I can—" He stops, looking at my crotch. At first, I think he's marveling at the sight of his come over my skin;

he flutters his fingers over the spot, smearing it. "Did I do this?"

Incredulous, I prepare to ask him who the fuck else came inside me, until I realize he's indicating the love bite, which, after a glance, I confirm has darkened into a crime scene-level bruise.

"Um, no. You didn't. That was..." My face flushes so suddenly I hear the blood rushing to heat my cheeks. Full understanding of what I've just done hits me like a blow.

I didn't tell him about Jesse and I. I *meant* to, but the information never made it all the way out, and now I'm stuck.

But I can't lie.

"That was Jesse. Last night."

Callum stares blankly until I start to squirm. Then he rises gracefully and puts his back to me.

"Callum, wait!" I stagger to my feet. My limbs are jelly, so I careen into the tree trunk. At least it gives me something to support myself against. "It's not— We aren't exclusive, and um." How can I explain that Jesse and I agreed to not let our relationship stand between either of us and a connection with Callum without it sounding really, *really* weird?

In the end, I can't.

"We should get you back to the cottage, Bennett." He collects my clothing and my boots, still not looking at me.

"I don't think I can walk," I say faintly.

Callum offers me the depressing lump of my belongings. He spots my phone and picks that up too, setting it on the small pile before hurrying to put distance between us.

I dump everything next to me on the spongy wood and proceed to use my shirt to wipe the come off my thighs. Then I tug on the wet pajama pants, cringing. There's no way I'm getting this damp binder on, so I shove it into one boot with my phone, and the defiled shirt into the other boot.

All throughout, I'm painfully aware of Callum's absence. I want to apologize, want to wrap my arms around him, but he's sitting on his heels with his back to me, elbows draped over his knees and head hanging.

"Callum?"

Instead of responding, he shifts back into his wolf form.

I stare into the lapis-blue eyes that've become so dear to me, silently begging for forgiveness. Callum ducks his head and, unexpectedly, butts it against my chest. I stagger back a step, confused, but when he nudges me again with his nose and a third time with his shoulder, I realize he's telling me to—

"Are you asking me to *ride* you?" My cheeks burn, even though I quite literally rode his face and knot while sprawled in the faerie circle.

Callum huffs an affirmative, so I hoist myself over his wide back and nervously take a handful of his thick scruff. My other hand presses my boots against my exposed chest. I clench my thighs around his ribs and lean forward, whispering, "I'm ready."

Callum trots forward, slowly at first, making sure I'm as secure as I claim to be. When I don't fall, he coils his muscles and breaks into a run.

25

DIRTINESS IS OKAY

As usual, I slump down in the passenger seat of Jesse's car when he drives by the Harris pack house. Before, I said it was because I didn't want word to get back to my mom, but the truth is simpler: I don't want to be around them. Or anyone. I've gone out of my way to avoid all Harrises, even Josie and Ms. Chen.

Over the last week, my social interaction has been limited to Jesse. I've been standoffish to Naomi, and Callum has been standoffish to *me*.

Jesse hasn't pushed for an explanation. He also hasn't seemed offended by my withdrawal back into our previous level of intimacy—hugs mostly, and a few safe, chaste kisses. It's obvious I'm not okay, but despite texting Jesse every minute we aren't physically together, I haven't been ready to talk about it.

We visited Callum's three days ago. He's been ignoring my texts, but I thought he might listen if I was able to corner him. He evaded my attempts to get him alone, practically gluing himself to Jesse's side for the first time ever. When

Jesse went to the bathroom, Callum had an errand he mysteriously needed to run, leaving Jesse confused when he exited the bathroom to find me sulking in the corner of an otherwise empty cottage.

I don't know if Callum told Jesse what happened between us that day in the woods. It certainly wasn't subtle when I rode into the front yard on Callum's back, half-naked and reeking of dirt and sex. I'd bolted to the shower, refusing to look in Jesse's direction in case I found hurt in his eyes. When I emerged, he'd been as sweet and affectionate as usual, offering me his shirt to sit in while Callum washed my clothes, but I've felt like an absolute monster since.

I should've told Callum that Jesse and I had slept together. I don't know if the point of contention was how recently it had happened, or that I didn't disclose how physically close Jesse and I had gotten during the conversation about both of us having feelings for Callum. Either way, it's obvious I fucked up. I thought I'd been transparent, but I wasn't.

Callum might even be upset at the possibility of me having "cheated" on Jesse, even though I'd never have jumped Callum if Jesse and I had been exclusive, feelings or not. I don't know the specifics of Callum's hurt because he won't fucking talk to me, even to hear an apology.

I wish I'd had a good excuse to beg off visiting the cottage with Jesse today, but I haven't had many options for where to spend my time. I've made an effort to not be home while my mom is awake, and Jesse hasn't wanted me to roam the city on my own like I used to. He hasn't brought up the rift between Callum and me, since I've made it clear I'm not ready for the conversation, but he's perceptive. Even if he wasn't, it's not exactly subtle.

A Fae's Two Alphas

Watching the trees pass as we near the cottage fills me with mounting dread. How can I keep facing Callum without any hope of resolution? How can I be near him when, above anything else, the stalemate has left me feeling *dirty*?

What kind of person fucks two different guys within the same twelve-hour period? I was supposed to respect and care for Callum and Jesse as friends, not use them as emotional vibrators instead of fully processing my issues. Callum was right—I *am* selfish.

The week has been mental torture, and with every day that creeps by, the names I call myself get worse. I don't think either of them would want me to feel this way, but I do, and I have no idea how to talk about it, so here we are, pulling up to the spot where Jesse always parks like everything is normal and fine.

Jesse jumps out of the car and slams the door. In my peripheral, I see him lift the key fob to lock the car before he realizes I haven't moved. Jesse's muffled voice questions me from outside the car; when I don't respond, he pulls the passenger door open and leans against the roof of the car.

"What's wrong, Benny?"

"It doesn't matter," I mumble, which puts me only slightly above Naomi in terms of communicativeness. She would have turned the question around rather than give any ground by admitting there might be something off. Functionally, the result is the same.

Jesse examines me. Then, with a sigh, he unbuckles my seatbelt and drags me out of the car. I sputter, doing my best to push him away, but all that gets me is his hand ruffling my hair until I can't see past my bangs.

I honk like a disturbed goose. Jesse only smiles as I pat myself back into order, and doesn't even flinch when I hiss at him. Unfortunately, I lack a serrated beak, so my intimidation factor is actually inferior to that of a goose.

How depressing.

Having failed to provoke any reaction despite my best efforts, I deflate.

"Ready to talk yet?" Jesse asks, folding his arms over his chest.

"Sorry, you're going to have to rough me up some more before I break," I say, heavy with sarcasm. I realize my mistake too late, but there's no time to dodge before Jesse snatches me up and throws me over his shoulder.

"I'm dumping you in the creek," he says.

"Jesse Nathaniel Chen!" I holler.

"Oh, you did *not* just middle-name me. You are definitely getting dunked now."

"Fuck you! Goddamnit, put me down. I'll talk."

Jesse stops walking. "You sure?"

"I promise, even though this counts as a confession under duress and thus is not valid evidence in a court of law."

"Don't act like you know things about human law, Ben." Jesse flips me over his shoulder and sets me, or the extremely rattled doll that took Bennett's place, on the pebbled ground.

I immediately tackle him around the midsection, but as usual, he doesn't have the decency to even pretend to stumble. Doesn't even sway. I wear myself out quickly, and with one final sigh of defeat, I say, "I feel like an amoral slut who irredeemably fucked up his most important friendships."

If Jesse's jaw could fall off, roll into the creek, and flow downstream, I think it would.

"You feel like a what?!"

"You heard me." I scuff my toe through the dusty rubble, then abruptly decide I don't want to risk seeing more of Jesse's confused expression, so I begin a stomping path toward the cottage.

It doesn't work. In my defense, I didn't think it would.

Jesse catches my elbow and spins me to face him, then seizes both of my shoulders so I can't turn away. "Please go back to the beginning of that statement and, like, say it again, but with context this time."

I run my fingers through my hair and frown downward. He can stop me from escaping, but he can't force me to meet his gaze.

"Bennett. Look at me." Nevermind, guess he can.

My face grows hot, but Jesse gives me an insistent little shake, and it's enough. "What the fuck else do you want me to say?" I snap. "I fucked both you and Callum in basically the same day, and now everything is ruined!" Emotion surges over me—a specific flavor I'd been trying to block out—and I have to clap my hands over my face to avoid humiliating myself with projectile sobbing.

"Why do you think—"

"Cal won't even look at me. He hasn't spoken to me other than 'here, I made tea' and 'damn, it sure is getting late,' which we both know is Midwestern speak for 'get the fuck out of my house.'" Jesse opens his mouth to interject, but I steamroll over him again. "And sometimes I'm glad you haven't said anything, but other times I worry you're secretly thinking the same thing. I know I fucked up, but I don't know what I should've done instead. Should I have waited until my fuck-meter recharged or something? Does having sex with two people I've been openly attracted to make me as greedy and thoughtless as I feel?"

The furrow between Jesse's brow grows deeper the

longer I rant. Once I've burned myself out, I simply stand there staring upward and silently pleading for him to bring an end to my misery.

"I didn't realize you were struggling so badly," Jesse says quietly.

A hysterical laugh bubbles up my throat. "You didn't realize? How could I *not*? I can't stop telling myself that you guys see me as dirty and slutty because I wasn't able to pick just one of you."

"Okay, first off"—Jesse puts a finger to my lips—"neither Cal nor I would *ever* call you dirty. And if Callum slut-shamed you, I'd break his fucking orbital."

"Please don't," I mumble. "He has pretty eyes."

"I'll make sure to keep at least one of them intact."

I really, really want to laugh. Instead, I just faceplant into Jesse's chest and wait until he wraps his arms around me.

"I can speak to Cal if you want," he says.

I give a vehement shake of my head, mussing my bangs against his shirt. "That would be so fucking embarrassing. Humiliating."

"You'd rather he ignore you forever?"

"No, but I don't want him to think I sent you to shake him down. If he doesn't want to talk, he doesn't want to talk."

Jesse hums, not sounding convinced.

"Not to mention, what would you say? 'Yeah, it's totally okay that Bennett fucked both of us. He's not playing with your heart at all!'"

Jesse squeezes me, then pushes me an arm's length away. When I stubbornly avoid his gaze, he gently tilts my chin up. "It *is* okay, though."

"It's not okay—"

"I mean, it's okay that you had sex with both of us. Callum shouldn't be throwing a fit over it. It's your body, and you can sleep with whomever you want."

"Just you two," I mutter under my breath, fully aware that Jesse will have no trouble hearing it.

"Aw, Ben..."

"What the hell am I going to do?" I hang my head and make my plodding way toward the cottage. This time Jesse doesn't stop me.

I slump into the cottage and kick off my sandals, unsurprised when Callum only spares me a brief glance, pointedly not meeting my eyes. I hover in the doorway, not sure what to do next.

"Please close the door, Bennett," Callum says evenly.

"Oh." I shuffle out of the way in time for Jesse to pop inside. The door creaks shut behind him, leaving me floundering while he unties his shoes. I take a few steps toward Callum, shyly suggesting, "Maybe tea?"

"Sit down," is all he says.

My shoulders droop as I drag myself to the couch, ignoring Jesse's concerned look.

"Do you need help, Cal?" Jesse asks.

Callum wrinkles his nose. "When have I ever needed help making tea? Go sit down. You two, I swear."

When Jesse sits on the couch, I mash myself against his side, clinging to his shirt. Anxiety pulses in my chest. I stay that way until Callum arrives with three mugs of tea, at which point I jerk backward into an isolated bubble, not knowing how he'll respond to seeing me flaunt my close relationship with Jesse.

Callum sets a mug in front of me—a white one, even though he knows the purplish-teal mug is my favorite—and sits stiffly across from Jesse and me. "I don't have much time to entertain today," he says. "I've an important commission that needs work."

"We've hung out while you worked before," Jesse says, unimpressed.

For once, I'm loath to be trapped in the middle of their bickering. I reach for my mug, but nervous energy has my fingers slipping on the unfamiliar handle. The mug clacks against Jesse's, sending a splash of hot tea over my wrist.

"Ow," I say without inflection, examining the blooming red spot of burned skin.

Jesse quickly pulls the mug out of my hands. He says something, but it's Callum's voice that cuts through the numbness that's taken over my brain.

"Bennett, are you alright?"

"Just a burn." I sound calmer than I should. Callum reaches for me, but I withdraw. "I'll be fine," I start to say, but he snatches my wrist anyway.

"Give me your hand, damn it." Callum wastes no time muttering an incantation, his callused palm squeezing uncomfortably over the burn. After a moment, the sting begins to ease, but even when the pain recedes fully, Callum doesn't release me. His grip relaxes until he's cradling my hand in his much larger one, eyes locked on where my lax fingers drape over his.

I have no idea how to proceed. All I manage is a quiet "Thank you."

Callum looks up sharply, then drops my hand like a dead thing. I let it fall, struggling to swallow as an even more vicious tension chokes the atmosphere around us.

Jesse clears his throat and rises. "I'll get a rag." Several long strides take him to the kitchenette before he returns to wipe the spilled tea from the coffee table.

"I'm going to wash my hands," I announce, then flee toward the bathroom.

26

PROVE IT

I HIDE in Callum's small, utilitarian bathroom as long as I can, until I start feeling suspicious of my *own* whereabouts. I'm surprised Jesse hasn't banged on the door yet, but I'm glad he hasn't, because all I'm doing is sitting on the side of the tub playing some tie-dye fractal creator game on my phone. It's supposed to be soothing, but right now, the swirling colors are only making me more anxious.

With a defeated sigh, I close the app and stand. I've already washed my hands, but I wash them again, taking my time just in case I missed a few germs the first go. Wouldn't want to leave my filthy, slutty handprints all over Callum's fixtures.

Okay, that's going a bit far.

I nudge the bathroom door open, wondering how much longer I have to stay before I can politely excuse myself. I'd make the *I want to take a walk* excuse, but of course I wore sandals today. My ankle felt fine days ago, but Callum still got snappish about me wearing boots again. Even if I was willing to risk ticks, I'd probably end up hogtied before either of them allowed me to walk through the field unprotected. Maybe I could get a head start by saying I'm just stepping out for some air. Not likely.

My half-hearted daydreams about running away dissolve when I step out of the bathroom to see Jesse and Callum inches away from each other's faces. Both have their eyes lit with the eerie alpha glow. Callum is baring his teeth while Jesse looms over him, his hands fisted tight in Callum's shirt.

They don't notice me standing there, frozen like a prey animal, trying to hear their argument over the pounding of my heart.

"—acting like a jackass," Jesse hisses, giving Callum a shake.

Callum seizes Jesse's wrist in a crushing grip. "How many times will I say it's none of your fucking business before you leave me be?"

"Don't bother trying, because it *is* my business. If you had a problem you should have come to me days ago." Callum opens his mouth, but Jesse raises his voice. "Don't you dare lie to me. I already know you're going to say you don't have a problem when you obviously fucking do."

"Even if it did concern you," Callum growls, "you have no right to demand anything of me."

"Fuck whatever rights you think I don't have. You hurt him."

Callum is silent for several seconds. "It'll pass."

"He shouldn't have to wait for you to communicate about your fucked up reservations. Do you know what he said to me earlier?"

Jesse's going to reveal too much. I need to break this up... except I still can't make myself move, or even speak.

"You made him feel dirty, Cal," Jesse snaps. He releases

Callum's shirt and attempts to shove the other alpha out of his space, but Callum grabs his wrist and holds fast.

Callum's voice is quiet and gruff when he asks, "He said *what*?"

"You've been acting like he's some kind of—"

"Jesse!" I finally yelp, launching forward to get between them. "You told me you wouldn't say anything!" I push at both of their chests, trying to force distance, but Callum refuses to let go of Jesse's shirt.

"I didn't promise anything," Jesse informs me while looking over my head to continue glaring at Callum. "He should hear it."

"He doesn't have to hear anything he doesn't want to." I cast a nervous glance at Callum, who's still meeting the challenge in Jesse's eyes. When neither of the stubborn, posturing alphas give up their battle for dominance, I drop my arms, giving up so thoroughly it steals my breath. "You know what? I'm just gonna stay away from now on. I didn't mean to ruin things between you two."

That commands their attention, leaving a symmetrical diptych of shock on both their faces.

Too late. I turn toward the door, already prepared for an argument and steeling myself against giving in. I don't expect to be snatched off the ground mid-step, both alphas pulling me between them once more. Incredulous, I try to glare in two directions at once.

"You did *not* ruin things," Jesse insists, at the same time as Callum says, "Don't leave."

I turn on him, and my voice cracks when I yell, "Why shouldn't I?" Beyond frustrated, I cast my arms wide, and nearly hit Jesse with the gesture. "You've been treating me like I have the plague! I don't know why, either, since I was very fucking clear that I have feelings for both you *and* Jesse, and if you didn't notice all the hickeys before screwing me, that's your damn issue, not mine."

I cross my arms to make a defensive shield in front of me and take a step back; this time I do run into Jesse. He puts both hands on my shoulders, holding me steady.

"I know I made a mistake," I say. "I hurt your feelings again, but I tried to apologize, and you wouldn't let me. If you didn't want me to feel like a ruined fucking slut, you should have at least talked about it." I want to level him with one of those bold, unwavering glares so I can see his reaction, but my gaze slides away. Jesse gives my shoulders another squeeze, but it barely helps.

Callum sighs. "Bennett..."

"Don't tell me you're about to make excuses," Jesse says harshly. He isn't having any trouble staring Callum down. At least one of us is brave.

Callum growls; one of those resonant ones that stirs the foundation of the cottage itself, making the cabinets creak and the salt shaker tip sideways onto the table. "I wasn't going to make excuses." Our eyes lock, and the anger in his posture dissolves until he looks just as tired as I am. "I'm sorry, Bennett. I don't see you... that way... at all."

"Were you jealous?" I ask.

"I don't know," Callum admits.

"Then why? Not knowing isn't good enough!"

The words leave him haltingly. "I didn't know what to do with my"—he swallows—"feelings."

"He has them so rarely, you see," Jesse says with a roll of his eyes.

I elbow Jesse, forcing my expression to remain serious even though I want to laugh hysterically. "Will you be able to do this, Cal?"

Callum's brows furrow. "Do what?"

"Me and Jesse. Me and you. *You* and Jesse." Behind me, Jesse sputters, but I ignore him, even though that's difficult with the heat of his body at my back. "I can't keep coming here if..." I let the rest hang.

"You really think all three of us...?"

I huff. "Want me to prove it?"

"How would you—"

My hands shoot out, grabbing the front of Callum's plain grey shirt and yanking him toward me. I don't have much leverage, but he steps forward like I've rewritten physics. I coax him into leaning down, his blue, blue eyes so bright, pupils contracted into pinpricks.

"Like this, Cal," I whisper. "I'll prove it like this."

Then I kiss him.

At first Callum doesn't respond. I haul on his shirt so he can feel my desire, and scrape my teeth over the corner of his lip, tugging gently.

Let me in.

Callum's wide, calloused hands enfold my cheeks, cradling my face for two, three seconds. I have just enough time to whisper '*please*' before he descends upon me. He kisses me hot and hard, mumbling something I can't decipher. Apologies, maybe. He doesn't need them anymore. I throw my arms around his neck, Callum catches my waist, and some combination of the two lifts me onto the balls of my feet, my spine arching as I struggle to get closer to him.

A second pair of hands settles on my hips. Jesse's. Big in a different way from Callum's, narrower and warmer; the soft palms of an idle scholar. I lean back to give Callum a moment to breathe, but I don't allow myself to take more than a sharp inhale before I turn over my shoulder. Jesse meets me halfway, our mouths sloppy and hungry, only in part due to the awkward angle.

There's Callum, hands framing my ribcage while his mouth enrages the faded bruises Jesse left on my neck. Then Jesse, pawing anywhere and everywhere, keeping me locked against him as he worries the shell of my ear with his canines.

I'm pressed so tightly between them I might as well be the gravity connecting two opposing forces. I cling, refusing to release my hold until we form our own galaxy, orbiting one another in a moment of perfect harmony.

I grope below Callum's waistband, finding his cock straining against the denim in a wanton bid for escape. Jesse's erection is pressed against the small of my back. The idea I get—Callum panting as I massage his cock through the heavy fabric, Jesse grinding against me, similarly trapped—is absolutely filthy and so wholly perfect I don't give myself time to second-guess it.

With one final kiss to both of their lips, I drop to my knees.

I made sure to get ahold of their belt loops to prevent either of them from backing away. Callum tries, but stops when I resist. He stares, slack-jawed, as I attempt to unfasten his jeans with one hand. Jesse, ever helpful, nudges me away from his pants so he can see to them himself, giving me the leverage I need to tug the zipper down on Callum's fly.

Jesse frees his cock, letting it brush my cheek, just as gorgeous and tantalizing as I remember. I meet Callum's eyes as I tilt my head to give Jesse's cock an experimental lick. Callum shudders like it was his, even though he's still tucked inside his pants. The root of his cock is visible, nestled among the silver hair, because he isn't wearing underwear. I huff a soft laugh, run my palms up his toned abdomen to push his shirt out of my way. Then I rain a series of slow, closed-mouth kisses down from his navel to his pelvis.

Callum shudders, eyes glowing bright, then fading, only to surge again like blinking fireflies. "Bennett, are you sure?"

Smothering a laugh, I wrap my left hand around Jesse's waiting cock and stroke from base to tip. Then, with a grin just as wolfish as any alpha, I say, "Let me have your cock, Callum."

27

IN WHICH TWO ALPHAS

With respect to everything that lead up to this moment, I find it of significant importance that Callum be the one to free his cock and offer himself to me. I have to remind myself that I'm holding Jesse's dick, not his hand, because I almost squeeze it from sheer nervousness.

What if Callum refuses? How will I ever get past this, other than going down to the creek and selling my soul to the river spirit?

Callum's hands don't shake, exactly, but they're not steady either. He eases his pants low enough that his erection slides out, but his face is blank. Caught in a moment of worry that I'm pressuring him, I hesitate to take him in hand.

Jesse looks at Callum, his gaze so intense I imagine it piercing through Callum's external layers, digging into the heart of him. Jesse's looked at me that way before, and it never fails. His lips form a half-curve as he says, "We've got you, Cal."

I can't help but snicker. "The sentiment is nice, but

please don't treat this like a trust exercise. I'm not doing anything life-changing—it's just a blowjob."

"Could be both," Jesse teases.

"I'm not *that* good at sucking dick," I say with a roll of my eyes. Then, before he can snark back, I twist to take the head of his cock into my mouth and suck as hard as I dare while warming up.

Instead of speaking, Jesse catches his hand in my hair and moans. Good boy.

I reach for Callum, painfully aware that the wrong shift of attention could alienate him past the threshold of shame, but he's slightly too far away. I pop my mouth off Jesse's dick to say, "You guys need to move closer. I'm not getting a twinge in my neck for this."

Callum stays where he is, looking panicked. I swat Jesse on the flank, prompting him to sidle up to Callum instead.

"Better?" Jesse asks, light dancing in his eyes.

"Yes. Thank you." My eyes settle on Callum. "Are you ready? Or, okay? Or…?"

"I'm fine," he says a bit too quickly.

I nuzzle my cheek against his hip. "Let me know if you stop being fine. Promise me." I catch his hand and kisses each of his knuckles.

"Bennett—"

"Promise me, or the date is off," I insist.

Callum's cock twitches. I grin and lap at the tip of his thumb, his blunt claw depressing my tongue.

Now he's shaking. Callum gently extricates his hand from my grasp, then traces the curve of my cheek before his fingers gently wind into my hair, tangling with Jesse's.

"I promise," he murmurs, voice beautifully husky.

A thrill runs down my spine when I clasp both of them like the internet's most amateur porn star, stroking cautiously. Callum's dick has a more dramatic upward curve than Jesse's. It's thicker, too, while Jesse's is straight and long and darker than the rest of his skin. They're both beautifully sexy, and even better side-by-side, waiting for me.

I ease Callum's foreskin back so I can lick the thick head. Nervousness has left my mouth dry, making my lips stick together even when I gather the first drops of precome. Meanwhile, my left hand is clumsy around Jesse's cock.

It's been forever since I last sucked a dick. The only thing encouraging me to keep trying is Jesse and Callum's fingers entwined in my hair. If not for that grounding me, I might have fled to hide in the bathroom again.

How do the twinks in porn make this look so easy?

I drag a calming breath into my lungs, then go down Jesse's length first, figuring it'll be easier to get it all the way to the back of my throat. I do okay until the pressure makes me feel like I have to sneeze. Panic makes me gag, which has the fortunate result of finally triggering my saliva glands. Spit fills my mouth and drips down my chin.

"You alright down there, Ben?"

"Shut up. I got this." Neither Jesse nor Callum look particularly convinced.

"You don't have to do this if you—" Callum begins to say.

I close my eyes, a hair's breadth from a complete meltdown. "If you two don't stop talking, I will bite them both off." My gorgeous alphas blink in unison, Jesse wincing while Callum's brow furrows, but neither speaks. "Good boys," I say, giving both their asses approving pats.

Jesse guffaws and smacks my hand away. "Stop it. I'm going to lose my boner."

"Haven't yet." I lick my lips, open my mouth wide, and swallow Callum as deep as he'll go. It isn't as far as I'd like, but my annoyed grumble has Callum's hand tightening in my hair.

My left hand is still awkward as I jerk Jesse off. I don't want to leave him bored while I focus on not choking unsexily on Callum's cock. I fist my right hand at the base so I can't accidentally slide down too far, and bob my head several times before I have to come up for air. Fortunately, I'm able to obscure my lack of breath control by switching to Jesse, who's already leaking as he waits for me.

Where Callum was patient and hesitant, not trying to steer me despite his grip on my hair, Jesse is... the opposite. He tugs firmly, dragging me further down his cock than I'd risked with Callum, murmuring, "You can do better than that, Benny."

If I was capable of coming on command, the combination of those words and Callum's gasp would have done it.

Tears spring to my eyes. I struggle to breathe through my nose, letting Jesse apply pressure in an agonizing build until I can't handle it anymore and have to slap his thigh to signal for a break. Jesse releases his hold immediately, untangling his fingers from my hair so he can trace them down my cheek, thumb passing through one of the wet lines streaking from the corners of my eyes.

"Did you already call dibs on 'good boy?'" he asks. "Just so I don't get the parts mixed up."

"I was being sarcastic," I inform him, pawing at my dripping nose. "Call me a good boy. Or a bad one. Just know I sure as fuck am not calling you 'daddy.'"

Jesse laughs and gives Callum a shove that puts Callum's cock directly beside my nose, which works just fine for me. I part my lips, dropping teasing open-mouthed kisses down the length of him before dipping lower, holding his cock out

A Fae's Two Alphas

of the way as I suck on his balls. I'm grateful for the hand he still has on my head, allowing me to gauge his quiet reactions by the clenching of his fingers.

I lick up the underside of his cock, using the moment to study his face: lips parted, those long, silvery eyelashes lowered in concentration. His cock is so heavy and sweet on my tongue. I take just the head between my lips and hum to get Callum's attention. His piercing blue eyes fly open. I wink my damp eyelashes, then nearly laugh at his appalled expression.

Before I come up for air, I cup Jesse behind the balls, guiding him close enough to switch between them seamlessly, my throat working open more easily this time. After the first few dips, I challenge myself to take Jesse even further—he doesn't need to pull me into place when his cock finds its way home at the back of my throat.

I still can't take him all the way, but I'm getting there. Jesse moans, low and intense, when I draw wet suction up his length. I do it again, flicking my eyes up to see Jesse clasp his free hand around Callum's arm, head hanging until their foreheads are just shy of touching.

I wish they would touch. Later, because Jesse grabs my jaw, thumb tugging my bottom lip. I open until my jaw aches, prepared but unable to avoid a shocked inhale when he thrusts into my mouth, neither shallow nor gentle. Staring up at him, somewhere between adoring and imploring, I welcome the friction, the thrumming sensation of being used.

"Knew you could do it, sweetheart," Jesse rasps as his cock disappears, fully and finally, all the way down my throat. With my nose buried against his dark pubic hair, all I know is the smell of him and the burning in my lungs.

When I can't handle another second without air, I jerk

back with a ragged gasp. Jesse doesn't remove his hand, allowing me all of two breaths before he curls his strong fingers at my nape and steers me toward Callum. My shaking fingers steady Callum's cock, allowing me a second to gulp one more lungful of air before Jesse pushes me down.

Callum sits differently in my throat, catching my upper palate with every stroke. It's sensitive in a weird way, ensuring I connect with him entering me every time Jesse puts pressure on the back of my head.

I prepare myself for another dive, ready to take all of Callum, but Jesse tightens his grip, refusing to let me move. I whimper, shooting him a confused, frantic look.

Jesse nudges Callum with his elbow. "Take him," he instructs, tipping his chin toward me. Ever helpful, he adjusts his hold, forcing me to arch my back and bare my throat.

Callum blinks, still wearing that vaguely appalled expression. "Jesse, that's not—"

"Callum, please?" I entreat, wanting it more than words can express.

My face is wet, spit and snot and tears having dripped down my neck to soak the collar of my shirt. It's uncomfortable, so I knock their hands away, giving myself room to grab my shirt from the bottom and tear it over my head. I shake out my damp hair, then tuck my fingers behind Callum's thigh, squeezing through his pants.

"You heard him, Cal," Jesse says, eyes glittering.

Callum runs the rough pads of his fingers over my cheek, hesitation palpable. I catch his index finger between my swollen lips, reveling in his gasp when I suck lewdly. He smooths my bangs away from my forehead, threading each digit of his hand into the sweaty mess before they close into a loose fist.

Encouraging and hopelessly eager, I let my tongue settle on my bottom lip, hanging open in invitation. With far more care than the act requires, Callum guides himself to my waiting mouth. I let him test out a few shallow thrusts, his thumb sweeping a soothing line over my brow.

"Are you sure?" he asks, worrying his lip with one fang.

It's adorable, and I have to stop myself from commenting on it. "Do I look unsure?" To demonstrate, I flick my tongue into his slit and taste salt, how he leaks with want.

Callum makes a breathy, wounded sound, and carefully guides my head forward to meet the first purposeful drive of his hips.

They take turns after that, fucking my mouth in long, powerful strokes until my throat burns and Jesse's cheerful control begins to waver. Callum grows bolder as Jesse's desperation mounts, though he's still achingly tender. He steers me to lave my tongue over Jesse's balls, which tighten under my attention as I jack the upper length of his cock with practiced flicks of my wrist.

"Make him come first," Callum instructs.

Jesse only moans—the lack of a quip is how I know how far gone he is.

I wipe a particularly flattering glob of fluid off my upper lip with the back of my hand. "If you insist." Then I swallow Jesse, moving of my own accord rather than responding to their directions. My other hand never leaves Callum, but I focus everything I have on Jesse's pleasure, responding to his tells, those twitching thighs and little moans.

Callum's voice rasps, "Go on then, pup." He snatches the back of Jesse's long hair, tugging backward until Jesse's throat is bared.

I almost lose my rhythm, stunned by the visual and hoping Callum will go further. Before we can find out, Jesse produces a broken cry. I move my hand as fast as my arm can withstand, switching my mouth to Callum, then back to Jesse, trying to keep them on the brink together. With one final sweep of my tongue urging him along, Jesse comes, releasing a thick spurt that's hot on my skin.

My throat vibrates with my own moan as I swallow Callum down. Each streak of come Jesse paints across my lips and cheeks ramps up my arousal until it's painful. I wring every drop of come out of Jesse, and with his stuttering sounds a backdrop for my rough voice, I whisper, "C'mon, Cal. Your turn."

One look at my face, dripping with Jesse's come, has Callum's mouth falling open. He spills himself over my tongue and chin, shaking with tiny hiccups of pleasure. I lick both of their cocks clean until my powerfully vulnerable alphas are easing away from any more stimulation. I release them, remaining posed on my knees, watching their chests expand with deep breaths as their eyes clear.

Jesse and Callum look at each other, then at me. I bite my lip to smother a smile, fail horribly, and settle for sweeping my middle finger over a patch of skin where their ejaculate has combined before sucking it into my mouth.

"You little imp," Callum says faintly.

Already laughing, Jesse snags my upper arm so he can tug me to my feet. "Get your ass up here."

28

DRINK MORE WATER

I'm naked before I have time to process what's happening. It feels more like a wet dream than reality, but the warmth of two hungry alphas pressing against me doesn't lie. No dream could feel this amazing.

Jesse and Callum roam every inch of my body, taking me apart like I belong to them. At some points the contrast between them is striking—Jesse's skillful teasing, Callum's burning intensity—but there are times when I can't tell them apart, where they're one wave cascading over me in glorious unison.

It's not until they're satisfied with having stripped me down and pieced me back together that Callum and Jesse shuck their own clothes. I make sure to explore them with just as much reverence: every contour, how they harmonize, how they diverge and come back together to form two aching halves of my heart. In these moments, it beats for them as one.

Then Jesse moans about how badly he wants to fuck me. Before we go down the "no condoms" route again, Callum volunteers his services and assures me his spell will be temporary. An odd pulse of magic low on my belly ensures there'll be no unfortunate surprises.

After that, I end up on the couch, splayed across Callum's lap with Jesse pinning one of my wrists against Callum's shoulder. My other hand fists in Jesse's hair as he eases into me, both of us moaning as our bodies join. The moment my cunt adjusts to the intrusion, I urge him to move, gasping at how deep he spears inside. Callum runs his knuckles up my throat, praising me in shy murmurs as I welcome every stroke of Jesse's cock.

That's only the beginning. All other responsibilities forgotten, my alphas take me in every way a body can be taken. Teeth and tongues leave marks on my skin, painting me with evidence of their desire. Together they bring me to unimaginable heights, again and again, until I find myself sprawled over the couch, consumed by a beautiful ache that reaches through my skin, deep into my core.

Never before have I felt so well and truly fucked-out. My consciousness hovers above my body, sated and unimaginably happy.

Jesse swats my hip. I didn't hear him approach, but I'm too tired to jump. "Up," he says. "You need to drink more water."

"You already made me drink water," I whimper.

"That was forty-five minutes ago."

I squint at him, struggling to remember what happened in those forty-five minutes. We were standing by the sink, all three of us stark naked, with Callum funneling water down my throat. Jesse had lifted me onto the counter made a tacky joke about dessert, since just before that Callum had cooked dinner. We'd been at it for a while.

But then I nearly fell off the counter, and Callum decreed sex officially over. I whined all the way to the couch.

Like a merciless tyrant, Jesse levers me upright enough to get the cup to my mouth. Once the first mouthful passes my lips, I realize I *am* thirsty. I chug the rest, gasping and wiping my mouth when I'm done.

"Feel better?"

I fake-scowl at him. "I feel *everything* right now. What counts as better?"

Jesse prods me in the side. "Can you walk yet?"

"Fuck you." I clench my pelvic muscles, then hiss. "I don't think I'm walking for another week."

"I'll have to carry you everywhere."

"Oh boy, what a hardship," I deadpan. He ruffles my hair and takes the cup back to the sink to refill. I stare at his ass the whole way.

The bathroom door opens, and Callum emerges, his lower body wrapped in a towel. Despite the summer heat, steam fogs the air around him. I peer over the back of the couch, offering him a weary but genuine smile. Callum tilts his head at me, eyebrows cocked, then snorts softly when I give him a thumbs up and collapse back onto the cushions.

Callum reappears above me and bends over the arm of the couch to press a soft kiss to my brow. I mewl, trying to reel him in for a proper kiss, but he pulls away before I can make contact.

"Your turn," he says, using his towel-covered knee to nudge my arm, which is hanging limply off the side of the couch.

"My turn to what?"

"Shower."

I groan, long and passionate, and not in the sexy way. "Callum, I don't want to *move*."

Callum folds his arms over his chest. "I'm not touching either of you until you're both clean."

"You're mean."

"You're filthy."

"Whose fault is that?"

"Jesse's."

Still in the kitchenette, Jesse laughs. He doesn't appear offended by Callum scapegoating him.

I scrunch my nose at Callum. "I'm pretty sure it wasn't Jesse's idea to stick a finger in my ass while he was fucking me."

Callum arches an eyebrow. Such expressive goddamn eyebrows he has, even being blessed enough to raise one of them at a time. "Did you dislike it?"

My brain blanks. "Dislike what?" I've already forgotten what we were talking about.

"Him putting a finger in your ass," Jesse reminds me.

"Oh." I scoff. "Of course I liked it, but you, Mr. Truett, have huge fingers!"

Callum hides his mouth behind his hand and turns abruptly to face the wall. I don't know what to make of it until I see his shoulders shake.

I bolt upright, ignoring the protests from every single one of my molecules. "Callum Truett, are you *laughing* at me?"

Callum fixes me with an incredulous look, but I swear there's still laughter in his eyes. "I'd never laugh at you, Bennett," he says, sounding very sincere—so much so I'm certain he's teasing. "Furthermore, if you're sore, I could make you a cream."

I launch myself off the couch, determined to tackle him, but the moment my foot hits the floor I yelp like a kicked dog. Callum catches me with the towel, seamlessly trapping my arms while I dissolve into giddy laughter.

"I'll throw you in the bathtub like this," Callum warns

before kissing me on the forehead a second time. He unravels me from the towel and gives me a gentle push toward Jesse.

I lean against Jesse as I stagger to the bathroom, my cunt protesting every step.

Jesse and I barely fit in the bathtub together, but he does a lovely job soaping me up and washing my hair while I stay plastered against the cold tile wall. I remain there, eyes closed as the warm water runs down my face, until Jesse runs a washcloth over my chest, aggravating my stinging nipples. At some point Callum decided he enjoyed torturing them. A *lot*.

I hiss and squirm against his front. Jesse apologizes for being too rough, but I'm distracted by his dick, now poking the small of my back. "How the fuck are you still going?"

Jesse snickers. "Chill, Ben, it's just a reflex. I'm not threatening your purity. At least not for the next couple of hours."

"Make that the next *several* hours."

The remaining ablutions, which include two new toothbrushes on the side of the sink, proceed uneventfully. Jesse whisks me out of the bathroom and into Callum's bedroom, where I've never been before. Curious, I look around, but find there isn't much to see. A queen-sized bed with plain maroon sheets; what I assume is a closet door; and a bureau. Depressingly empty, but not unexpected. I don't suppose Callum uses his bedroom for anything other than sleeping.

I wonder if anyone other than Callum has ever slept in this bed. I develop half a mind to ask him, but when he enters the bedroom, he reveals that while I was in the shower he actually did make a cream. I smack him with a pillow in mock offense, then apply it generously between my legs, on my tits, and over the various bite marks and hickeys scattered over my body.

Within a few minutes, I feel much more comfortable. When Callum brings me tea, I express my gratitude a very enthusiastic kiss.

Jesse kisses me next, just because, then sits beside me and absently finger-combs my wet hair while I drink my tea. Callum leans against the wall, watching.

None of us have bothered with clothes, and as the night winds down, so does our conversation. Callum closes the curtains and locks the cottage door, then brings me another cup of tea. Jesse makes a joke about my raspy voice, and Callum threatens to make him sleep on a bed of pine needles outside.

The room goes quiet in a different way, with Jesse and Callum silently regarding each other. They hadn't discussed sleeping arrangements beyond "get Bennett horizontal."

"I could," Jesse begins, hooking his thumb toward the door.

I interrupt before either of them can make any ridiculous suggestions. "If both of you don't jam your giant muscular bodies into this bed with me, I will cause problems on purpose."

"Can't have that," Callum says quietly.

Jesse looks at him for a long moment. "Guess we can't."

It takes some finagling to fit all three of us. Three people on a queen isn't impossible, but Callum is on the bigger end of above-average, and Jesse's the kind of person who stretches data points.

"How tall are you even?" I mumble sleepily while he perches on his side behind me.

"Six-four," Jesse says, kissing the back of my neck.

I hum in acknowledgment and tighten my arm around

Callum's waist. I can barely breathe, wedged between the two of them, and I'm sweating despite the cooling spell Callum cast.

After a bit more squirming, we settle into a comfortable three-part knot. Between Jesse's breath ghosting over my shoulder, and Callum stroking my hair, I can't think of anywhere I'd rather be.

29

MAKING DEMANDS

Morning comes harsh and ugly, in the form of loud voices rising above the hazy border of my unconsciousness. Bleary-eyed, I blink first to my right, then my left, and sit bolt upright when I find myself alone in Callum's bed.

The mattress is still warm on either side of me, meaning this was a recent evacuation.

I don't have a scrap of clothing in here, so I yank open a random drawer in Callum's bureau, revealing several neatly folded shirts, all in muted tones and similar styles. The room is dark and the air is still cool, so I dig for one of the longer-sleeved ones and tug it over my head. Unlike Jesse's shirts, it only just barely passes my ass-cheeks, but it'll have to do.

Shoving the sleeves up to my elbows, I peek out the door, which has been left ajar. The light is low, but I can see Jesse and Callum's outlines. They're shoulder-to-shoulder at the entryway to the cottage, arguing with someone outside. Both of them are shirtless and disheveled, wearing only pants.

I'm too tired to decipher anything that's being said.

Their voices are overlapping, and Callum is growling, but the higher register sounds familiar enough for curiosity to draw me farther into the room.

Far enough, apparently, that the third figure, whose head rises almost as high as Jesse's, sees me over Callum's shoulder.

"Bennett Chiston, call your mother. Right the fuck now."

My jaw drops. "Josie?"

Callum growls louder, and the cottage starts doing that foundation-rattle thing again. Jesse leaves him at the door, then tries to corral me back into the bedroom.

I bat Jesse away because this is absurd.

"Stop it, both of you," I say, projecting as best I can after having recently had two dicks jammed repeatedly into my throat over an extended period of time. And also being sleepy or something, but probably mostly the dick-sucking. "What the hell is going on?"

Josie frowns at me over Callum's head. She moves as if to cross the threshold, but Callum slams a hand against the doorjamb, a warning snarl crackling through the cottage.

"For fuck's sake, Truett," Josie snarls back.

"This is my territory, and you have no right—"

Jesse tugs at my shoulder. "Just leave them to argue, this isn't—"

I suck air into my lungs until they strain, then holler as loud as my abused throat will allow: "Please, just fucking tell me what's going on!"

It doesn't go silent, but the noise lowers enough for me to hear Josie's voice above my personal bodyguards' fretting.

"Naomi Chiston has been ringing Mom's phone off the hook for the past fifteen minutes, demanding to know where her *son* is."

My mouth opens, then closes as I consider my words

carefully. "I'm trans," is the carefully-thought-out declaration that emerges.

Josie pauses in the way people do when they're trying not to commit a crime. "Thank you for the information, Bennett. Mom didn't know, which is the fault of *someone in this room* who is not you." She turns her glare over my head.

"What does my mom want?" I ask, uninterested in discussing the nuances of my gender transition while trapped between a pair of unhappy twins.

"She wanted to know where you were and why you weren't answering your phone."

Naomi and I haven't spoken much since she threw herself at Jesse like a rabid grizzly. Until now, the standoff has been mutual, but I'm not surprised she's broken it. I should have thought about her sooner. I'm usually still in bed when she gets home from work, and she's always paranoid about my safety. Of course she'd fly into a panic.

I sigh. "Where I am is none of her business."

Josie's response is frosty. "It's none of my business, either. Or it wasn't until your mother made it *my* mother's problem at five in the goddamn morning."

I press my palms over my face. "Tell her to leave Ms. Chen alone. I'm going back to bed."

"Bennett." Josie's inflection carries all the command of an alpha pack leader. Even though I'm not part of her pack, or even a shifter, I freeze. This might be Callum's territory, but Josie's voice makes me want to roll over in submission.

Would I feel the same if Jesse or Callum spoke to me that way?

My brief horny fantasy is ruined by Josie saying, "You need to go home."

"The hell he does," Jesse snaps.

"This is non-negotiable," Josie says, a warning rumble framing her words.

Callum rumbles right back. "You don't get to tell my—tell Bennett to go anywhere he doesn't want to."

"No, but he should handle his mother. She sounded frantic."

I don't miss Callum's slip-up. Josie's refusal to leave gives me no opportunity to grill him on it, which causes irritation to prickle down my spine. "Mom can deal with her own feelings."

"I'm not asking," she says.

I take a few steps forward, tilting my head so Josie is no longer enrobed in shadow. She's almost as tall as Jesse, with a face that would be just as affable if she wasn't scowling. Josie was always the more serious of the twins. Her black hair is short and neat, so at odds with Jesse's free, uncontained waves. Was she this tense, this demanding, when I knew her ten years ago?

"I have no obligation to obey you," I say finally. "Maybe just ask politely instead of yelling at me."

Josie blinks like that never occurred to her.

"'Bennett,'" I prompt, "'Will you please address your mother's unhinged behavior so we can go back to sleep?'"

"Joze?" Jesse places a supportive hand on my shoulder. I fold my hand over it, interlacing our fingers.

Josie tracks the movement, staring for several beats at our connection. Then she purses her lips and, like she's being forced to chew something bitter, says, "I'd appreciate it if you could speak to your mother about this." A pause. "Please."

I slump back against Jesse. "Yeah, okay. Whatever." I scan the dark expanse of the cottage, then mumble louder than I meant to, "Where are my clothes?"

Understanding finally crosses Josie's face. She looks first at Callum, wearing pajama pants, then at Jesse, in the jeans he abandoned before noon yesterday. Her gaze returns to me, naked under Callum's shirt, my hands half-hidden by the long sleeves spilling past my wrists.

I twist my fingers together nervously. This is not at all how I wanted my morning to progress. For starters, I hadn't planned on waking up for hours yet, and when I did opt to join the world of the living, I'd assumed it would involve more orgasms.

Grumpy about those hopes being dashed, I grind the heel of my palm against my eye and mutter, "Don't think about it too hard."

Josie massages her temples. "This is a fucking headache. I'll wait outside."

"You don't have to wait at all," Callum says. "Feel free to leave."

"I'm taking Bennett home."

Jesse pulls me against his chest possessively. "I'll take him."

Sensing another flurry of arguments, I hold up a hand to halt him. "Okay, just let me get dressed." I pry myself out of Jesse's arms, then decide I don't give a single shit about Josie's opinion and rise onto my toes to kiss him. "Find my clothes?" I entreat.

Jesse growls low in his chest; an intimate sound compounded when he presses his forehead to mine. With one more glare at his twin, Jesse stalks off to gather my discarded belongings. Callum stays in the doorway, unwavering gaze fixed on Josie.

I trot over to him and tug his elbow so I can kiss him on the cheek. The ice blue glow in Callum's eyes fades just a bit, enough for me to see the cerulean beneath. He lets me hug him, but doesn't hug me back.

They're overreacting. It's just Josie, who is grumpy about being woken at five in the morning, which I can understand. I'm grumpy too, so I make it easy as possible by quickly collecting my clothes from Jesse before tottering away. The surge of adrenaline is fading, leaving me conscious of my incredibly sore legs. And other parts.

I check my phone, which was in my pocket and on silent. Seven missed calls. Sweet fuck. I shoot off a text to Naomi.

> Bennett Chiston: Stop bothering Ms Chen
> I'm omw

Then I rustle around to find the cream Callum made. I apply a liberal amount to the worst of my sore areas, before easing myself into my cutoffs, forgoing underwear. I also decide to not put on my binder, despite feeling awkward about my unflattened chest. Callum's shirt is soft and comforting, so I leave it on, then bundle my abandoned shirt and underwear with the pot of cream and clutching them to my chest when I exit the bedroom.

When I kiss Jesse goodbye, I press my cheek against his bare chest. I listen to his strong heartbeat for a long moment, then kiss him again. Putting on my shoes is a silent affair, as is nudging Callum aside so I can leave the cottage. I kiss him too, ignoring Josie, who is staring from a few paces away.

"My car's right here." She tips her head toward the Jeep she's parked dangerously close to Callum's garden.

"Could've run something over, parking this close," I mumble under my breath.

Josie doesn't respond. She unlocks the car, and I make a

valiant effort not to hiss when I climb into the passenger seat. I spare one last look at Jesse and Callum, affection surging inside me when I see them still hovering in the doorway. I offer them a weak smile before closing the car door.

Josie hops into the driver's seat and begins backing out of the clearing without waiting for me to buckle my seatbelt. I wince as the tires tear up the ground.

We drive in silence. I hug my belongings hugged tight against my chest, trying to imagine Callum's shirt as an embrace. I lose myself in an exhausted daydream until Josie pulls up to the curb outside my house.

No, *Naomi's* house. Not mine. Never mine.

The front door is unlocked, which it rarely is. I enter to find Naomi sitting on the couch, looking a wreck. She shoots to her feet the moment she sees me.

"Bennett!"

"What was so important?" My voice is flat.

Naomi tries to approach me, but I sidestep her open arms and cross the room to dump my stuff on the kitchen table. She narrows her eyes. "I wanted to know where you were."

"I was at a friend's house. Why did you call Ms. Chen?"

"You weren't answering your phone."

"It was five in the fucking morning," I grumble, trying not to lose my calm.

Naomi sucks her teeth. "I thought you'd be with Jesse, so I called Maria."

"Please don't ever do that again."

Naomi folds her arms over her chest, then looks warily over my shoulder. I glance behind me to see Josie in the doorway. She enters without asking, coming to a stop in front of Naomi with her arms folded in a similar fashion.

"Ms. Chiston," she greets. "I fetched Bennett because I

understand you being concerned about your son. Don't disturb my mother again."

A stalemate makes the air crackle with ungrounded electricity. Despite looking haggard in jeans and a camisole, shoulders slumped so her bear tattoo is partially hidden by shadows, Naomi doesn't cower under Josie's commanding tone. In other circumstances, I'd be proud; no one tells my Mama Bear what to do.

Unfortunately, this situation is fucking bonkers, and Naomi should feel at least a little bit ashamed.

"Thanks for bringing me home, Josie," I say when Naomi doesn't respond. I don't have time for this—I just want to go back to sleep. "We'll make sure it doesn't happen again."

Josie shoots me a dubious glance. "I'd appreciate that. Goodbye Bennett, Ms. Chiston."

I roll my eyes once Josie's back is turned. She isn't behaving much better than my spoiled, stubborn child of a mom. I can understand being pissed at Naomi, but rudely ordering everyone else around isn't particularly endearing either. Though, judging by what Jesse's said about the Harrises, she might have to be a hard-ass to command the respect she deserves as the pack alpha. Regardless of the reason, once she's off the porch, it's no longer my problem.

I close and lock the door, then turn to Naomi. "What was so important?"

Naomi's face contorts in an unfamiliar display of emotion. I have no idea how to interpret it.

"I missed you," she admits.

My teeth clench and grind. It's difficult to keep my temper at bay. Naomi acted like this all the time when I was a kid, but even with her clinginess the past two years, this is an escalation. I partially suspect she's jealous of me having someone other than her to spend time with.

"Bennett, I'm sorry." Naomi grabs my shoulders before I can duck out of the way. "I shouldn't have behaved the way I did with your friend. I just missed you. I want to spend more time with you. You've been so distant this week."

"Because of what you did," I remind her. "You caused it."

"I want to un-cause it," she whispers, eyes so sad and tired I think she might cry, which alarms me on a molecular level.

"Mama Bear…" Sighing, I clasp her shoulders in return. Not quite a hug, but close enough to forgiveness to pass as one. "You're fucking ridiculous, but I do love you. I'll try to be around more. However, right now I need to sleep."

Naomi nods limply, like a broken bobblehead. Her lank brown hair flops over her eyes.

"Mama Bear, you need to shower," I chide gently, nudging her toward the bathroom. "Go get clean. I'm going to sleep, okay? We can talk more tomorrow."

I expect her to argue, but Naomi walks down the hallway without a fight. She stops right at the open bathroom door and gives me such pathetic puppy eyes I allow her to kiss my forehead.

I forgot to remove my sandals when I came inside, so I abandon them in the hallway as I drag my feet toward my room. I barely manage to close the door before collapsing in bed. Exhaustion consumes me, and I don't even have enough energy to pull up the sheet before falling unconscious.

30

ONE BIG TANGLE

Despite my desire to remain comatose, I wake up a few hours later, just after ten thirty. My head throbs, along with the rest of my body. First thing I do is crawl—yes, on all fours—to the bathroom, followed by wobbling into the kitchen to retrieve my phone and Callum's magically soothing cream. After I apply it under my slept-in clothes, I prop myself against the wall and look at the notifications on my phone.

A few from Jesse, one from Callum. I create a group chat to inform them both that I'm okay, then drag myself upright with a groan. Coffee. That's what I need.

Unfortunately, when I paw through the cupboards, I don't find any. I stand with my forehead pressed against the side of the cupboard for a while before deciding I *need*-need coffee. There's a small café not too far away from the house, just past the 7-Eleven. They close at two, so I have plenty of time to fetch breakfast if I can survive the walk.

Marathon sex with two alpha shifters is great, but next time I plan on having absolutely nothing to do the following day.

Next time. Shit, there I go... thinking. Assuming.

Maybe it's not assuming to suppose they'll want me to stick around, but it won't last. I'm still determined to return to Faerie. Unless I'm starting to accept the reality of it never happening. Maybe I'm subconsciously reaching for things that'll keep me from losing myself to despair.

Callum's slip-up earlier, the way he stuttered 'my'... His what?

I stand in line forever, glad I popped a few ibuprofen before leaving, then slump into a seat to wait for my bagels and a large box of hot coffee—yes, the ones people order for their entire office. I'll need it. I'm aware of people glancing at my throat, particularly the employee at the counter, who doesn't meet my eyes when I thank her and collect my purchases. I haven't studied my reflection yet, but a glance this morning suggests I look like I've been choke-slammed, when really I was just thoroughly chewed on by two wolves. Does that make it better or worse?

By the time I get back to the house, an hour has passed. I creep inside quietly because Naomi shouldn't be up for another couple of hours, and she'll be even more of a wreck if she doesn't get enough sleep before work.

I set down the bagels and coffee, then give in to curiosity. I tiptoe into the bathroom to look at myself in the mirror. My tits were too sore to be squished under a binder, so I put on two baggy shirts. I remove them now, then gasp at my reflection.

From neck to hips I'm a disaster, marked in every way. Nipples puffy and red; the curves of my breasts patterned with faded pink rings of teeth imprints; mottled purple-and-red splotches down my sternum and pelvis. I have even more under my cut-offs.

It's *thrilling*.

A Fae's Two Alphas

I've never felt so utterly claimed. For the first time ever, I feel at home in this mundane body. I explore the lingering sensations by running my fingers over the tender spots. My aching muscles and bruised skin are intimate reminders that I belong to someone—two someones.

That's when I hear voices.

The elated bubbles in my chest pop, becoming soap scum inside my ribcage. I prowl down the hallway, finding Naomi's bedroom door cracked. I attempt to rationalize—*maybe she left the TV on?*—but that's definitely her voice, and she sounds angry.

"I haven't slept," she's saying. "I'm so stressed I'm losing my mind. God damn it, Brann, this is your fault."

My spine goes ramrod straight when I hear my father's name. I inch forward, trying to get a look inside her room without alerting her to my presence. On her bed I can see the upturned corner of the thick parchment, knowing the rune circle written over it will be lit by the magic transference.

"How is it my fault?" My father's voice, rounded syllables and sharp consonants, wavers as it's transferred across the veil.

As I predicted, Naomi had no trouble finding the circle to communicate with Brann when *she* wanted to talk to him. Meanwhile, I haven't heard his voice in almost two years.

It takes everything within me to resist barging in to yell at him, at her, at them as a unit. They're always playing games with each other and dragging me into the wreck along with them. I only hold back because I need to know more about Naomi's angle.

"It's your fault because you took him from me," Naomi snaps.

"I didn't take Bennett anywhere he didn't want to be," Brann responds crisply. *"It's your fault he's miserable now."*

I clap my hands over my mouth. What does he mean about it being her fault?

"If you hadn't taken him, I wouldn't have had to bring him back."

My mind races. Tears well up in my eyes, hot and anguished, but I hold my palms tight over my face to keep silent.

"Bennett isn't a toy to be fought over, Naomi."

"Then stop fighting me."

"Have you told him yet?"

"Told him what?" Naomi's voice is sharp.

"I'll take that as a no. Has he asked to speak with me?"

Naomi is silent for several moments. "No," she says finally. "He's angry with you."

"I'm sure you love that," Brann starts to say, but gets nothing more out because I slam the door open.

It bangs off the wall and swings back to hit me in the side, but I don't even wince. I should be crumbling. My body has already been used and abused—in the best way, mind— but emotional shock smothers all other sensations. It takes over my senses, clouding my head until I can barely see.

"Why are you lying, Mom?" I hate that my voice is so raw, quivery rather than strong. "I asked to speak to Dad. What does he mean by 'it's your fault'? Dad, why did you—?"

"*Bennett*—" is all my father gets out before, with a howl of rage, Naomi sweeps the square of parchment from her bed. I watch in horror as she tears it down the middle.

Static.

That's all I feel, all I hear. Numb, I look at the torn halves of parchment, the delicate pattern of runes wrinkled and fractured. It was the only sure way I'd ever have of communicating with Brann directly.

Naomi pants as she stares at me, face lined with fear. She clenches her hands into fists, crumpling the parchment even worse. "Benny, you need to understand—"

Sick of unfinished sentences, and of lies, and of being yanked around like a resisting cat on a leash, I grab the door and slam it behind me. I run to the bathroom, desperate to climb into those shirts again so I can escape before Naomi comes after me.

Just after I get the shirts over my head, hiding the worst of my alphas' love-bites, Naomi appears in the doorway, eyes wild.

"Bennett, please listen."

"No. Let me through."

"Brann wouldn't understand."

"I'm not interested in hearing it. I need to get to my bedroom. Please move."

Naomi tilts her head. "What's on your neck?"

I clasp my hand over the area she's looking at, but there are more on the other side.

Her brows knit. "Did someone hurt you? Was it Jesse?"

"No one hurt me," I snap. "Get out of my fucking way!"

"No! You're bruised. Let me see."

"Fuck off and let me leave!" Naomi takes a step forward, and I counter it with two steps back. "I swear, Mom, if you put one fucking hand on me, I will leave and never come back. You'll never see me again."

That's what puts real terror in her eyes. "I just want you to listen to me."

"I don't want to listen to you. Move out of my way."

"You're my baby." Her voice emerges a scratchy whisper.

Naomi is shattering. I can see her center through the

cracks—my anxious, paranoid, obsessive Mama Bear—but I can't muster even the tiniest bit of sympathy.

"I'm going out."

After a stretch of brittle silence, Naomi presses herself against the bathroom wall, out of my way but just barely.

I cringe against the door, sliding along the wood to get out of the bathroom without touching her. Her eyes burn on my back as I walk calmly into my bedroom, then lock the door.

Finally alone, I find myself too panicked to cry. Nothing is ready to be let out, not yet, so I grab a backpack from my closet and stuff it with a pair of shorts, long cotton pants, underwear, and my binder. I add my phone charger and rarely-used laptop, the pot of cream, and a few other things I might need. Finally, I snag a warm water bottle, chug half of it, and shove the remainder in the backpack, which I zip up tight.

Swallowing hard past the lump in my throat, I grab a pair of old chucks from my closet and put them on, regretting that my boots are at the front of the house. I don't even want to open my bedroom door enough to grab my sandals from the hall.

I brace myself, then open my bedroom window and ease my backpack to the ground. The rest of me follows with far less grace. I land so hard it briefly knocks the wind out of me, but I force past the discomfort. If Naomi sees me outside the window, this will become far messier.

My body protests putting the heavy backpack around my shoulders, but I don't stop. I gather the last dregs of my strength, and break into a run.

I barely make it to the 7-Eleven where I usually meet Jesse. When I get there, I'm gasping and sweating from the oppressive summer heat. I'm still wearing Callum's shirt under one of my t-shirts, which does okay at concealing my chest but has consequence of making me overheat. I slump onto the curb, then pull out my phone to text Jesse. Then, deciding it'll take too long for him to get here, I summon a rideshare instead.

The drive to the other side of Marquette is filled with the driver's country playlist and intermittent beeps of Jesse and Callum texting the group chat, trying to find out what's going on. Unfortunately, I'm not especially coherent, so all I manage is reassuring them I'm not dead.

When I get out of the car by the liquor store nearest the Harris pack house, Jesse's car is already in the parking lot. I mumble thanks to the driver and trudge toward the car, then receive a surprise in the form of Callum, popping out of the passenger door. I blinking vacantly, sorting through relief, surprise, and grief—not in that order. Callum reaches me and proceeds to herd me into the passenger seat. While Callum climbs into the back, Jesse snags my seatbelt and buckles it for me, even though I don't need the help. Jesse eases out of the parking lot like a someone's grandma, but despite his efforts the car bounces on the cracked driveway. I slosh against the car door and moan.

"What happened?" Jesse asks as soon as we're on a smoother road.

I'm vaguely aware of Callum shaking his head at Jesse. "We can talk when we're home."

I let my hand fall onto the car's center console and stare dully out the window. When my brain comes back online, we're driving down the road on Harris land, almost at the place where Jesse usually parks. Both Callum and Jesse have twisted their hands around the one of mine, creating a three-way tangle of fingers that squeezes my heart in a comforting vise and doesn't let up.

31

A TETHER TO WHOM

I'VE NEVER BEEN STARED at during a shower before. If I had to imagine a situation in which that might happen, it wouldn't have involved two alpha shifters fretting at me like mother hens.

Jesse and Callum barely fit in the bathroom at the same time, but they make it work with Callum sitting on the toilet and Jesse propped against the doorjamb. They watch me through the clear curtain while I describe the conflict with Naomi. I'd prefer to be showing off for them rather than talking about my mom, but neither of them are in the mood to play right now.

I don't blame them, because I'm not either. I'm just desperate for a distraction.

Afterward, we discuss what to do next. We need more information. It won't come from Naomi, and I can't get it from Brann, which leaves only one option:

Snooping.

As a child, I never went through my parents' rooms. It was a combination of genuine respect for privacy and accidentally having walked in on them having freaky sex when I was nine. Some secrets are not meant to be shared. Since returning to the mundane realm, I've never had a reason or the desire to infringe on Naomi's privacy.

Until now.

It takes a bit of arguing before Callum and Jesse agree to my plan. They want me to rest, but I maintain that we can't afford to lose time, and I wouldn't be able to sleep anyway. So, after gulping down one of Callum's spelled tea blends, we load into Jesse's car and drive across town to Naomi's house.

By now she's left for work, and the wolves confirm no signs of life before I'm allowed out of the car. Callum stands guard outside, just in case.

I'm quiet unlocking the front door, but I shouldn't have bothered. Jesse tromps inside like he's daring Naomi to pop out from the floorboards and try to stop him. We go down the hall, straight to Naomi's bedroom. Nervous, I prepare myself to dig through her belongings, possibly unearthing some hidden chamber full of cursed weaponry. Or a box of severed human feet. Maybe she's a serial killer.

It's almost anticlimactic when Jesse opens the door and my eyes are immediately drawn to an open shoebox sitting on her dresser. The torn halves of wrinkled parchment have been tossed atop the contents.

"Take it," Jesse says before I can touch anything.

"Shouldn't we look through it first?"

"No," he says. A shiver runs through him. "That thing feels weird. If it's not anything useful, we'll deal with that, but I'd bet my tail this is what we're looking for."

After a brief scan to see if there are any other items of note, I close the shoebox and tuck it into my arms. Jesse shuts Naomi's bedroom door behind us, then waits patiently for me to grab my toothbrush and other toiletries

I had to leave behind when I escaped this morning. I shove them, my shoes, and some extra clothes in a big garbage bag, which Jesse ties up and throws over his shoulder.

Then we leave.

I stand in the doorway, looking at the home that was never mine and knowing I'll never come back. Jesse gives my elbow a light tug. With a heavy sigh, I close the front door, lock it, and set my key in the mailbox.

And like that, it's over. I stare out the window, refusing to look back at the house as Jesse drives off. We don't converse during the drive or the short walk to the cottage. It's not until we're inside and I'm curled up on the couch that Callum breaks the silence.

"Bennett, is your mother a witch?"

My spine straightens. "No. I mean, I guess she could be. I've never seen her use magic, but with all the shit she's kept from me, anything could be possible."

"There's magic in here," Callum says, indicating the shoebox. His gaze flicks between me and Jesse, who's leaning over the back of the couch. "Strong magic."

"The only time she's ever used magic around me was when we were summoning my dad with the rune circle."

"Do you have access to that circle?"

"It's in the box, but she ripped it in half."

Callum frowns. "I could repair it, maybe."

"Open the box first," Jesse suggests.

After a second of hesitation, Callum says, "I think Bennett should do it."

I cringe. That's not what I wanted to hear. "Why?"

Callum carries the shoebox over to the couch and sets it on the coffee table in front of me. "Judging from the energy alone, it's plausible we'll find answers inside. But"—he looks uneasy—"the energy signature is reacting negatively to my aura."

My mouth has gone dry, tongue sticking to my cheeks when I try to speak. I swallow several times before I'm able to choke out, "You think it'll be safer if I open it?"

"Yes. If I sense anything that might harm you, I'll intervene, but I don't think your mother would keep something that could damage you."

"She's way too possessive for that," Jesse adds, lip curled in distaste.

I squeeze my eyes shut, count to three, and open them again. My vision blurs, spots flickering in front of my eyes.

"Okay," I say. "Let's do this."

The cardboard lid comes off the box easily, feeling utterly normal and insignificant in my hands. The first glimpse inside reveals the torn parchment, which Callum cautiously picks up to inspect.

I dig further, finding an antique-looking mirror; bits and bobs of sticks, herbs, and marbles; and something inside a worn velvet bag. Carefully removing it from the shoebox, I set it on the coffee table.

Callum runs a claw over the faded black material. "This is where the energy is coming from," he murmurs. "The aura is immense."

"Are you sure you don't wanna open it?" I ask, shifting nervously.

Jesse nudges my jaw with his knuckles. "You can do this, Ben."

With a deep, preparatory breath, I gently untie the strings cinching the bag closed and ease out a plain wooden box, roughly hewn from dark wood, as if made by a careless hand. I fiddle open the tiny metal latch and flip the lid, revealing...

"What is this?"

A frown twists Callum's mouth. "Rosewood," he says. "A hand-carved receptacle." He traces the air over the box, naming the items. "Rock salt, tarragon, birch bark, and ginger root." He taps a small glass vial with his claw, disturbing its contents. "If the recipe is correct, this will be toenails, blood, and spit."

"What recipe?" Jesse enquires.

"Patience." Callum glares at him, then grumbles, "It's a tether."

"What's a tether?" That one's me. He doesn't glare this time.

Callum eases down next to me on the couch, folding one leg underneath himself. "It's a collection of items that allow the holder to exert magical influence over an individual. This specific recipe forms a contract that can only be done with the knowledge and consent of the target. Hm." He gestures for me to set the box down, then knocks a few chunks of salt aside, revealing a dirty slip of paper. "*Rest, deceit, insurance,*" he reads. "These are the terms, written in the words of accord. Bennett, will you?"

I cautiously peel the tiny piece of paper off the bottom of the wood, noting the texture of thick pieces of wood pulp with dirt ground into the fibers.

Callum peers at the back. "*Control.* That's the intent." He looks at me. "Who would your mother need control over?"

I don't have to think very hard. "It'd have to be my dad. He said it's her fault I'm unhappy, but I didn't hear why." Because I barged in like an idiot rather than waiting to hear more.

"It's something," Jesse says. "Do you have any ideas how we can use this?"

"I need to think. I need... to make tea." Callum snags the tether and drifts toward his tea cart.

Jesse sends me an amused look, but I can't reciprocate. Responding to my distress, Jesse sits and pulls me into his arms until I'm nestled in his lap, my ear pressed over his heart.

"It'll work out, Benny."

I don't have energy for conversation, so I sit in Jesse's lap until Callum returns, carrying only one mug of tea—my favorite one, purplish-teal. He pushes it toward me. "Drink. I have an idea."

Jesse perks up. "I knew you wouldn't need long."

I crawl out of Jesse's lap to grasp the mug, sampling the tea. It tastes bizarre. Like no tea I've ever had before. Grimacing, I ask, "What is this?"

"It's a conductor. Stop delaying."

I stick my tongue out at him, then do as I'm told. It isn't the first time Callum has had me swallow something foul. I gulp the tea as fast as I can, and when I get to the dregs, Callum picks the tea satchel from the bottom of the mug and drops it into the tether box. That's when I notice the missing contents.

"Did you just make me *drink* that? Who knows how old that was?" I'm incredulous and more than a little grossed out.

Callum doesn't even look at me. "Do you want magic or not?"

My mouth hangs open as I process. "You've figured it out?"

He grunts. "I've a theory."

"That's promising," Jesse says, so cheerfully it has to be sarcasm.

"No one asked you, pup. Bennett, come outside. Jesse, you can join us if you're silent."

"I wouldn't bet on those odds," I say. My various aches protest when I haul myself off the couch, but I'm determined. Callum opens the door for me, and Jesse follows on my heels.

The evening air has an unusual chill. Today was hot, but now I feel as if I need a jacket. Shivering even under Callum's long-sleeved shirt, I follow Callum to the table. He sits me down where we were the night of the solstice, during those long hours surrounded by fireflies. None are out tonight.

Jesse props his hip against the table, and Callum drops into a crouch in front of me. It takes him a moment to speak. We consider one another in the interim, leaning into the tense knowledge that something is about to change.

Callum sets the box on the ground between my feet and opens it with the contents facing me. "When it happens, Bennett, breathe in as deeply as you can."

"When what happens?"

"I'm going to destroy the tether." Callum rubs at his forehead, heavily-lined from the force of his concern. "If our conclusions are accurate, this will sever any contract there is between Bennett's parents. With the aid of the conductor, Bennett should receive a moment of control over his father before the contract fully dies. If Brann has possession of Bennett's magic..."

"I'll be able to make him give it back?"

"You'll have to feel that out in the moment," Callum says with a sigh. "Either way, the conductor should give you the power to do *something*. Regardless of what that is, Bennett, you'll need to trust your instincts and follow through."

"I haven't had magical instincts for two years, Cal."

Callum puts a hand on my shoulder. A second later, Jesse's larger hand lands on the other one. "We believe in you, Ben," Callum says quietly. They both give me a squeeze before letting go. "Ready?"

"I'll have to be." My voice is terribly faint. "I love you both. Thank you for this, and... everything, really. I'll love you no matter what."

Jesse scrubs his hand over my hair, and Callum offers me the smallest, most fragile, heartbreaking shadow of a smile. Just a twitch at the corner of his mouth, there and gone, but it's enough.

They are more than enough.

"Let's do this."

32

FLAMES OF THE UNEXPECTED

ALL CALLUM DOES IS SNAP, but the instant one icy blue spark of his magic touches the slip of paper bearing the contract terms, smoke billows up and out, carrying a pressure that throws Callum off balance. Behind me, Jesse starts to cough, but I can't see to either of them because I'm...

Choking.

Something's in my throat, crawling up my sinuses and down into my stomach, scorching everything in its path. I gag, but can't puke, as if a stopper has been shoved in my mouth, so hot it sears my tongue. In the last moment before my body gives out, I remember Callum telling me to trust my instincts.

I squint through the putrid smoke. The tether burns angrily, the fire now arterial purple rather than Callum's ice blue. Those flames lick at the tiny vial containing pieces of my father, heating the glass to molten orange. There won't be much more time.

I pull the conductor's magic to the forefront of my mind, begging my instincts to do something. A phantom sensation makes the hair on my arms stand on end. It draws my gaze to the magic contract, fluttering in the churning smoke. The corners are starting to crumble. Before I can interrogate why, I snatch it from the flames and blow at the corners to stop it from burning further.

Now that it's in my hand, I can feel fine threads dripping from the paper. I rub it between my forefinger and thumb, and some of the threads fade into whispers of ash. The rest are unstable, but I follow them anyway, needing to know where they lead. My consciousness rides the threads through pinpricks in the veil. Immediately, a force attempts to drag me back to the mundane. I reach with all my strength, and through the agony of stretching myself so far, I feel the familiar coolness of my father's energy.

There. *There!*

I paw around inside him, unable to stop even as the slip reignites. There's pain when the flames lick my fingertips, but I have no time; I have to find my magic before the paper burns to nothing.

When the strain is seconds from making me snap, I expand my consciousness through my father. I force my energy into his pores until something feels like me, and as hungry purple flames begin to eat at my mundane skin, I fucking *yank*.

Suddenly, I can feel it. Spicy and sharp like tamarind, sparkling on my tongue, is the magic I've sought so ardently. Exactly what I wanted, what I needed, a bitter razor's edge that shrieks along my nerve endings as it floods my cells, running through the conductive thread formed between myself and the tether, and now Brann. I steal back my magic in greedy mouthfuls, swallowing past the blockage that had choked me.

I release the burning note—I don't need it anymore.

When my eyes flutter open, things are different.

I see Jesse, doubled over coughing, while Callum tries to corral the wretched fire that's spread past the tether, sprinting along the dry pine needles to the ivy climbing the stone walls of his cottage.

I pluck the withered tether from the ground, barely feeling the flames kiss my skin. Opening my mouth, I suck in long plumes of screaming fire, breathing them in and in and in, until the drained husk of a tether crumbles to ash in my hands. I look to the cottage, soot-stained but safe, and listen as Jesse's coughing eases.

I've *done it*.

When I regard my lovers, it's to find them looking back with trepidation. Callum steadies Jesse, then opens his mouth like he has something to say. No sound issues forth.

"It worked," I tell them, wondering why they aren't happier. It *worked*. I feel different—isn't this how I've always felt? "Is everything alright?"

Jesse coughs behind his hand. "Bennett, are you okay?"

Tilting my head in confusion, I ask, "Should I not be?" Long, oily hair spills over my shoulder, vibrant like wet ink in the last rays of the setting sun. "I feel like I can breathe again."

"That's... good," Callum says. "You look different."

"That's to be expected," I inform him. "I never looked like that. That mundane form." My voice crackles with the force of my distaste. "This is how I always was."

Then I look down at my hands, greying skin and long fingernails, pointed and sharp as talons. Much more powerful than the blunt stubs of mundane flesh. I curl my lip, rage creeping up my esophagus. All that fire I swallowed looks for a way out.

"Bennett—"

I bare my teeth. "I need to find my father."

Jesse grips Callum's arm, but Callum catches my gaze and holds it.

"Maybe you should think more," Callum says. "You don't seem stable right now."

"I'm exactly the way I'm meant to be," I insist. Even if they refuse to see reason, I don't have to listen to them. I show the wolves my back and call upon the veil. Ready to go home. Ready to hunt down Brann and tear him to shreds for what he did to me.

Something gives me pause.

I glance over my shoulder at the wolves, my lovers. "Thank you," is all I can think to say. "This couldn't have happened without you."

Satisfied, I watch the darkness in front of me go gauzy, the singed garden warping and shifting like a heat mirage. I take a step forward, eager to taste the crisp Faerie air. The Summer Court awaits—

Before my eyes, the veil tears.

Everything tips sideways. My vision wobbles as if I'm in a barrel rolling down a hill; my inner ear spins and spins, until I fall to my knees. I prick my fingers on pine needles as I dig into the rocky ground in an attempt to anchor myself. I'm peripherally aware of loud clattering and an oppressive pressure, but my mind won't focus. Bile claws its way into my mouth, sour and thick as sap, and when I shake my head to escape the taste, the nausea causes my stomach to revolt.

My gut spasms, my throat contracts, and a spurt of something passes my lips. I heave again, and my eyes water as more of it splatters between my hands, fouling the rents I've torn in the ground. I attempt to wipe the gritty residue from my mouth, but it sticks like tar. Digging my nails into my cheeks doesn't remove it either, and when the black substance comes in contact with the shallow scratches, my skin begins to burn.

I try to cry out, but the sound gets trapped.

"Bennett, Bennett—what's happened to you?" A large hand lands on my back. Another pushes—no, two more, tucking my hair behind my shoulders, trying to get it away from the worst of the putrid vomit.

"It didn't work," I say, enraged. My lip catches between my teeth, which are much longer and sharper than my mouth remembers. Blood drips down my chin while I snarl. "What the fuck is this? I'm—" I barely have time to bat someone out of the way before another wave hits. More of the dark substance shoots from my mouth, igniting my torn lip with radiating pain.

I pant, staring at the puddle of whatever is being forced out of my body. Footsteps grow distant, whoever they belong to disappearing into the distance. I don't know how long it takes before they return, but that when they do, I'm crying again. Furious tears run over the smears of burning tar searing my skin, joining the blood dripping off my chin.

"Hold still, Bennett." My head is turned with a firm hand, and an unfamiliar substance is applied to my skin. It's fragrant and tacky like old honey, but it eases the stinging. "Can you look at me?"

I squint upward, hissing at the glaring sunlight until a very blurry Callum manifests. He's crouched beside me, trying to keep his bare feet out of the black sludge while his gloved hands rub more of the off-white medicine over my chin. Jesse must be the person holding my hair back.

"I need to cross the veil," I say as I try to stand.

The image of a frowning Callum wobbles in my fractured vision. "You'll do no such thing."

I rock onto my haunches in an attempt to escape his reach. "You have no right to order me around."

"You just blew a hole in my cottage, so I disagree. Now *hold still*." Callum rips off the gloves and seizes the sides of my head in a hold I can't break. Without warning, his magic plunges into my mind.

I scream and thrash, but he doesn't let go. Jesse uses his hold on my hair to assist him, his other hand heavy on my shoulder, keeping me in place.

For a long stretch, I think I've never felt anything more painful than Callum violating my energy by forcing himself into my head. Then, abruptly, it stops, and I blink several times in alarm.

"Cal?" I squeak, then immediately clutch my stomach as another fountain of putrid fluid gushes from my mouth, spattering over Callum's feet. "Fuck!"

Callum reels back, hands and eyes glowing. I watch in horror as thin curls of smoke spring from the spattering of vomit. He quickly wipes it away with one of the abandoned gloves, but pink spots remain where his skin has been seared.

"I'm so sorry, Cal," I sob. I choke back more vomit, then something he said occurs to me. I look past Callum's shoulder and am horrified to see a massive chunk of wall missing from the side of the cottage. Broken stones scatter the hardwood floors; one of the chairs at the dining table has been upended, its leg broken; and a large pile of rubble has crushed half the couch and annihilated the coffee table. Callum's armchair didn't survive either.

A horrified sob catches in my throat. "The cottage—"

"Don't worry about the cottage right now, Ben." Callum scrambles further backward to avoid a new splash. The tar has thinned into a dirty grey slime peppered with flecks of coal-black.

"What can we do?" Jesse asks, frantic. His big hand strokes my back, up and down, up and down.

I reason he means to be soothing, but all it's doing is giving me motion sickness. I attempt to bat him away nicely, but all I do is smear a combination of Callum's medicine and the mess ejecting itself from my body onto Jesse's shirt. The fibers hiss where the sludge touches them. Jesse shoots to his feet and rips off the shirt, leaving my long hair to fall. It sticks to my face and neck, and judging by the locks pooling around my wrists, its length seems to be increasing.

"I don't know what to do," Callum says grimly. His eyes glow brightly, sweat catching the light as it drips down his brow. "I was able to create a barrier to protect your mind, but something else is flooding through you, and I can't stop it."

"It's okay," I mumble, wiping my mouth. "It'll be okay, Cal." To prove my point, I hurl so violently it spatters upon my exposed knees. Callum lunges in with the salve once more.

Just when it seems there's nowhere to go but down, a shimmer from the veil appears inside the cottage. Between one blink and another, a figure appears among the rubble, then immediately staggers into the table. The silhouette is familiar: tall, with long green hair that spills over broad shoulders like vines in a stiff breeze.

The person turns, and a jolt runs through me. I struggle to my feet. "Dad?"

Brann turns to face me. He looks exactly the same as I remember him except for his eyes, so bloodshot his sclera look red. "Bennett," he says, a trail of blood dripping from the corner of his mouth. "What have you done?"

A Fae's Two Alphas

"Better question, Mr. Chiston," Jesse says, coming to hover behind me. "What the fuck did *you* do?"

Brann picks his way around the broken chunks of cottage. He frowns at the missing wall, then, with visible reluctance, submits to the degradation of crawling through the hole.

"Firstly," he says, addressing Jesse. "Chiston is Naomi's last name. And she's the one you should be asking."

My chest goes cold. I stare at Brann with wide eyes, only vaguely aware of the argument continuing around me.

"Bullshit," Jesse snaps. "You're the one who took away Bennett's magic."

A bitter laugh escapes Brann's blood-flecked lips. "If you think I wanted to separate my son from his magic and our home, you're mistaken. I'd never commit such a despicable act, were it not for his mother forcing my compliance. Now," he says, kicking a rock out of the way as he walks forward, gesturing at me. "Who's responsible for this?"

Callum says, rising to his full height, just a bit above Brann's. "Instead of demanding answers, maybe you should explain yourself further."

"And who are you?" Brann enquires archly.

"Callum Truett, magewolf and owner of this land."

Brann sneers. "Would I be correct in pinning responsibility on you, then, *magewolf*?"

"Don't talk to my boyfriend like that!" My voice cracks to an embarrassingly high shriek. The combined weight of their gazes is mortifying beyond belief, but this is about more than my pride. "He was trying to fix this whole shitfest by destroying that, that um, the thingy box."

"Tether," Callum supplies.

"Yes, that. Destroying the tether Mom had on you."

"I suppose I should be grateful," Brann says, tone dry,

"except your version of 'destroying' the instrument my former partner was using to control me ended up funneling the energy into my son, whose body is unequipped to handle full fae magic."

Callum, Jesse, and I exchange alarmed looks.

"That wasn't Callum," I hazard. "I did that myself. Can... Now that you're here, you can fix it. Right?"

Brann is too silent for too long. Eventually, he admits, "I cannot."

"Why?" Halfway through the word, I burp up another mouthful of gritty slime. Disgusted, I spit it in the approximate direction of the existing puddle.

"Because it isn't mine to control," Brann says through gritted teeth.

Callum growls, sending a rumble through the rocks beneath our feet. "Explain."

Brann's hands are fine-boned like mine, and tendons protrude when he flexes his fingers in anger. I'm overcome by the urge to hug him, but he's already bleeding, and I don't want to smear whatever-the-fuck this is all over his clothes.

"When Naomi first birthed Bennett, her condition for being a part of our child's life was... insurance," Brann begins. "I agreed to the creation of a tether, which she insisted upon so I couldn't overpower or trick her. I didn't expect a human to create a tether as powerful as Naomi's became."

While Brann speaks, Jesse sidles up to me with his half-burned shirt. He dabs at my face, careful not to let the sludge touch his skin while he cleans it off me.

Brann continues, "Naomi could use her influence over me any time I was in the mundane realm. After Bennett and I left, I took pains to avoid her notice, but"—his brow creases—"one miscalculation was all she needed. I underestimated her a second time, and paid for it. Naomi demanded I bring Bennett back to the mundane and keep him from returning to Faerie. I had no choice.

"Now that it's gone, I'm no longer under her control. The more pressing issue is that Bennett has been infused with a substantial portion of my magic. His body is half-human; it's not equipped to manage the power of a full fae." Brann pauses to cough harshly, blood flecks spraying over his palm.

Terror makes my already-sore stomach clench. "Will you be okay? Why is it hurting you so much?"

"I'll recover," Brann says. "Magic being ripped from oneself isn't pleasant—"

"Go figure," Jesse mutters.

"But it won't kill me," Brann continues, his voice hard. Then he looks to me, and his face transforms into an expression of unfiltered grief. "If we can't close the conduit flooding Bennett with my magic, it will overwhelm his body."

Jesse and Callum inhale sharply. I don't have it in me; I simply blink up at my father, lips parted as I try to fit them around the right words. "Can't you take it back?"

Brann rakes his hands down his face. "Without your own magic, I'd leave you with nothing. It would scrape you raw, leaving you empty of your life force. My magic is already eating away at you. It will continue until there's nothing left."

"There has to be something one of you can fucking do!" Jesse tugs me against his chest as he looks between Brann and Callum.

"I sincerely don't know what I could try. I told you both from the start, fae magic is different." Callum's expression is raw, exposing too many emotions for me to identify. Shock. Regret?

Jesse growls, his gaze swinging to Brann. "Who *can* fix this?"

"The only way Bennett has a fighting chance is if he regains his own magic. To do that, you'll have to talk to the person who has possession of it." Brann sighs heavily. "His mother. Naomi."

33

DUMPSTER CONFLICT

When we pop out from the brief trip through the veil, we're greeted by the dumpsters behind the home goods store where Naomi works. It's got to be around ten by now, which means she's only been on her shift for about three hours.

Vertigo overtakes me so powerfully I have to stagger out of Jesse's protective grip to prop myself up beside one of the dumpsters. I lean forward so I can vomit as far away from myself as possible.

"Where is she?" Jesse demands.

"Doing her job, I presume," Callum says.

Jesse storms toward the back door. I scramble to wipe my mouth with what's left of his shirt and rush after him, but I trip on the long black hair that has grown all the way to my knees. "Jess, you can't just barge in there! She could lose her job."

He laughs just once, a callous bark. "I do not give a single fuck what happens to that bitch when your life is on the line."

My hand flutters over my mouth. "Don't talk about my mom like that."

"Bennett," Brann says on an exasperated sigh. "There's no point in defending—"

The back door swings open, and out runs my mother in a bright blue polo shirt. "What the absolute hell is going on?"

"Question of the day," I mutter.

Callum, who also seems uninterested in being nice to my mom, storms up to her and snags her by the elbow, yanking her toward me. "You. Fix this."

Naomi puffs up like a wildcat, and before my eyes, jerks forward and *tries to bite his hand*.

"Mom!" I shriek. "You can't just bite people!"

"Bennett," Brann sighs.

"Can you guys all stop being shitty so we can"—I hiccup hard—"figure this all out? I don't— I really don't want to die." And then I'm bawling like a child, greasy slime still dripping down my chin as Jesse presses against my back.

Jesse can't embrace me fully due to the corrosive sludge, so he instead jostles me in light reprimand. "You're not going to die."

Naomi looks like a caged animal, throwing suspicious glances between the three strange men surrounding us before she eases closer to me. "Benny, what happened?"

"It's all your fault," I wail. "We found the tether in your room, and Callum destroyed it thinking he could get my magic back but instead I just took a bunch of *Dad's* magic, and if we don't figure out how to get it out of me, I'm going to die! And it's all your fault!"

"You destroyed the—" Her eyes go wide, pupils contracting.

"Focus, Naomi," Brann says.

"Do *not* tell me what to do," she hisses back.

"He'll tell you whatever he goddamn wants if it ends

with you fixing this," Jesse growls, his entire body trembling with repressed rage.

Naomi tugs her ponytail and sends me an imploring look. "I don't know how to fix whatever's happening. I'm not magic."

"You're good at manipulating it though, aren't you," Brann says dryly. It's not a question.

"I did what was best for my family."

"Did you?" Brann takes a threatening step toward her.

Naomi shrinks like she's been slapped. "I—"

I pry myself out of Jesse's arms so I can turn on her. "Don't lie, Mom. You did what was best for you, not anyone else. Do you even care that I've been miserable here for two fucking years? You made Dad take my magic so, what, you could see me more? Why didn't you just *ask*?"

"I didn't think you'd agree," Naomi whispers.

"That's..." I swallow, nauseated by the grit still on my tongue. "That should have told you something."

"Where is Bennett's magic, Naomi?" Brann says, stepping forward. "I tire of hiding your secrets. Where did you put the token?"

"What token?" Callum asks.

Brann frowns at him. "When I took Bennett's magic, I put it in a token, which I gave to Naomi."

All eyes swing to her.

"I don't—" Naomi begins, hugging herself. "You can't... Don't take my son from me."

"You'll be taking your son from everyone. Permanently, if you don't get your head out of your ass."

"Jesse!"

"Fucking hell, Bennett, forgive me for not wanting to see you die!"

"Jesse," Callum growls, "you are not helping. Can you shut up and *stay shut up* for once?"

Jesse's reply is lost to me. I give up on trying to stop the bickering. This is between me and my mom.

I approach Naomi, holding my grimy hands out in supplication. "Please. You'll lose me forever if you don't give up control. Try to think."

Naomi's eyes grow glassy and wet. "I just wanted my baby back."

Then she tugs down the collar of her hideous blue polo, exposing the open-mouthed roar of her bear tattoo. She folds one palm over her chest and closes her eyes. I don't risk taking a single breath, watching in a mix of horror and awe as the lines of Naomi's tattoo begin to glow. There's one bright pulse, and then I see it: a small, hand-carved box resting in her palm.

"What is that?" I ask, voice rasping as it pries itself from my scratchy throat.

"This is another tether. I made it when you were a baby." Her eyes flutter closed as if she's steeling herself against the backlash.

And backlash there most certainly is.

Brann's voice rises above the rest. "You made a gods-damned tether for our son without telling me?"

"He needed protection!" Naomi yells back.

"In what way?" Brann demands. "Nothing in that town was more than we could handle, yet you forced Bennett to hide himself his entire childhood. You wouldn't even let him have magic friends." He casts a look at Jesse.

"It wasn't safe," Naomi says, as if she hasn't heard. "I had to know if he was near magic or accidentally using it, so I made the tether to alert me."

Suddenly her paranoid texts all those times I was with Jesse and Callum start to make sense. She didn't know exactly where I was or who I was with, but it alerted her when I was doing something she didn't want.

"Where were you keeping it all this time?" Brann asks. When Naomi touches her tattoo, Brann huffs like an angry bull, sending a fresh trail of blood dripping from his nose, over his lips. "In the space I made for you, Naomi? You betrayed me *and* our son."

"Wait!" I try to rewind. "Your tattoo? How did you keep it there?"

"A pocket dimension," Callum says, eyebrows high on his forehead.

I perk up, alarmed. He can't be talking about the same thing, but I'm sure I'm not misremembering. Only a couple of weeks ago, we were on the couch in Naomi's living room, Jesse and Callum and I dancing around one another, drenched in so much sexual tension I'd completely forgotten that silly video we watched. Sarah the magician teaching viewers how to use a pocket dimension for a few seconds to create a convincing magic trick. Callum admitting to using one to hold his belongings when he shifted.

Callum continues speaking, running over my thoughts. "The power necessary to keep an item of such importance in a pocket dimension indefinitely would be immense."

Brann sends him a grim look. "I thought the same when she summoned me. I'd never heard of a human, a non-magic user at that, being able to maintain something of this nature."

Jesse wrinkles his nose. "And she used it to fuck over her kid?"

"Wonderful to get to the bottom of that," Callum deadpans. "Open it, Naomi."

She bares her teeth at him but doesn't argue. With shaking hands, Naomi pries open the box and removes an insignificant-looking twist of metal. "It's in here," she says, cradling it in her palms. "Bennett's—"

A bright flash sends the box flying from her hands. Naomi grabs for it with a shriek, but it clatters across the pavement, smoking from the spell Callum projected. The token locking my magic away lands in Callum's outstretched hand.

He closes his fist around it and murmurs something under his breath. "Bennett," he says, but I'm already in front of him, watching light pour from the cracks between his fingers.

"What do I do?"

Callum doesn't have time to answer. Curls of warm yellow-green magic burst free, twisting around his wrist and climbing his arm. I open my mouth to ask again, not expecting his hand to shoot out, strong fingers latching onto my jaw.

It hurts at first, the scorch of magic flooding my mouth and nostrils, mixing with the churning tide of my father's foreign magic. Fire ignites in my veins, coursing through my body until I'm digging my nails into Callum's wrist, silent tears dripping down my cheeks as I'm stuffed so full I might burst. I would collapse onto the grimy pavement if not for Callum's grip on my face.

The remaining black residue on my skin sizzles, then lifts from my skin, dissolving into black smoke until shallow pink burns are all that remains.

Eventually it ends, as most awful things do. With one final, desperate gasp for air, I slump into Callum's arms.

I feel woozy and wrung out. My breathing evens, leaving me hollow yet too-full at the same time. I allow myself to think it's over… before a shock of severe pain wrenches a scream out of me. I writhe against Callum's chest, abused throat scratching as I howl.

"Brann's magic," Callum says urgently. "It's trying to reject Bennett's."

Brann shoves Callum aside so he can guide me down onto the cement, my aching body crumpled between his knees. He cradles my cheeks in his cool palms. "I wish I could spare you more pain, my son."

It's all the warning I get before the overstuffed sensation shifts, becoming an awful sucking whirlwind. Just as I yanked the full-fae magic from my father, he rips it back out of me, leaving my life force struggling to keep energy flowing through shredded channels.

In this moment I believe I really will die—the desperate bid to save me has failed, and I'm going to die behind a home goods store next to a fucking dumpster.

Then my magic starts to fight back.

I gasp a breath of relief as the lost part of me runs through my system, soothing the ache. It'll take time before everything heals, but as my magic caresses the abused spaces inside me—spaces that have been empty for so, so long—an ecstatic hysteria rises within my chest, bubbling up my throat as a relieved laugh.

Inky black hair brushes my ankles, but when I run trembling fingers through it, the strands smudge like charred paper, disintegrating to expose what's hidden beneath: a dirty blonde, overgrown mess that once was a purple and teal mullet.

I struggle upright, knocking my father's hands away until I'm on my own two feet. My body remembers what it was like to be whole, and magic sparks within me so sudden and powerful I hug my chest. Then I inhale deeply, and without giving anyone the chance to stop me, disappear over the veil.

34

THE LOST DANDELION CHRONICLES

Returning to Faerie is anticlimactic.

Maybe because my mom betrayed me by lying to and controlling my dad, then let me believe he was the person responsible for my pain.

Maybe because I hurt my dad by taking his magic, even though I thought it was mine to reclaim.

Maybe because I just puked up at least a gallon of that full-fae magic, physically manifesting after being rejected by my halfling body—magic that would've killed me had it not been removed. Would I have continued to heave out that black tar until I disintegrated into a lifeless husk?

Maybe the bitterness I feel is because, after all they did to protect me, I left without even a word of thanks to Callum and Jesse. No *'thank you for saving me,'* no *'I love you both.'* No *'thank you for loving me back.'*

The first thing I do, after stumbling and falling to my hands and knees in the fragrant grass, is shift into my fae form. It's the body I lived in for years—chest flat without a restrictive binder; hair bright and colorful without quickly-fading dye; eyes bright above my rosy cheeks. I stare down at my hands, at the way my skin looks pearlescent under the warm summer sun. It's been so long.

Now I'm free.

So why don't I feel happy? Elated?

I sit at the base of a tree, surrounded by the brilliance of a Faerie forest. It's too beautiful for the mundane realm to emulate, the colors too bright, and with impossible hues.

I'm just overwhelmed. That's all. It's a lot to take in at once, and when the shock wears off, relief will set in. For now, my thoughts make it impossible to sit in peace.

Callum's siphon theory was correct—I knew he would figure it out. Meanwhile, he had faith in my instincts.

Yes, the ones that almost *killed* me.

Groaning, I drag my fingers through my hair; they emerge with a stalk of puffy dandelion seeds caught under my middle finger. I twist it, watching each fluffy segment sway.

Suddenly, I'm no longer alone.

Brann materializes in front of me. The frantic expression and bloody mouth are gone; he looks composed, the way I remembered him while stewing in my anger.

After considering me, Brann kneels. "How are you feeling, son?"

"Awful," I answer without hesitation.

Brann nods. "I'm sorry, Bennett. If I could have done something differently—"

I shake my head. "I don't blame you. You were being manipulated, and I should be apologizing to you for assuming..." Bile rises in my throat, but I choke it down. No more of that. "I should've known Mom would have something to do with it. I didn't want to think either of you would hurt me, but I had no answers, and I was just so upset."

The worst part is how unsurprised I am. While I never would've guessed the full extent of Naomi's betrayal, I tried to stay objective about her flaws. Naomi is cunning and manipulative and, apparently, has the strength of an actual, literal bear in her life force—strength she used to lie and deceive and harm, all out of selfish paranoia. If she'd asked to see me, of course I would've said yes. I love my Mama Bear.

Loved her.

"Did you know she was lying to me when I was a kid?" I ask.

Brann hesitates before answering. "Somewhat. She didn't want you around magic, and I wasn't able to interfere with her decision to shelter you."

"Of course not. And you really didn't know she'd made a tether for me?"

"No." A scowl twists his features. Brann typically keeps his appearance simple, maybe because he spent so long appearing human in the mundane realm. In Faerie, he's recognizable as fae, but not to the degree of some. As he speaks, I see cracks in his façade, the shark-toothed monster he could be peeking out. "I would've killed her. After you left, I almost did."

"What?!"

"She manipulated me. She blamed me for harming my own son while exposing him to torment for years. That—" His hands clench against his knees. "We stayed together for thirteen years, during which I made sacrifices I'll regret for the rest of my life. She wasn't this bad at first. It got worse as you aged."

I don't think I've ever seen my father so badly shaken.

"We didn't love each other, but I cared about her. More importantly, I wanted to stay in your life. Eventually, it became too much. She cares about no one's happiness but her own."

"I don't think she's capable of feeling happiness," I say bitterly. The more I ruminate, the angrier I get. "What stopped you from killing her?"

"One of your wolves. The silver one."

"That sounds like something he'd do."

According to fae law, Naomi would deserve a wicked fate, but the idea of my dad killing my mom sits oddly in my stomach. I'm glad Callum intervened.

"Both of them were distressed by your departure."

"I knew they would be."

Brann prepares to speak, then hesitates. "You're staying here, Bennett?"

"Of course I am." I'm shocked he'd even ask. "I spent months trying to get my magic back so I could come home. Why wouldn't I stay?"

"I was just asking. I thought you might split your time."

The implication seals my lips into a tight, pained line. I made it clear that when I got back to Faerie, I'd never return. "They'll be fine," I murmur, skipping several lines of conversation because they're too painful to say out loud.

Jesse and Callum will be fine without me. They will. And me? The aching hollow inside me will fill with time.

Brann shifts his weight until he can press careful lips to my forehead. "I've missed you, my son."

Warmth surges from my throat to my fingertips, and before I know it, I'm bawling, crushed against my father's chest.

"I was so fucking lonely," I sob.

I didn't realize how deep a relief it'd be to settle into my dad's embrace again. Brann wraps his arms around me and squeezes, holding me like a child until the heaving gasps calm and the tears slow. He doesn't speak, only wipes my cheeks with his sleeve and strokes my hair.

Eventually, Brann decides I've cried enough. He stands me up and straightens my clothes, murmuring about getting me something decent to wear. I offer him a wavery smile as I follow him toward our village—where I belong.

I'll be okay.

Won't I?

※

The fae in my father's village—my friends—welcome me back. They get me drunk and high, celebrating my return, but I suspect they were looking for a reason to get drunk, high, and rowdy anyway. A 'welcome home' celebration is as good an opportunity as any.

I attempt to ride a horse for the first time in two years. The other fae laugh at how clumsy my equine handling has become. After the run, my thighs burn badly, underused muscles sore. I had thought all the walking I did in the mundane realm would make riding easy. Unfortunately, it didn't.

While I'm trying to adjust, Brann is so attentive it embarrasses me. I never needed to be fussed over, even when I was a child. Naomi was clingy and controlling, but I'm the one who monitored her, making sure she didn't go off the deep end. Since Brann pointed it out, I can't stop thinking about how she worsened as I grew more independent. By the time she figured out how to drag me out of Faerie, she was an utter wreck.

Everything is just as beautiful as I remembered. The forest and flowers, the rolling hills. I share tables with fae who have wings like orchid mantids and converse with tall, antlered forest dwellers. One of my regular companions, the person who treats me the least like a novelty, grows long trails of bluebells over their body, tangled in their long hair and twisted around their limbs like vines on a trellis. The town butcher has four arms, and the seamstress who made my new clothes first assessed me with three of her six eyes. Hunters return from the woods with braces of rabbits, venison, and all types of fowl—filling my plates with the best meat I've ever tasted.

Brann invites me to join the hunts now that I'm older, but I've found myself disinclined to try horseback riding again after everyone mocked me. It's strange how much has changed in two years. I've forgotten things, misremembered others, and feel I spend more time being laughed at than laughing with anyone.

Did this town, these people, always make me feel so utterly, hopelessly, *alone*?

The days spin together like colorful ribbons of paint, stretching into marbled patterns that never mix, never creating something new. The land of the Summer Court is perpetually warm and sunny, but as the mundane season draws closer to fall, days here shorten in preparation of the Winter Court's ascension. Even though it hasn't yet arrived, I find myself perpetually cold.

I shift on the riverbank where I'm sitting and heave a disappointed sigh—something I've been doing with increasing frequency. Behind me, Damhnait clucks their tongue.

"You're restless today." Their fingers remain steady and nimble as they braid wildflowers into my hair. I've maintained my preferred style, shearing the sides and leaving the rest as long, wispy strands framing the points of my ears.

"My ass just hurts," I say sourly. Damhnait tugs the unfinished braid, plucking the bud off a dandelion that's sprouted from a teal lock. I duck my head, pulling out of their grasp. "Ow."

Damhnait drops the dandelion bud into my palm, then tightens their hold on my hair and resumes braiding. "Remember that pain, and hold still."

I stare at the little flower. It blossoms before my eyes, exposing fluffy yellow petals. I rub them gently between my thumb and forefinger, sighing once again.

"You know," Damhnait says, using a tiny sprout from their fingertip to tie off the bottom of the braid. "Dandelion seeds are good spies."

My brows furrow as I turn to face them. "Spies?"

"Yes. They can cross into the mundane through thin spots in the veil, and you can follow them. See what they see, hear what they hear."

"Why would I need to know that?" I ask, carefully neutral. "Am I meant to be spying on someone?"

Damhnait smiles, secrets closed firmly behind rows of short, needle-thin teeth. "I'll teach you, if you can think of anything you might need it for."

I tug at a string of bluebells descending from their earlobe. "You're terrible at feigning innocence."

"Maybe," they allow. "But no one here is worse at lying than you are."

Damhnait folds their fingers over the flower still resting in my palm, and when they withdraw, the yellow petals have dried, exposing a puffball in their place. I allow Damhnait to steer my smaller hand, bringing the seeds to my lips. "Blow. Then follow them with your mind, and listen."

After that, I return to the river with increasing frequency, often waiting until Brann has gone away on hunts before I sit by the mossy bank, running my fingers through my hair until tiny sprouts turn into dandelion buds. They come off easily with a gentle nudge from my magic, blooms maturing more quickly with the shortening of every day. I don't know exactly how long it's been since I left the mundane realm, but they're somewhere in September. The reminder makes me shiver.

With a puff of breath, I send seeds from the latest flower into the brisk fall air, watching as they spiral in the air before disappearing through the veil with brief winks of light. I close my eyes, focusing on what the flying seeds tell me of the mundane.

It took a few tries to find the right place. I poked at different places in the veil, with Damhnait monitoring my progress. Finally I located a small, unattended circle of mushrooms, forgotten in the woods of Michigan's Upper Peninsula. After a few successes, Damhnait stopped accompanying me to the riverside hill.

Sometimes I don't see them for days on end. Whatever the seeds show me is pure chance; they're at the mercy of wind currents and the forest's many obstacles. Most are caught before even approaching their goal, lost to iridescent spiderwebs and dewy grass. Those times, merely seeing the familiar surroundings has to be enough. Of the few that make it to the small clearing, fewer still catch sight of my targets.

On very special days, the ones I cherish when I'm at my most empty, I hear their voices. Bickering, as usual. It makes me smile—an occurrence that grows rare as time continues to filter through my fingers.

When a seed landed on the carved wood bench, I was

able to see them working on the cottage wall, heaving new stones into place. I watched until the image grew blurry, the seed's power fading. After that, I could only listen until the magic ran entirely dry.

The sound of footsteps has my eyes popping open. I swivel to regard the approaching person, trying not to show frustration at having been interrupted. Ashamed heat gathers in my face when I see my father—possibly the worst individual to catch me in this act. He lowers himself gracefully to the riverbank beside me.

"Hello, son."

I do my best not to squirm. "Hi, Dad."

"How are you today?"

"Um." Do I lie? "I'm okay."

Brann gives me a skeptical look but doesn't call me out. "You've been coming here quite often."

"Yeah, I... like the sound of the water." That's not a lie; I do. I like it almost as much as the babbling of the creek near Callum's cottage.

"It's soothing," Brann agrees.

My eyelids flutter as I try to maintain awareness of the dandelion seeds, afraid they'll make it to their targets while I'm not able to focus.

Brann's voice interrupts again. "Son, are you happy here?"

I shift restlessly, insisting, "Of course I am. I did nothing but miss this place, especially you, for years. I'm glad to be back." The words sit heavily in my stomach.

"Bennett..." He pauses long enough for me to catch a glimpse of the seeds' paths—nothing so far. "You don't have to lie to comfort me, you know."

I straighten from my slouched position. "I wouldn't! Fae can't lie." Which is true, but I suppose having a human parent who operates exclusively on deceit allows me the gift of dishonesty. Regardless, Damhnait says I'm horrible at it.

Brann's unwavering gaze communicates the same sentiment.

Finally, I begrudgingly admit, "Being in Faerie isn't like I remembered."

"I had wondered if the adjustment would be difficult."

"It's not just the adjustment. I thought I fit in when I was younger, but now I feel like they see me as a toy. I'm a halfling who doesn't understand things full-blood fae consider a given."

"You're of age now. They expect you to conform in ways you didn't as a child." After weeks of tiptoeing around my feelings, Brann's frank words surprise me. "If you don't find that comfortable, maybe this isn't where you're meant to be after all."

My face falls. "Dad, I..." I curl in on myself, arms tight around my knees.

Brann sets his hand gently on the back of my head, a comforting touch that fills me with unexpected grief. Not because I don't want him to touch me, but because I'm reminded of the weight of Jesse's fingers ruffling through my hair.

"You don't have to worry about me, Bennett. Now that both of us are untethered to Naomi, we can cross the veil to visit whenever we want. Your decision doesn't have to be one or the other." When I don't respond, he sighs and squeezes my shoulder before rising to his feet. "Think about it, son. For now, you should return to your observation."

I flinch, but maintain my silence. I can't bring myself to seek out the seeds until his footsteps recede entirely, and when I reach for them across the veil, it's without hope there's enough magic left to catch anything.

It's a windy day, and the majority of the seeds have scattered far. None of them report movement or sound other than the wind, which is blowing in the opposite direction from the cottage. I scrub a hand over my face, ready to give up until the stillness of the mushroom circle is interrupted by light footsteps.

Surprised, daring to hope, I push my awareness into the nearby seeds caught in the grass and listen attentively. I pick up two sets of footsteps—no, more than that. Disappointment fills me. It's probably just a few deer.

Then the figures step into view of the dandelion, wrenching a gasp free from my lungs.

Two wolves, one brown and grey, the other larger and silver. Their thick fur gleams in the sun.

Callum sniffs a mushroom at the edge of the circle while Jesse paces restlessly around the perimeter. I watch them inspect the surroundings until, far too soon, the magic in the seed begins to run out.

"No," I whisper to myself, heart clenching in my chest.

But it's too late—the scene goes dark, leaving the extension of my consciousness empty and still. I come back to myself, my hands shaking terribly.

What the fuck am I doing here?

I don't give myself time to deliberate. No thinking, no hesitation, no wasting time. I push through the veil, uncaring when the brilliance of Faerie fades into the simpler colors of the mundane realm. When the fluttering edges of the veil clear from my vision, I come to full awareness of my new surroundings—directly in the center of the faerie circle, crouched on the spongy tree trunk, staring down the surprised faces of two wolves.

A slow grin pulls my face into an unfamiliar shape, and all I can think is: *This is what I've been waiting for.*

The brown wolf leaps over the line of the circle, bolting like no obstacle could keep him away. I open my arms, grunting when Jesse slams into me. He rises onto his back legs so he can press his front paws against my shoulders, yipping excitedly. I wrap my arms around him and bury my face in thick brown fur.

"I'm sorry," is the first thing out of my mouth. "I'm so, so sorry. I missed you more than I can describe. So fucking much."

Jesse pulls back enough to lick my cheeks, cleaning away tears I didn't realize I'd begun to shed.

The silver wolf stays back, outside the circle, but his laser-blue eyes are trained on Jesse and me. I nudge Jesse aside and climb off the log, bare feet sinking into the familiar moss. Heart pounding, I pad toward Callum with outstretched hands.

"C'mere, you beautiful, feral man."

He snuffles, then steps delicately through the flora, careful not to crush anything beneath his large paws. The moment he's through, I lunge. In the time it takes me to cross the space, the wolf disappears in a shimmer of magic, so that I land in the embrace of a very strong, very naked man. Callum crushes me against his chest while Jesse barks behind us, then the beat of pawprints transitions to footfalls, and a second pair of arms fits around our bodies, pinning me between them.

Then I'm being kissed, two pairs of lips warring for possession of my own. Their tongues tangle, pushing into my mouth at the same time. I do my best to respond, messy and careless, digging my nails into their skin to ground myself since they aren't wearing clothes for me to hold onto.

"You're back," Callum whispers when I draw back for a breath, panting hard, my eyes watering with joy.

A Fae's Two Alphas

I cradle his face in my palm, stroking silver stubble with my thumb. "I couldn't leave you. Either of you." Jesse dips to kiss my temple.

A sudden gust of wind blows through the clearing. The alphas are both naked, but I'm the only one who shivers.

"Are you cold?" Callum asks immediately.

"We should get him back to the cottage," Jesse says without waiting for me to answer.

I place one hand on each of their chests and grin. "Some things never change."

35

ENTHUSIASTIC HOMECOMING

I RIDE on Callum's back, with Jesse running alongside us. My stomach churns with excitement to be at the cottage again, to see the work they did on the walls, inside and outside, repairing my awful, reckless mistake. The moment Callum skids to a stop in the front yard, I hop down, moving eagerly toward the familiar front door.

By the time I make it inside, both wolves have shifted and are close on my heels. The door slams shut with my back against it, alphas crowding me from each side.

They kiss me again, even messier this time, and begin exploring my body like it's new. Which, I guess, it is. Callum traces the point of my ear with his tongue while Jesse reaches under my shirt to circle my nipples with his fingertips, thumbs exploring the contours of my flat chest. Then my shirt is gone, laces loosened until it can be tugged easily over my head. Jesse fists a hand in my hair, tugging me forward so Callum can insert himself between me and the door. He's hard already, velvety soft length pressing against the small of my back. Having missed the weight of him in my hand, I reach behind me, but Callum

A Fae's Two Alphas

drags my arms up and wraps them behind his neck instead.

I don't have time to question them.

Jesse divests me of my pants while Callum runs his palms from my throat to my hips and up again, stopping periodically to circle and pinch my nipples between his claws. Then Jesse sinks to his knees and throws my leg over his shoulder. I wobble, trying to balance on one leg, and have to dig my fingers into the back of Callum's neck to support myself while Jesse buries his face into the apex of my thighs.

I rock onto the ball of my foot, pelvic muscles flexing as Jesse fucks me with his tongue. Callum spreads my labia with his fingers, holding me open so Jesse can tongue directly at the head of my engorged clit.

We haven't even made it past the front door and I'm already overstimulated, squirming as Callum squeezes my clit. The shock mounts upon the pleasure of Jesse sucking around Callum's merciless fingers. Without warning, Jesse slips two of his own fingers inside me and crooks them.

My hips buck wildly, both toward and away from the rhythm of Jesse's fingers and insistent tongue. Vocalizations escape unbidden, tearing their way out of me in squeaks and whimpers and agonized, needy moans.

Callum licks up my neck. "Come for us, Bennett." He has a firm grip on my hips, holding me steady despite my badly trembling leg. It has the added effect of keeping me from squirming away from Jesse's lashing tongue.

I spasm and thrash, cry and curse, and with a final, tortured groan, I throw my head back and surrender to an orgasm so powerful it reaches into my soul.

Jesse doesn't let up until I beg him to stop, chanting *fuck* over and over again until he slowly removes his fingers.

Then he sits on his heels, mouth and cheeks wet with my come. He helps Callum ease me into some semblance of uprightness, supporting me when I wobble and moan.

"One hell of a homecoming," I mumble, swooning against Callum's chest.

Jesse stands and takes my chin. "You just wait."

"Oh no," I deadpan, half meaning it. "However will I survive?"

Callum noses at the back of my neck. "You've been through a lot."

"He can take it." The slick on Jesse's face catches the light when he grins broadly.

"Thanks for the vote of confidence." I smile back, then try to wipe the mess off his cheeks. It's hopeless, so I withdraw. Then Callum catches me by the wrist and draws my fingers into his mouth, sucking the taste off them.

Jesse's eyes fix on Callum's lips, wrapped around my fingers. "That's hot as fuck."

I nudge him. "You could do it too, you know."

"Suck your fingers?"

"No, let Cal suck yours."

Both men fall silent. I wait expectantly, almost laughing when Jesse studies the fingers he had inside me like he's never seen them before. They glisten, slick stretching between them. Callum's gaze is trained on Jesse as if he's transformed into prey. Ever helpful, I take Jesse by the wrist and guide his hand close enough to Callum's face that if he tilted his head forward, he could pull Jesse's long, golden-brown fingers between his lips.

My alphas stare, wild-eyed, measuring each other like they're approaching a great battle. I do my best to hold my tongue and let them figure it out, but the seconds stretch too long, and finally, I roll my eyes and say, "God, Cal, just do it."

I extricate myself from between them, bumping Callum with my hip just hard enough to give him plausible deniability. My stomach tightens with arousal when Callum goes, tongue first, for Jesse's outstretched hand.

Callum licks at the seam, rubbing his lips down the length of Jesse's fingers before dragging back up. After catching Jesse's wrist with a steadying hand, Callum sucks his wet fingers into his mouth.

Jesse inhales sharply, his other hand twitching. I snag it and twist our fingers together, giving them a reassuring squeeze. Callum gets a better grip around Jesse's palm, tonguing more obscenely than he did with me. He dips his head, taking Jesse's fingers to the second knuckle, and draws back slowly before going down further.

"Fuck, that's hot," I say, echoing Jesse's earlier words. Thoughts of Callum going down on Jesse for real fill my head until it's spinning with the force of my desire.

Callum doesn't stop. He moves to Jesse's palm, licking down the sensitive skin until he reaches his wrist, where he sucks lightly. Then he tugs Jesse closer. They stop only a handful of inches away from each other, gazes locked. Jesse chuckles, tense and uncertain.

Again, I wait. I hold my breath, anticipating them finally —fucking *finally*—kissing. Jesse clenches his hand tightly around mine until I give in and whisper, "You both want this."

Callum and Jesse come together like a surging wave, dropping all pretense as they fall into each other's arms. Callum fists a hand in Jesse's hair, holding him close while Jesse clasps both sides of Callum's face like he never wants to let go. I curl against Jesse's side, watching with satisfaction that almost feels as good as the orgasm they dragged out of me barely five minutes ago.

It's not until Callum starts fucking his tongue into Jesse's mouth that Jesse breaks away, panting. "What the hell are we doing?" He sounds lost.

I tilt my head, giving him a curious stare. In my peripheral, I see Callum looking very much like he wants to escape, so I loop my elbow through his and hold his arm tight against my chest.

"What do you think we're doing?" I ask carefully.

Jesse shakes his head. "I don't know."

"I assumed it was mutually understood that the three of us were becoming a Thing."

"Are we?" He looks at Callum with trepidation.

Callum opens his mouth, then turns to me for help.

"You've wanted each other since before I came into the picture," I remind them. "I don't want you to share me. I want this to be all three of us, together. Equal. Can you boys handle that?"

"I mean..." Jesse's brow furrows. "Cal?"

"It's a mutual decision." A gentle smile curls my lips. "One of you can't take the lead on the other."

Jesse scuffs his bare toes on the wood. "Cal *does* take the lead."

I snort. "Is this one of those shifter things?"

"Yes," Jesse responds, just as Callum says, "No." Then they stare at each other.

Careful not to spook either of them, I catch Jesse's arm and pull it to my chest alongside Callum's, holding them both so they're still facing each other. "Callum," I start, "Do you want Jesse? Are you attracted to him?"

Callum's throat spasms, lips opening and closing. "I... Yes."

I kiss Jesse's shoulder. "Jess, do you reciprocate Callum's feelings?"

Watching Jesse's teeth sink into his bottom lip, I resist the urge to give a little cheer of victory. His gaze dips to Callum's mouth, swollen from kisses, then back to his eyes. "You know I do."

"I do know." Callum's voice is steady, but he's shaking.

"Kiss?" I suggest, after too much time passes without either of them giving up ground.

"Not without you," Jesse says, shifting to cup his palm around the back of my neck. I soak up the warmth, the weight.

Callum agrees, "Never without you."

Their mouths meet slowly this time, tongues curling together. I squeeze them both, welcoming my beautiful alphas back into my arms when they descend upon me in mutual agreement.

36

THE MOST MAGICAL SOLUTION

"I like the new couch," I comment. It's bigger than the last one, with one side protruding into a chaise lounge. I try not to read too much into that.

"Jesse picked it out," Callum grumbles from the kitchenette. He's making tea, because of course.

I turn my grin on Jesse, who merely shrugs. I let it go, choosing to snuggle into his side instead. The leather creaks under my shifting weight, and I resist making a joke about breaking it in.

Callum returns with three mugs. I beam at him, accepting my usual mug and blowing on the steaming tea inside. Callum moves to sit across from us, like he always does, then stops. I realize he hasn't replaced the chair that was destroyed in the explosion.

Jesse pounces on the opportunity. "Sit next to us." He leans back against the couch, stretching his arms along the back. One hand tucks me against his left side while he pats the cushion to his right. Callum hesitates long enough for me to loose a pathetic whine. That motivates him to ease himself onto the cushion next to Jesse. He attempts to keep

A Fae's Two Alphas

some space between them, but it doesn't work. Jesse catches Callum around the shoulder and yanks him against his side. Then, after a moment of contemplation, he nuzzles his nose into Callum's hair.

The gesture stops Callum from lurching away. I watch with interest as they square off, the stalemate only breaking when Jesse lowers his eyes and tilts his head back, exposing his throat. Callum examines the display, then slowly leans forward, exhaling against Jesse's bared skin. Wanting a better view, I squirm in Jesse's near-unbreakable hold. He's remaining still for Callum, but is clutching me like a comfort stuffie.

Callum's lips part, revealing fully descended fangs. If I had enough breath I'd gasp, but Jesse is holding me too tight. Jesse vibrates with tension, but when Callum nips his throat, not drawing blood despite his sharp canines, Jesse's melts with a soft moan. Callum bites him a few more times, leaving red marks that'll fade quickly.

"Okay, I changed my mind," I say, finally free of Jesse's grasp. I kiss the other side of Jesse's neck, then Callum's cheekbone. "The shifter powerplay stuff isn't dumb at all; it's way hot. Like, super hot. Feel free to keep going." Callum strokes my bangs aside, then kisses my forehead. I notice his fangs begin to retract, so I grab his face. "Don't do that. I want *all* of you. Both of you."

Jesse rubs his cheek against mine. "You've made that pretty clear, Benny."

"You need reminding." I kiss him, then Callum, quick and meaningful, then rock back to study them. Before I lose myself to insecurity, I blurt, "I want you both to fuck me."

"That's direct," says Jesse, lip quirked. "But we can work with it."

Callum shoves him. "He can be as direct as he wants."

"It was a joke, asshole."

Callum palms Jesse's face, shoving him back against the couch. "What do you want to start with?"

"Whom," Jesse corrects, ignoring Callum's scowl.

"Both of you. At the same time."

"What, like we did—"

"Not that combination of holes," I specify, fully aware I've gone bright red. It sounded smooth in my head, but without the frantic tension of a mid-fuck confession, it's just awkward.

What I'm trying to convey hits Jesse before it hits Callum. They look at each other in alarm, like I've requested something unreasonable.

"What's wrong?"

"Ben..." Callum winces.

Jesse spits it out: "You're so *tiny*."

"Smaller people have taken two dicks," I insist. "I see it in porn literally all the time."

Callum slaps his free hand over his face in an effort to hide how darkly his cheeks flush. I attempt to ignore how I just exposed my taste in porn. They'd learn about it eventually if this Thing is going to work.

"Please? I'll speak up if anything is uncomfortable. And..." I hesitate. "I've got my magic back, you know." I reach for a lock of my long hair, stroking it rapidly. Embarrassment floods through me when a dandelion sprouts beneath my fingers, too obvious to hide.

On cue, Callum knocks my hand away so he can cradle the tiny bud. It blooms, bright buttery yellow, in the center of his wide palm.

"You do have your magic back," he says. "I noticed."

Jesse adds, "You look like you fell into glitter. Like, all over."

I tuck the lock of hair behind my pointed ear and pluck the dandelion from Callum's hand. "Yeah. So, I can take it," I finish without flourish.

Callum examines me dubiously until a vague almost-smile twitches the corner of his mouth. "Okay." His gaze swings to Jesse. "Pup?"

"We'd better figure out how this is going to work," Jesse says. "I don't want to crush him."

"You'll be on the bottom," I say. "We should probably-definitely get lube." Callum leaves without a word, giving me an opportunity to manhandle Jesse into position. "I like the lounge," I say, shoving him until he stretches out on it. "Was it your idea?"

"That obvious, huh."

I hum, then climb astride him, wasting no time grinding against his cock, thick and hot. He filled me so deeply, all by himself. Even I don't know how I'm going to fit him and Callum at the same time, but I trust my body to make it happen.

What's magic good for if it can't help me take two dicks from the alphas I desperately love?

Jesse moans, wrapping his long fingers around my hips and squeezing, just hard enough. He rocks up against me, not breaking our shared gaze until Callum returns with the lubricant, drawing both of our attention.

I grin. "My holes thank you."

Callum's face screws up. "Please don't refer to it like that."

"How else am I supposed to phrase it?"

"By not referring to your body parts as individual entities," he says firmly.

Then Callum palms the back of my head and pushes me forward until I'm face down against Jesse's chest. The couch leather creaks under his weight as he props one knee on the chaise. I wait as Callum hovers over me, kissing the base of my spine.

Then he spreads my asscheeks and circles my hole with his tongue, reducing me to a trembling wreck. I've never been rimmed before, but it feels incredible, especially with Callum's skilled mouth.

Callum tests the ring of muscle with his forefinger, his mouth shifting. Beneath me, Jesse moans. I wonder what he's doing. Laving over Jesse's balls, maybe pulling each one into his mouth and sucking. I grind my cunt along the length of Jesse's cock, drawing out a desperate little squeak. Callum returns to me, pushing the tip of his tongue into my ass, fucking in gently to soften me up.

Jesse strokes up the length of my spine. "How does he taste?"

"Fucking amazing," Callum answers. He squeezes my thigh when I go rigid with embarrassment. "Relax, Bennett." Then he reaches for the lube, briefly leaving me to Jesse's gentle, soothing ministrations.

Sudden panic mixes with anticipation, churning in my stomach. I bury my face in Jesse's neck and try to breathe.

Callum places a kiss on the back of my thigh. "Do you need to stop?"

I shake my head. "I want to keep going," I assure him. "It just... This means so much to me."

"We love you." Callum wraps his arms around me, pressing close against my back. "*I* love you, Bennett. You brought me joy, when I thought companionship was beyond me."

Jesse pushes up on his elbows so he can kiss Callum over my shoulder, slow and thorough. "I've loved you since

A Fae's Two Alphas

we met," he says, his tone mock-serious. "You were just playing hard-to-get."

Callum huffs a laugh that, for once, he doesn't attempt to smother.

After giving Callum one more kiss, Jesse switches to me, nipping my bottom lip. "You know I love you in ways I can't verbalize. Do you want me to try anyway?"

"No, I believe you." I bite him back, leaving teeth imprints on the line of his jaw. "Right now I would prefer you just fuck me."

Callum hums. "Alright. Deep breath, then." Slick fingers probe my hole, their usual claws absent.

Despite the warning, I gasp, my whole body clenching.

"Shhhh," Callum rumbles, almost a purr. He licks the side of my neck, nuzzles it, nips at the crook of my shoulder like he did with Jesse. As I relax, he teases with one finger. He's done that before, and I remember how to take it, so I do, groaning at the intrusion. Callum rumbles again and begins to move, worrying my skin with his sharp canines. "I'm going to do something. It'll tingle, but only for a second."

I trust Callum implicitly, so all I do is nod, my forehead brushing Jesse's collarbone. The sensation comes and passes, leaving me shuddering in his wake. Callum adds a second finger, stretching me further. It goes in easier than the first, with no discomfort at all.

Jesse joins in, tucking his hand between my thighs so he can play with my clit. When I shudder, he says, "Lube, Cal."

Time passes in increments of me saying *'fuck,'* Jesse exploring my cunt while Callum works a third finger into my ass. I'm briefly overcome by the magnitude of my ask. I've never been filled like this, will never be fucked this way unless it's by them.

I love the sound of that.

"Now," I whisper. "I'm ready."

Jesse manipulates my body into place and Callum positions himself behind me. Late afternoon sunlight pours through the window, bathing the three of us in filmy gold. Jesse's eyelashes flutter, casting shadows across his cheeks. I kiss his eyelids, then freeze up, mouth hanging open as Jesse guides me down onto his cock in a steady, merciless slide.

I celebrate with a tremulous moan. "God, you're huge."

"You still want two?" Callum asks, wet sounds indicating he's slicking his cock thoroughly.

I nod. "Just go slow."

"Of course," Callum says. "We'll take care of you, love."

"I know you will."

It takes a few tries and a lot of deep breathing before Callum is able to seat himself fully inside me. When it finally happens, when both of my beautiful, trembling alphas have their hips as close to flush with my body as the position allows, I signal for them to move.

Painstakingly careful, at first. Cursing to themselves while they figure out a comfortable rhythm, while I mutter a string of profanity and do my best to hold still.

As our collective confidence grows, the *in-and-out* slide of them melts into smooth indulgence, frictionless other than the barrier between my ass and cunt where I can feel them rubbing together. It's weird in an amazing way, and when I find my voice, it's to beg for more. My body breaks out in a sweat as I'm rocked mercilessly, Callum's hands clamped on my hips.

Jesse strokes the damp hair at the base of my skull, whispering toe-curling, sexy words of praise. "You like that, babe? Such a good boy. You're so beautiful, Ben. So incredible. Look at how well you take us, filling you all the way. You feel amazing."

Callum catches one of Jesse's hands, interlocking their fingers and holding tight. He plasters himself along my back, each thrust measured and precise. My nerve endings are on fire already, but it doesn't stop me from begging, demanding they fuck me harder.

"Fuck," Jesse groans. "I'm close. Cal?" Callum only grunts, and Jesse lets out a breathless laugh. "You sure you're ready for this, Benny?"

My whole body is thrumming with restless energy, and there's a smear of drool on Jesse's shoulder. I slur, "Ready for you to fuck me for real?"

Callum snorts against my shoulder blade, his pace slowing.

"You're going to regret being this cocky someday," Jesse warns.

Fae magic sharpens my teeth, and I bite his collarbone. It turns his snickering into a yelp, then a moan when I lick up the pinpricks of blood.

Jesse pinches one of my nipples—*hard*. "Okay, sweetheart. Have it your way."

My ability to have coherent thoughts cuts off there. All I know next is screaming—my own—and the slap of skin on skin on skin, my alphas forcing themselves into my welcoming body over and over again. I become vaguely aware of tears leaking from the corners of my eyes, dripping down my nose onto Jesse's chest, as the brutal onslaught of stimulation grows to be almost too much.

"Bennett," Callum rumbles in my ear. "You're coming first. We'll fuck you the rest of the afternoon if that's what it takes."

"Speak for yourself," Jesse gasps. "Fuck, I didn't think he could get any tighter."

"Haven't even—" I break off into a sharp cry, digging my nails into whatever parts of Jesse's flesh I'm holding onto. It takes work to force out the rest. "Knotted me. Yet."

Callum jerks to a stop. "You can't take both knots."

"I can and I will." I glare at him over my shoulder, jaw set stubbornly. "You asked me what I wanted, and this is it. Please." They still seem hesitant, so I add, "I need both of you. Fill me, come inside me, hold me down... *Own* me."

A loud, resonant growl makes my limbs thrum. It comes from both of them: Callum and Jesse, in unison, responding to me pleading, begging them to possess my body, my everything.

Fully aware that I'm teasing a pair of predators, I prepare to say something even filthier, but Callum shoves his fingers in my mouth before I can. Jesse pulls my hair, forcing me to arch my back, and thrusts sharply. Callum keeps my mouth open as I wail, unable to do anything but submit as they take up a brutal pace.

My orgasm doesn't so much mount as it creeps up on me in a herd of other wild, powerful sensations. I cry out some abused attempt at their names, syllables running together into a weepy mash. I think Callum comes first, or maybe they come together, voices harmonizing as they empty themselves into my body over the course of several frantic thrusts.

As fucked-out as I am, I nearly forget about the next part: the base of their cocks growing inside me, pushing all the way past my rim until I'm aware of nothing but the weight between my legs.

Pressed between their sweat-drenched bodies, I weep

helplessly, mumbling something along the lines of *I love you, I love you both so much*.

Jesse's body goes lax, unmoving other than his thumb sweeping back and forth against my throat. He kisses the crown of my head, soothing me with soft noises.

Callum has tipped himself against the arm of the chaise to avoid crushing me, leaving our combined weight on Jesse's torso. He submits to the affection when Jesse threads the fingers of his free hand into his hair, combing through the silvery strands.

Then Callum murmurs, "This is new."

"What is?" I ask.

"Open your eyes and see."

I squint, trying to clear my vision. My mouth rounds when I see dozens of dandelion seeds spinning through the air, catching the bright streams of sunlight like little gemstones. Callum's fingers disturb more of the rapidly blooming flowers as he continues petting me. The buds explode from shaggy yellow petals into fluffy seeds that join the rest in spinning around the room.

Closing my eyes again, I mumble, "That's embarrassing."

"It's cute," Jesse murmurs, drowsy. "I'm sleeping for a century. Goodbye."

"Not like this you aren't." My back is starting to protest, so I shift into a different position. Soft sounds escape both Jesse and Callum in response, and I join them a second later, cunt throbbing from even the lightest stimulation. "How long do you think it'll be before we can go again?"

"You're ready for more already?" Callum asks.

"Maybe not this exact configuration, but I sure have more orgasms in me."

Jesse hums. "Get Bennett off twenty more times, *then* sex coma. Got it."

When their knots go down, Callum is the first one to pull out, followed by Jesse, who sighs. The sensation of being emptied is accompanied by the wet trickle of semen dripping down my perineum and inner thighs. I shiver when Callum pushes me further up Jesse's body, giving him enough space to drag his tongue over where his come has intermingled with Jesse's.

It's so filthy-hot I feel as if I could come again from the thought alone, but Callum kisses up the cleft of my ass, then my spine, until he can take my mouth with his come-slick lips. Jesse leans in, too, all three of our mouths creating a sloppy, perfect afterglow.

For about three minutes, anyway, until the endorphins fade and our bodies need to stretch. As Jesse sits up, I spill off the couch, ending up moaning softly while facedown on the hardwood. I feel physically empty, even if my heart is just as full and heavy as my holes were a moment ago.

"Can I take a raincheck on the next bout of fucking?" Jesse stretches his arms above his head with a yawn. "I'm cooked."

Because he's a gentleman—feral or otherwise—Callum scoops me up from the floor. "I think we all need to rest."

"Fine with me." I curl against him, nuzzling happily into his neck while petting his silvery chest hair.

37

POSSESSED AND POSSESSING

"No, you cannot carry me. I'll be fine. Stop fussing."

In Faerie, moping by the river and spying on Jesse and Callum was the most stationary part of my day. Meaning that, after a nap, I was up and active again. I milled around the cottage, looking for something to occupy my mind. Aside from the new couch and repaired wall, nothing was different.

Once I confirmed there wasn't anything new to discover on Callum's land, I shoved them both out the door, insisting we go to the creek before the sky grew fully dark.

"Bennett, you just got railed within an inch of your life," Jesse protests. "You shouldn't be walking this far."

I roll my eyes, then shoot Callum an amused look, which he returns. "You didn't hurt me, first of all," I say, ticking it off on my index finger before extending another. "Second, I was way more banged up last time we fucked, and I still managed to *run* afterward." Not that it was fun, but I don't mention that. "Third, I've got my magic. You know that means I can heal just as fast as you now, right?"

Jesse whines. Yes, he actually whines, like a puppy upset at not getting his way.

"Would you rather him not heal, pup?" Callum asks, apparently coming to the same conclusion. I grin when Jesse turns on Callum, clearly offended.

"I never said that."

"Let the little imp walk if that's what he wants."

They bicker all the way to the creek. My lower body does twinge a few times, but I don't let on to it, and I'm fine otherwise. When we arrive, I strip my shirt and kick off the sandals I'd dug out of the bag of my belongings Callum still had in his closet. I'd almost teared up again when he hauled it out.

But no. Aside from good, fucked out tears, there's no need for any more crying. I'm happier than I could have imagined, even though I'm in a mundane forest rather than Faerie. I did love it there, but Faerie lacked two very important elements that were critical to my happiness.

I roll my pants up, cuffing them above my knees. Then I straighten with a deep stretch, arms over my head, delighting at the freedom of a flat chest and no binder restricting my motion.

"Anyone joining me?" I don't wait for an answer before plunging into the creek, sighing in pleasure as the cool water flows over my bare feet. When I turn, it's to see Jesse and Callum wading in after me. Callum reaches me first, tugging me against his chest so he can kiss the crown of my head. I hum, letting my eyes drift closed as I nuzzle his chin.

Something occurs to me, then, and my eyes pop back open.

"Hey, Cal? Remember when we were doing the firefly ritual during the solstice, and you were reading to me from the River Spirit's book?"

One more squeeze, and Callum releases me. He acknowledges my question with a nonverbal sound.

"I don't know if you could have guessed, but that last story? About the boy and the wolf? If you recall how I freaked out during it, well… that's because the story was about me and Jesse."

Callum's eyebrows climb incrementally as he turns over this information, piecing things together in his head. "Interesting choice," he says, the words resonating in a way that suggests he isn't speaking to just me. The wind picks up, rustling the trees and shaping the whisper of leaves into a sound suspiciously akin to laughter.

"You guys got *spirits* gossiping about us?" Jesse asks, his grin crooked.

"I guess the River Spirit was projecting how horny I was for you that day onto how horny I was for Callum during the ritual."

Their expressions go bashful, and I laugh at the sky in delight. How can they be willing to jam their dicks into my body while I'm making a mess of myself begging for it, but be shy outside of the moment, and over far more tame phrasing?

I take a moment to revel in how happy they make me before shaking head clear and leading them downstream. The three of us walk mostly in silence, listening to the chattering of nature. When I stop at the edge of a small incline, so do my wolves. Water spills over the rocks, creating a small fall surrounded by bubbly foam.

"The leaves are starting to turn," I say softly, studying the hints of red and orange peeking through the green. "And I keep hearing this obnoxious fucking honking because all the geese are migrating."

"They do that in fall, yeah," Jesse says. He picks his way

over the slippery rocks until he's at my side. He strokes leftover dandelion seeds from my hair.

I go silent, gnawing on my lip.

"Bennett?" Callum asks once he's alongside us.

"I just realized I don't have anywhere to go." I sink onto the flat rock at the top of the shallow waterfall, heedless of the cold current rushing over me and soaking my pants. "I've lived with my parents my whole life. That's pathetic, isn't it? I'm pathetic."

Callum and Jesse lower themselves at either of my sides, neither of them looking pleased.

"You aren't pathetic," Jesse says. "It's completely normal for shifter packs—"

"You'll live with me," Callum interjects.

I blink up at him, eyes wide.

He huffs. "I don't know why you'd think any different."

"I didn't want to assume—"

Callum folds his arms over his chest, intimidating even while sitting on his haunches with water flowing over his knees. "I take care of what's mine. I'd never let—" He shakes his head. "You're ours to protect."

"And love," Jesse adds.

"I don't need *that* much protection, guys," I say, a small smile chasing away the brief but intense flash of insecurity. "It's not like I'm a getaway driver for a vigilante organization. No bank robbery or anything. I don't even steal candy from the grocery store."

Jesse snorts. "Doesn't matter. We're never letting you out of our sight again."

I consider it, looking to Callum for further reassurance. "You two really..."

Callum nods firmly.

A Fae's Two Alphas

My cheeks flush with pleasure, toes curling against the smooth rocks. "My alphas," I whisper.

The words trigger something primal in the men beside me. I'm not snatched up and kissed—it wouldn't have surprised me, but I suppose even shifters should be careful while perched on slippery rocks. I end up held, though, with Callum seizing my wet pantleg, then placing a slightly gentler hand possessive on the back of my neck. Jesse's claws lengthen, brushing my skin—not as a threat, but a reminder of his strength. He's a creature of power, an alpha capable of neutralizing threats, capable of starting fights *and* finishing them...

But most importantly, capable of working with Callum to possess me so wholly, I feel it deep in my marrow.

A shudder overtakes my body, combining the thrill of their claiming with the chill of the breeze grazing over the cold water. Neither alpha asks before they pull me to my feet and start the walk back to the cottage.

Back home.

I shudder again, in pure pleasure this time, because it's been years since I truly belonged somewhere.

We reach the bank, where Callum uses a spell to dry my pants so I don't have to walk back to the cottage in wet fabric. He leaves Jesse wet, though.

They jostle each other over the snub, then out of nowhere, Jesse says, "We have to build a second floor."

Callum's face scrunches. "We?"

"Yeah. I mean, who else is gonna help you?" Jesse's eyes sparkle with mischief. "Ben needs a place of his own. For fuck's sake, there's one room, and every corner is filled with your stuff. You can't expect him to hole up without any room to himself."

"Hm." Callum looks at me, then back at Jesse.

Suddenly shy once again, I say, "You don't have to do all that for me. I don't need much space."

Callum shakes his head. "No, Jesse's right. I'll... We'll draw up plans."

"We also need to get a bigger bed," Jesse adds. "I don't think I can survive wedging myself onto that queen-size indefinitely."

Grumbling, Callum says, "Who says you're invited? There's plenty of room for Bennett and me."

I smack his arm. "Enough."

"Don't worry, Cal. I'm staying at the pack house for now." Jesse swings an arm around Callum's neck and yanks him close. "But I'll be visiting for frequent sleepovers."

"And more than sleeping," I say.

Jesse laughs, entirely unbothered when Callum shoves him away with a growl of warning.

Shaking my head and chuckling to myself, I head back to the cottage. My pants are dry, but with this wind my skin is verging on freezing, and I want to curl up on that squeaky new couch with a blanket, mug of tea, and two wolves tucked against me, one on either side. Someday I'll get them to cuddle each other, but for now, I'm more than willing to soak up the warmth and attention.

We pass Jesse's parked car and cross the humble road, walking in comfortable silence through the red-tinged trees. When the cottage comes into sight, I pause.

Then I turn to Jesse and Callum, beaming so brightly I suspect I'm glowing from it. "I need to make something clear." Their eyebrows rise in question simultaneously, and my smile grows even wider until my cheeks ache and my heart throbs in my chest. "I'm both of yours, to protect and love and fuck, and all the rest. But mostly, you two are mine. Don't forget that."

With that said, I take off, bolting for the cottage and laughing in pure joy when my alphas break into a run at my heels.

fin.

Thanks so much for reading!
If you enjoyed this book, join my Facebook group to keep up with my current and upcoming projects. You can find **jem zero's author box** here: https://www.facebook.com/groups/jemzeroauthor/
If you'd like more of Bennett, Callum, and Jesse, sign up for my newsletter to receive a free bonus story in which the alphas reconcile their hierarchy issues so the three of them can form a mate bond.
Sign up here: https://jemzero.com/newsletter/

ACKNOWLEDGMENTS

I'd like to thank my family: Mum, my wife Tora, and my sibling for supporting me while I write my silly little gay stories. I would not be able to learn and grow without y'all.

Then I'd like to celebrate the skills of my brilliant developmental editor Guindo (he/him); line editors Charlie Knight (they/them) and Sara LaCroix (she/her); and beta readers Felix Graves (he/him), Eliot Grayson (she/her), and Elle Porter (he/they).

Much appreciation for Skye Kilaen (she/her), who very patiently formats my manuscripts in exchange for cute queer stickers, and the cover artist, Samantha Santana of Amai Designs.

Finally, Donyae Coles (she/her) is the absolute best for supporting me while I whined through every single stage of edits.

ABOUT THE AUTHOR

jem zero (ze/zir) is an autistic and disabled transmasculine person who lives with zir family in a house built by zir great-grandfather. Ze primarily writes queer Sci-fi/Fantasy with strong themes of romance and social justice.

Zir sci-fi erotic flash fic, A Study In Circuits And Charcoal, published in Erato by The New Smut Project, won the award for Best Feminist Sex from the Good Sex Awards. Ze has other published fiction, creative nonfiction, and further eccentric nonsense listed on zir website:

jemzero.com

twitter.com/jem_zero
instagram.com/jemzero